I0658920

Rescue Me

IGNITING LOVE

SARA OHLIN

Igniting Love
ISBN # 978-1-83943-927-8
©Copyright Sara Ohlin 2020
Cover Art by Erin Dameron-Hill ©Copyright November 2020
Interior text design by Claire Siemaszkiewicz
Totally Bound Publishing

Published in 2020 by Totally Bound Publishing, United Kingdom.

Totally Bound Publishing is an imprint of Totally Entwined Group Limited.

IGNITING LOVE

Dedication

For the amazing and powerful single moms everywhere who create magic all by themselves. And for Lisa, a wonderful friend and fierce supporter of women. I love your tush!

Chapter One

"Penny, I'm here!" Katie shouted into the seemingly empty penthouse apartment twenty-five floors in the sky. She lugged in her bags overflowing with groceries. "Penny?" There were several boxes, some open, strewn across the entry hallway, and packaging popcorn left a trail toward Penny's office.

It wasn't uncommon for Katie's clients to be gone when she arrived. As a personal chef, she mostly cooked alone. But Penny Jager, successful sex therapist-turned-author, worked from her home, with its stunning view into Corvallis. Today, however, clouds hovered around the building, blanketing the town below, thickheaded and still, like a pouty six-year-old determined to wear her pajamas to school. The lack of scenery outside the floor-to-ceiling windows unbalanced Katie. *Surreal to be up so high and not see anything but puffs of white.*

"Be out in a minute!" Penny yelled from her office. "Sorry for the mess!"

I wonder if those clouds are as stubborn as my six-year old? It sure was a relief not to have to be at a job exactly on time. As a widow and a mom of three girls, Katie was never on time. She had barely dropped her youngest, Cece, off at the elementary school this morning before the bell rang. One more tardy and she'd be getting the dreaded note home about how attendance matters. *Gah! And it's only October.*

Katie unloaded food and supplies and jotted down her task list. First, she checked the coffee — nearly empty. She ground beans and brewed a fresh pot for Penny who mainlined caffeine during the day. Next, Katie boiled water for the baked pasta she'd pair with meatballs and homemade pomodoro sauce.

She measured breadcrumbs and chopped fresh parsley. The repetition, the way Katie coordinated everything, brought her a level of comfort and energized her. *Or it used to.* She glanced up to the still-shrouded view. *Out of balance, and not just from the clouds. More than out of balance. Needy, wanting.*

She used her hands to mix the ingredients together then rolled them into meatballs and placed them on a plate to chill in the refrigerator. "It's not your fault, guys," she said to the food. Cooking wasn't the problem. She still loved making food. It was just that, lately, her job, her *life* felt —

"Oh, thank God you're here. I'm starving! We're socked in like a cock in a too tight condom, I imagine. And look at you talking to balls." Penny sailed in, barefoot and wearing what looked like a long fuchsia caftan over lounge-type pants.

Katie wouldn't tell Cece that some people did get to wear their pajamas all day. Penny was nothing if not dramatic and blunt, both of which served her well in her profession. Luckily for Katie, she was also kind, full of compassion and had offered friendship as well as a paycheck in exchange for Katie's meals. She was Katie's favorite client.

Penny grabbed the enormous twelve-cup pot. "Coffee, love?" She grabbed a mug for Katie. "And please tell me you're making those chocolate chip muffins this morning."

"Better," Katie said. "I made them at home." She unwrapped a huge muffin and plated it for Penny. "Might still be warm."

"Heaven." Penny sighed after swallowing a bite. "Tempt me with the rest of the week's menu."

"Steak salad with farfalle, spicy chicken for tacos and I'm not telling you any more." Penny was also her favorite client because she let Katie surprise her each week. Several of Katie's clients ordered the exact same meals. Every time.

"Mmm-hmm, what's got you sighing and lamenting over balls? Or is it the lack of balls in your life?" Penny's laugh was full and deep, like a jazzy lounge singer in a smoky bar.

Katie's face heated. "Hah! I was thinking how much I enjoy cooking for you because I get to interact with you."

"And have me drool over your creations."

"That doesn't hurt either." Once the cans of tomatoes were open, she chopped onions. "I never see the rest of my clients. After John died, when I started personal cheffing, the solitude wasn't a problem. I looked forward to it, for the calm compared to the rest of my life and because I was barely keeping my head above water. I didn't have time to get bored. Things were crazy busy, as they are now."

"I bet, with three young divas at home."

Katie laughed. Her daughters *were* divas. One teenage angsty diva, one serene know-it-all middle-kid diva and one loud drama-queen-six-year-old-going-on-twenty-six diva. "But now, I notice empty spaces. Does that make sense? I don't mean to sound ungrateful. But I want connection, more adults in my life. I want to share my love of food and cooking with people, not just cook by myself all the time."

"You're lonely. How could you not be? You're raising three girls on your own, you work your butt off as a mom and business owner and you have so much to give the world. Bet you're feeling lonely in the bedroom, too."

"Oh no you don't." Katie raised her hand. "I'm not one of your patients."

"You're my friend. And you don't have to be one of my patients for me to see you're in a sexual desert."

"What, parched? Searching for my oasis?" Katie smirked.

"Exactly. Needy, unfulfilled. Wanting and enjoying a healthy sex life is normal, Katie. How long has it been?"

She didn't hide her sigh. *Way too long.* She did miss sex lately. Jeez, was it written on her face or did Penny have a *sex* sense? "Since John died."

"Five years? That's no desert—that's Mars!"

"Calm down." *Should I laugh or cry?* "When should I have found the time, running my three divas to their activities, keeping them from killing each other, saving the house from my brother's ridiculous decision to toss a puppy into the mix, working full-time, scheduling one more stupid car maintenance appointment?"

"Single parents date, Katie. You just have to make the effort. Figure out what you want. There are such things as babysitters. Mmm. Do you want to find someone again? Enjoy sex again?"

Yes, and yes, please. Too choked up all of a sudden to voice the words, she nodded. She wanted both. Hot oil from the sautéing onions zapped her hand when Katie stirred the garlic in. "Ouch!" she yelped and ran her hand under cold water.

"That's a sign to take a break. Come with me. Wouldn't you know these boxes arrived today of all days."

Katie turned off the burner and followed Penny down the hall.

"We might need some whiskey in our coffee to have this discussion," Penny mumbled to herself. "My agent seems to have a fortuitous sense of humor."

Katie stepped into Penny's bright office. Boxes similar to those in the entryway sat open with packaging strewn over the floor. Brightly colored items shaped like rods o...*oh!*

"A company called Love Handle wants me to review their new products."

"*Sex toys?*" Katie asked.

"Honey, people don't come to me for tax help. They want to enjoy life, find pleasure in the bedroom again. Or on the dining room table or in the sauna. With or without a partner." Penny calmed her laughter before taking a sip of coffee.

Katie picked up a silver dildo bigger than any real cock she'd ever seen. "'Lonely Lady's Friend.' It's apropos, but the name certainly doesn't make me feel better."

"That's just it. It *might* make you feel a whole lot better. Look, there's something for everyone's tastes. Pun intended. Musical themes like The Slow Jam, mmm-hmm. Or A Day's Hard Night. How about a fantasy line to tickle your fancy? A bit expected calling this one Unicorn, but look at the rainbow ribbed feel."

Penny was having way too much fun with this.

"And good Lord, even techies need their toys—The Code Hacker. Oh! Here's the box for you—food themes. Delicious."

"God, don't tell me they're all different sausage names?" Katie couldn't help her grin.

"Oh, no, much cleverer than that." Penny wiped the tears of laughter from her eyes. "Oh, I do love my job." She handed her a shiny gold vibrator. "Butter Finger."

Katie's neck was warm and she knew it bloomed bright red.

"Tell you what," Penny said. "As much as I do enjoy a healthy sex life, there's no way I can test all of these products myself. I think you should pick a few sexy toys and give them a go. Then report back."

"No way. I can't just try out a"—Katie held up what looked like a sparkly pink set of silicone beads connected on a chain—"on command."

Even Penny blushed. She took that one out of Katie's hands. "We should start you on some more familiar play. I'll keep the butt toys for later."

Butt toys? Katie buried her face in her hands, which only made Penny laugh harder. "I'm going to need an instruction manual for these tools."

"Ooo, good one—you need to handle a man's tool all right."

Penny's teasing and innuendos could make anyone laugh, Katie included.

"You're suggesting I need to spearhead my own research," Katie said. Maybe she could get the hang of this.

"Exactly, find someone to shuck your oyster."

"Oh! Stop!" Katie said, choking on her own laughter. "Too far."

"Okay…" Penny got more serious. "I think you do need more than toys. You need emotions and desire. Your assignment is to go out at least once before I see you next week. Schedule a blind date. Head out to a fun bar for girls' night. Sign up for online dating. Talk to a hot guy. Flirt your cute butt off. Anything for adults. Leave all your responsibilities at home and start taking care of your health. Practice, practice, practice."

* * * *

She had picked the easiest suggestion — meeting her girlfriends at Lachlan's Pub. But Katie still felt nervous. The sneaky sex therapist had snuck a few toys into Katie's purse. Katie had immediately stuffed them into her dresser drawer. Even picturing them there made her blush. Five years with only a handful of self-induced orgasms did seem like more than a tiny drought.

Ever since their sex conversation, steamy fantasies had interrupted her thoughts. Surprisingly erotic images involving muscled men ready to pleasure her. Not one reminded her of her husband. Maybe she was ready to move on.

She missed John, but they'd been so young and naïve, together in their teens and married by twenty. She'd never even seen a sex toy. After he died no one was having sex, except oh, the rest of the world! Penny was intuitive — Katie did want to find love again. And pleasure. Good Lord, would she even know how to have sex after so long without?

When her husband's death had been fresh, she'd been too tired to notice anything about herself aside from the pain of grief. The last few years, her body had resurfaced from its own sort of burial. *I miss sex. Can I miss something I only ever had with one man? And the memories as faded as a warm breath outside on a winter's night. Am I allowed to want again?* Things often felt like a betrayal to her dead husband, even her own confusing desires. But after this week of hot fantasies, she was almost ready to dig out the Butter Finger.

She was also nervous because she was running late. Again. Not that her friends would care, but she wanted to enjoy every moment of her night. It *had* been too long since she'd made time for herself. Plus, it was knitting night at the pub, an idea that sounded ridiculous and tons of fun.

Katie pulled open the door and walked into the charming dark entryway of the bar to scan for her girlfriends, but instead came face-to-chest with one enormous man. His hand shot out to steady the door behind her, which put his arm against her cheek. She sucked in a deep breath and was met with a deep woodsy, spicy scent that zinged right to her core and set the week's fantasies in motion. She leaned her face closer to his arm, his scent calling to her.

"Hey." A deep voice coaxed her gaze to meet his as neatly as if he'd reached out and tipped her chin up. And *whoa!* The entryway shrank from charming to cozy—his presence sucked the air right out of her.

Hey. Too busy panting, she couldn't get her words to work. A dark beard and mustache nearly hid the tilt of his full, lush lips. He had mysterious eyes with a hint of spark and was dark and moody, blending right into the midnight alcove. A winter beanie covered his head. *I want to run my hands under that hat, feel his hair in my hands, see if it's the same shade as his beard.* Was this what Penny meant when she talked about emotions and desire? Because Katie was a churning ocean wave of desire.

Towering. His perusal of her zapped over her skin as if he'd used his hands again. The man had silent voodoo powers over her body.

She came back to his eyes, which were laser focused on her face, specifically her lips. He was zoned in on her mouth like he was a wolf and she were little lost Red Riding Hood. He licked his bottom lip. *All the more perfect to ravish you with,* that slick of his tongue said. Jolted, he caught her eyes, smoothed his smile away and pulled a veil over his eyes to shut out the hint of spark.

Nope, he'd never blend in anywhere.

"Excuse us," he said. He removed his hand from the door but didn't step back. Music from the bar and the din of people talking drifted into her hearing. A woman clung to his side, a petite woman with gorgeous hair, flawless makeup and an enormous chest. Katie sighed. She'd always wanted big boobs. *Are luscious endowments what it takes to walk arm in arm with a man like that? I'll have to stick to my fantasies.*

"We're leaving." He made to walk by her.

"Right. I'm in your way." Shifting to the side, their bodies brushed against each other. Hard, warm planes molded into her, and she wanted to close her eyes, breathe him in, discover all his secrets. Give hers up to him. For a dreamy second, he paused too in that tiny zap of connection.

They turned at the same time, him into the night. Instinctively her body moved with his. She reached out. It seemed imperative she stop him, use her words, communicate her desire. "I…"

But he was gone, leaving her standing there in a crowded bar full of people, alone and shivering.

Chapter Two

"Katie, Katie! Over here." Ruby's loud voice carried across the conversations and laughter and dragged her back down to this planet. Her dream world snuffed out, the wisp of swirling black smoke its only reminder. Her heart still raced. *Did that really happen?*

She wove her way through the crowded room. The sauna-like air quickly overwhelmed her shivers, or was it the heat of embarrassment? *It did happen.* And cue utter mortification. She'd nearly pulled that gorgeous man to her, even though he was a complete stranger *and* was with someone else. To taste his lips. Maybe sex toys were the way to go for her. She felt like a bird figuring out how to fly from the nest. *Baby steps.*

"Ladies," Katie said, giving air kisses to Ruby, Ellie, Natalie and Sasha who were snuggled into a comfy round booth toward the back of the pub.

"You okay?" Ruby asked. "You're all flushed."

Well, if she couldn't tell her girlfriends, who could she tell? "I. Am. Not. Okay."

"We ordered your Shiraz." Natalie pushed a glass of wine her way. "What's wrong?"

I nearly kissed a strange man. Maybe she'd ease into things. "Not wrong exactly. I feel like I'm having a mid-life crisis or an awakening. I think I'm ready to date again," she blurted out then put a glass of iced water against her cheek.

"Oh, goody!" Natalie rubbed her hands together, the matchmaking gears turning in her friend's head.

"Perfect night to be at Lachlan's then," Ruby added and shimmied in her seat.

"For knit night?"

"Mmm-hmm." Ruby smirked her perfectly red lips and nodded.

Katie had walked into the wrong bar, or some alternate dimension, no doubt about it. It had been years since she knitted. And it had been *never* since she'd been to a knit night in a pub, let alone one that would help her in the dating game.

"Check out the hosts." Ruby gestured toward the back of the bar where the bands usually played. A long table draped in red velvet stood before a matching red curtain. Different colored yarns spilled from pretty baskets, knitting books and pairs of needles scattered in between the balls of color. However, as ridiculous and cool as the seductive table of knitting supplies looked, it was the three gorgeous people standing by it that held everyone's attention. They'd just finished giving an introduction.

The only woman was petite, in a black A-line dress paired with a blood-red cardigan, which might pass for a demure look if it weren't for the sexy v-neckline and the fishnet stockings plus high black heels she rocked. Her black hair was curled up at the top of her head, rockabilly meets Ella Fitzgerald. She stood between two tall, very fit, handsome men, one in tight black jeans and short-sleeved black T-shirt showing tattoo-covered arms, and the other in a blue chambray shirt with the sleeves rolled up, whose faded jeans fit his legs in all the right places. He donned super-sexy Clark Kent glasses and winked at Katie who'd been staring. *Whoops…hopefully I'm not drooling.*

"Holy cow!" She fanned her cheeks and faced Ellie. "Those are the hosts from…what's the name of the new shop next to your clinic?"

Ellie raised both eyebrows like she had a huge secret to share. "Knitting Takes Balls."

Katie laughed. She was surrounded by sexual innuendos, ever since she'd even entertained the topic again.

"They'll instruct you too, if you know what I mean." Ruby wiggled her eyebrows. "Seriously, though," Ruby continued, "look around. The bar is full of hotties, obviously here to meet all the sexy, smart knitters. We'll look out for you. Time to get your flirt and knit on! In fact, would you look at that. I just dropped a stitch. Maybe Max can help me."

Ruby had *her* flirt on. She swayed her hips and sashayed up to the host in the black T-shirt and jeans who might be a professional knitter but whose smirk had *dirty talk* written all over it. Katie watched them interact, their faces close, smiling. Max took Ruby's hands and moved her fingers over her needles. Katie could feel the heat between them from where she sat. *Seduction by knitting, that's new.*

If only I could learn how to flirt from watching Ruby. I'd be a pro. Natalie was an expert knitter and Ellie was just learning, but neither of them would be dallying with the teachers tonight. Their men, Jackson and Gage, sat together at the bar and beside them Katie's brother,

Connor, who'd offered to not drink tonight in case she needed a ride home. *Sweet of him.*

Sexy Rocker Chick, as Katie had dubbed the female proprietor of Knitting Takes Balls, walked right up to Connor with her needles and yarn and struck up a conversation. Ever so briefly, Connor's eyes flicked to their table and settled on Sasha before he turned back and engaged in conversation at the bar.

Interesting. Sasha sat at the other end of their booth. Her huge dog rested at her feet and her purse strap crossed over her body. *Ready to bolt at a moment's notice.* Katie couldn't blame her after the nightmare of abuse she'd lived through. It was rare she came out to the bar with the girls at all.

"And what are you working on tonight, gorgeous?" Clark Kent glasses slid into the booth by Katie. Large sculpted fingers held tiny needles attached to fluffy pink yarn. His tattooed arm rested against hers and their thighs touched, but when she looked up into his hazel eyes all she saw was the midnight stare from the dream man she'd nearly kissed at the door. She closed her eyes for a second to hold in the heady memory, the rush of sensations he'd sent swirling through her blood as they'd hovered close to each other.

"I'm Declan." The man's Irish accent was as thick as Guinness pouring from a keg and startled her back to her seat. He held his hand out.

"Of course you are." Katie raised an eyebrow, and he barked out a laugh. *You're here to have fun and practice.* She shook his hand, shrugged off her coat and dug out the scarf she'd started last night. "Katie. And it's nice to meet you, Declan."

He introduced himself to Sasha, who didn't return his handshake, quickly mumbled goodbye and got up to leave.

"I'll walk you out and wait for the Uber with you, honey," Natalie said. Ellie scooted out too and made her way to the bar to hug Jackson. Those two were never far from each other.

Katie sipped her wine. *Ahh, they scattered like the wind.* Subtle her friends were not. "Well, Declan, I'm working on a new scarf. I'm a novice knitter." She started on a row of purls. "And my flirting skills are ancient."

His smile was wide and genuine. "I'll take your warning under consideration. How about we chat and knit, and you can practice on me?"

If he only knew.

"I couldn't resist such a lovely table of Ellie's friends. Although it looks like it's just the two of us. This must be your first time at Lachlan's knit night. One does not forget a siren like you."

"A siren, huh? More like a hot mess."

Nudging her shoulder, he chuckled. "Okay, lesson number one, and it has nothing to do with knitting." He flirted his cute eyes behind the dark glasses. "Best not to admit to being a hot mess on the first date."

"Is that what you'd call this?" Katie said.

"A man can hope." A man who looked like he was fifteen years younger than her, at least.

His banter? Not one bit rusty. Giving her compliments, asking her what wine she liked when her glass was empty, leaning in and gently coaxing her hands into a more relaxed position when her fingers slid too close to the tips of her needles.

At the end of a row, Katie set her needles down and ran her hand over the soft hat he was making. "Looks a bit tiny for you."

"It's for my soon-to-be niece."

"That's lovely," she said. Inwardly she sighed. She smiled and enjoyed the evening even while her thoughts wandered to the mystery man in the entryway. There was not one lovely thing about him. Power, passion, maybe even a hint of danger had surrounded him, pulsed from him. She remembered the way his gaze had sizzled over her body. *I want to know what his hands feel like. On me.* She was going to need a pitcher of iced water if her thoughts kept going in that direction. At least her libido still worked. She gave herself a silent cheer and enjoyed her wine.

Who knew knit night would be hopping? Declan eventually got dragged over to a table of ladies in their early twenties. Lachlan was busy behind the bar, but his gaze followed Ruby with military-like precision, a scowl on his face every time she enlisted Max for a tutorial. And Sexy Rocker Chick, who'd eventually given up trying to get Connor's attention, was surrounded by a beginning knitters group, all making moony eyes at her. Aside from Natalie and Gage, who danced and flirted like they were still on their honeymoon, the night might have been more aptly titled *unrequited love night.*

* * * *

"You had fun." Ruby hugged Katie goodbye. "I want details in the morning." Katie climbed into Connor's truck and waved as Ruby headed back into the pub. The Knitting Takes Balls team had left a while ago.

The night had been fun, Katie could admit, chatting, flirting. It had been nice to have a hot guy's attention, even if he was a little clean-cut for her tastes.

Where did that thought come from?

One hot, secretive glance with a sexy stranger and suddenly everyone else was too clean-cut?

"So, should I run a background check on the Irishman?" her brother asked.

"Funny," Katie said. *He's not the one I want.*

"Looked pretty serious."

"Honestly, it was like hanging out with you all night." Which was the absolute truth.

"No sparks, huh?"

Not from him.

"You ready to date again?" His tone was serious now.

"I think so. The girls and I can't live with you forever. Helping us after John died…I can never repay you for that, but…"

"Never asked you to."

"What I mean is, I think we're enabling each other not to move on. We're both stuck in a rut since his death. Long time to be stuck. Don't you want to find love and start your own family?"

"Hmp," was all the answer he gave.

She was ready to move on. Tonight had been an easy reintroduction into the dating pool. Declan had kissed her hand and given her his number before he left. But she didn't suspect she'd be calling him.

Connor dropped her off and went for a drive, something he did often in the middle of the night. He pretended carefree nonchalance, but she saw deeper. *Such an unsettled man.*

After checking to make sure all her girls were asleep, Katie climbed into bed, still dreaming of how that man's lips might feel on hers. She really didn't have a clue when it came to dating or sex, but, as Penny suspected, she recognized desire. Her body lit up with it every time she remembered the man's smoky, penetrating stare. She couldn't shake the feeling he'd silently spoken to her, whispered tantalizing secrets for only the two of them. One precious instant and her lust for him hummed through her blood as if she needed contact with him to survive.

It was surreal, unnatural. It was amazing. Even the memory made her shiver in a wonderful way. Like a mystery disappeared into the darkness, but whose remnants lingered in all her hushed places.

Just because she'd never see dream man again didn't mean she couldn't indulge in more fantasies. She quietly uncovered the Butter Finger. With images of his lush lips surrounded by a thick black beard and mustache, and those sizzling eyes, his giant body over hers, Katie thoroughly enjoyed practicing, just as her sex therapist had advised.

Chapter Three

Taking pencil to paper wasn't helping. Unsatisfied with all his sketches, Leo tossed them in the garbage, pulled on his thick work gloves and began searching through the piles of metal scraps instead. If he could focus on a new project, maybe it would smother the restlessness that had crept upon him, subtle and slow over the last few months. He'd gotten to the shop early this morning to play with some ideas before the workday started.

"Appreciate you coming home to help, man." His brother Matt ducked into the last garage bay where they stored what Leo liked to call every piece of crap on the planet. But he wouldn't criticize. His brother had a way of salvaging unique, random pieces parts to fix anything mechanical. People visited from all over the city to have more than their cars fixed by Matt. Even as a child, his brother had known his way around mechanics. *Born with the instinct of how things fit together.*

"Glad you finally asked me," Leo said.

"I know fixing cars isn't your favorite thing, but you're the best welder out there. Once we have the team trained, I won't need your help. Whatcha looking for? I know where everything is."

He probably did, the way Matt's mind worked— once he put something away, he kept a photograph of it stored in his mind and could pull it back out in an instant.

"Not sure," Leo said. "Inspiration. My hands are itching to create again. Been a while." *My hands are more than itching after seeing her.*

"I've got tons of scraps saved, been putting more away once you came home."

"Thanks, man," Leo mumbled. More distracted than usual, he moved a huge piece of aluminum to get to a stack of bronze pieces. Friday night, as he'd been leaving Lachlan's, his restlessness had blown into an inferno in that enclosed space. When he'd escaped outside, where the breeze swirled and wet colored leaves littered the pavement, he'd tried to suck down the rain-dampened air to ground himself. Instead, the cloying scent his date had been bathed in had clouded his nose and frankly pissed him off. Which was why he'd left her at her car and walked home alone.

Pretty women were everywhere, but the first swell of autumn only came once a year. Fall was his favorite, in the moment, as it settled in. The scent of wood fires and dried leaves, a nip in the air, hot apple cider with lemon. But as soon as the first snowstorm hit in winter, he was like a kid in the Lego store, silly with joy. And, unlike most people who bitched about it, he welcomed the layers of pollen and rain in spring. On a hot summer night, watching the sunset with a beer, well, there was nothing better. Unless of course he had a warm naked woman to go to bed with after said sunset. Preferably one not drowning in perfume.

Friday night, the seasonal air hadn't calmed him one bit.

It had taken him the entire fifteen-block walk home to get the perfume out of his nose and, while the exercise should have calmed him, he'd been more annoyed, more fidgety than when he'd left the pub. He hadn't slept well all weekend, and he'd been pissed at himself…because he couldn't get that last-minute encounter out of his mind.

"Where do you get your inspiration?" An easy one, Matt's question.

Swirled gray-blue eyes on the most stunning woman I've ever seen. Leo stopped himself short of admitting his idiocy. But it was the truth. Ten, maybe twenty seconds in the beauty's presence and he wanted to sketch her, sculpt her with his hands and his mouth. His mind raced with thoughts of her.

He'd been so close he could have kissed her. *Ached* to lean in and do just that. Had completely forgotten the other woman hanging on his arm. It was only at the last second, when those eyes had felt like they'd reached into his soul and squeezed it back to life, that had jolted him out of his fascination with her lips.

"Leo?"

"What?" His tone was sharp, not at all how he intended. Leo shot his gaze to his brother's and dragged his mind back to their conversation. *Restless indeed.*

Matt studied him. "Nothing. I can see you're preoccupied."

"No, I…yes…distracted. Zoned out for a minute," he admitted. Jesus, he could even feel the softness of her skin, even though he hadn't touched her. Seductive.

He ran his hands over his face and let out a breath. He faced his brother. "Honestly it's been so long since I created for the love of it, I've forgotten how to get started."

"You seemed lost somewhere nice for a minute, if it's any consolation. You had a peaceful look about you. Maybe use that for inspiration, whatever it was."

Peaceful? Not the word Leo would use to describe how that woman made him feel. Worked up. Itchy. *Hard*. He again refrained from admitting an *it* wasn't stealing his attention, but rather a *who*. An extremely curvy, sexy, intoxicating *who*. No reason for him to mention he wanted to sculpt a woman he didn't even know. Even if it was the truth.

Leo dug out several large flat pieces of metal and ran his gloved hands along the sides. searching for guidance through the medium. He wanted to take his gloves off and caress her skin, see if it really was as soft as he imagined. *Mine*. He'd cement every curve of her into his mind and recreate her beauty through his art. He'd never do it justice…but that didn't mean he wouldn't rise to the challenge. Jesus, even imagining sculpting her had him adjusting himself.

"Well, Good chat," Matt said, dragging Leo's attention to the present once more. Leo could feel the sarcasm like a clip on the head. They hadn't had a good chat in years.

"My mind is elsewhere, confused about something," Leo offered. *Jesus, that the best you can do?*

"Yeah, I get it." Matt hesitated. Unspoken words sat heavy in his expression. "Good luck with your project, whatever it is," Matt said, extending his version of an olive branch.

Leo watched his brother head to the garage's office. A part of him longed to call him back. *What would I say?*

It was like he'd lost the power of intelligent communication with those he loved. He and his siblings hadn't been close this last decade at all. It was one-hundred percent Leo's fault. Stupid of him to think coming home would simply sew up all his relationship problems. Maybe getting back to his art, his passion would help. He'd always been a better man when he was creating.

But it had been a long while since he'd felt compelled to dream, to imagine, to sculpt.

Maybe my dry spell is over. He'd ease into it. Familiar exercises he could do without a sketch. A series of stars in the night sky. Light beautifying the darkness. He pulled his welding mask down and lit his torch. The hiss of sparks leapt and struck him like the woman's luminescent eyes had last night.

A Welsh goddess who could chameleon into a raven and fly away in an instant. A murmur or beating hummed inside her wanting to break free. It was written all over her nearly stoic face and wide-open vulnerable eyes. Ancient pools of fresh spring water. Pure beauty. She gave no smile, emanated no serenity, only pure want. And like his torch, he wondered if she was equally capable of creating and destroying.

Enough now, he told himself, as the thought of past destruction sank in his gut. His work and hopefully his family were his life and the only commitments he needed. He'd learned the hard way. A bad relationship was worse than a crappy weld on a car and could leave a man in pieces on the highway, gutted, totaled.

But as Leo watched the blue flame dance before him, waiting for guidance and control over how much power it possessed, he couldn't get the blue of her eyes out of his mind. A captured flame, waiting to be set free. Free to fly and shine and conquer. And for the first time in years, Leo turned his welding torch to metal with the intent to recreate those eyes that both haunted him and for some crazy reason gave him hope.

* * * *

I can think of better ways to spend my lunch hour. Katie drove her clunker to the mechanic on Monday afternoon. Well, it wasn't exactly lunch and she wouldn't call what she was doing driving, more like swearing to the gods of shitty cars while simultaneously urging hers on to the auto shop. It was making that horrible grinding sound, and she had a feeling the starter had crapped out. Again. The *again* being the important word and the only reason she even knew a car had a starter, because the one in her van continued to throw hissy fits.

Living with her brother the last few years, Katie had learned how to fix numerous things around the house. She was quite proud of her ability to snake a toilet and wire an electrical outlet. She could even stain floors. But cars were her nightmare. Even Connor sucked at fixing cars.

She pulled into Trevi's off Logan Avenue, the auto shop she'd been using for years. The adorable owner, Matt, humored her, but winced every time he saw her van. He'd been urging her to get a new car and put her nightmare to rest. Easy to say, "Get a new car." The reality was she did not want or need a new car payment. She was saving for a down payment on a house for herself and her three girls. Three expensive girls. Money bled out of her on a regular basis. Most days she felt like she should park a camp chair on her curb, shake herself a cocktail, don sunglasses and toss money to everyone who passed, because having kids basically meant hemorrhaging cash.

She'd thought she'd love a minivan, when she and John had bought it. She was a stay-at-home mom with a toddler and a newborn. When she'd gotten pregnant with Cece, she couldn't wait to buckle in a third car seat. It had been one of the more exciting parts of her life. Yep, once upon a time, a car big enough for all her babies had made her feel like a princess.

Five months after Cece was born, she'd become a widow and felt like the gods doubly hated her because around the same time her beautiful minivan had turned into a demon. Now Katie hated every minivan on the planet. When both the car owner and the mechanic hated the sight of the vehicle, she knew it was cursed.

Now she lusted after a Toyota 4-runner or one of those gorgeous Pathfinders. She slammed her door and noticed an enormous yellow Hummer in the lot next to her. *I'd look cool in a Hummer.* "Ha!" She kicked her van. "I'm having an affair on you with a Hummer. No more pansy-assed sissy rust clod for me."

"Sissy rust clod. That's a new one," a man's voice murmured behind her. There was humor in his tone as if whoever it was found her hilarious. "Never heard a woman say she was having an affair on her car."

Great. One of Matt's mechanics had heard her swearing at her pile of crap. And he was laughing at her. She couldn't be the first person to swear at a dead-beat auto. She couldn't take any more today, but, dammit, she needed help. So, she tamped down her hissy fit, plastered on a smile and turned around. "I really need…*you?*" Katie sucked in her breath and braced against her van. Struck dumb or alive, she wasn't sure, only that she'd been punched.

She'd been incorrect at the bar on Friday night. He wasn't a *bit* larger than other men, he was from another planet. Maybe he'd been a gladiator in a former life. Through the hazy sunlight, he carved a path of absolute darkness. A black jumpsuit covered his body. Long legs ended in enormous black boots so worn they might have come from the gladiator age. *Is there such a thing?*

"Hi," she said, and smiled. Like he was familiar, like he was *hers*. She sounded different. *Am I high?* She raised her hand up to brush her bangs across her sweaty forehead. *Gosh it's hot.* It had been a mistake to leave her hair down, but the morning had been cool, deceiving. Katie tilted her chin up and studied him. *Don't you recognize me?* she wanted to say. But her own overheated, sluggish thoughts were caught by the anger on his face.

Whatever teasing he'd had in him at her car antics was long gone. He pulled long leather gloves off, planted massive hands, carved by Michelangelo, on his hips and glared at her silently. Only nothing in the air between the two of them said *silent*. A million words thrummed between them, a foreign language. One of secrecy? Hope? Belonging? No. More like ruin and anger. *I'm so confused.*

"I, you, can, I…car. You're not Matt?" *What is wrong with my voice?* Was it the scorching sun or the man standing before her? Lordy, she couldn't even speak the one language she knew.

"Nope." One clipped word.

"Huh?" She brushed her hair out of her face. *Is he mad?* He was hot, though. *Have I ever thought a man hot before?* And not only because of the ninety-degree heat beating down on them. She fanned her face with her keys, which did absolutely nothing to help the beating she was taking from the sun's rays. The force of his beauty made her dizzy. She leaned against the van for stability.

He was so fierce and striking, almost a mirage as the heat swirled around him, and something pulled her to him, almost as it pushed her away. Fire, flame and heat and it was all consuming and not enough at the same time. She dragged her arm up and pushed her hair back off her neck. *Gosh I'm hot! Is the entire fricking sky the sun? It's relentless.* "Um." She smiled because for some reason her body whispered ancient words, *You know him.*

She wanted to run her hands all over him. See if he felt as beautiful as he looked. *Oh my God.* She smacked her hand over her eyes. She was having a conversation with herself and she wasn't sure how many selves were involved. Her brain was trying to talk her down from the cliff of ridiculousness, but her soul was electrified for the first time ever. Or was it woozy, icky and hot? *I don't feel so good.*

"It's hot out." Wow, she was such a stellar linguist. But she didn't dwell on how stupid she sounded, because his eyes blazed over her, like he wanted to devour her, but would hate every second of it. *He is angry.* The veil was back from the other night, and not a hint of a smile graced his beautiful face...more like scorn. His weird demeanor was one more thing she could add to the crazy list of things happening at the moment. She liked lists. *Car in ruins, check. Feel like I might faint, check. Sweating like pig, check. Beautiful mystery man I can't stop dreaming about from the bar Friday night glaring at me, check.* She unstuck herself from her car and tried to communicate even while her thoughts tornadoed together.

"I need a mechanic," she said, taking a step toward him. She wanted to be closer. "My uh..." She gestured to her van. "I think my starter's having a tantrum again." She wiped the sweat off her forehead. Not one single muscle moved in his body. He waited, his arms tight across his chest. She couldn't even tell if he'd heard her. "Can you, uh, are you... Do you work for Matt?"

"Nope." That one word, again. She wasn't sure whether to feel lucky, relieved or insulted. Why did she feel such burning around him? And why did he glare at her like he hated her?

"Did I, um, do something?" she asked. Lordy her tongue was like sludge.

He pulled a water bottle out of his back pocket and guzzled some down. *Oh, cold water.* "We're booked up. You'll have to take your infidelity and your piece-of-shit car somewhere else." And with his final punch thrown, he tossed the empty water bottle in the dumpster, turned and walked away.

"What?" she whispered. Standing there boiling under the sweltering day on asphalt so hot it even smelled like fresh tar, with sweat sticking her curls to her cheek and forehead, his words hit her like a lance. A hidden thorn from the most beautiful rosebush. Unexpected pain.

Her Beyoncé ringtone blared. "Shit!" She fumbled her phone out of her purse. The number for the high school was on the screen. Before she answered, she glanced once more at a man she'd never officially even met and wondered how someone so stunning could make her feel like complete crap with so few words.

"Hello," she said and climbed back into her van, dizzier than before. *What the hell just happened?*

"Hi, Katie, it's Sherry, from Principal Oscar's office. There was an incident with Rosie and another student today at school. The principal needs to speak with you. You'll need to take her home after the meeting."

"What?" Katie said, all the air sucked out of her. And she flew into mom mode. "Is she hurt? I'm on my way." Praying to all the saints that her car would last a few more hours, she headed in the direction of her oldest daughter's school with a throbbing headache and insults churning in the pit of her stomach.

* * * *

"Hacking?" Katie said, deathly quietly, to her pissed-off fifteen-year-old. "Answer me, young lady."

"I'm sorry, did you ask a question?" Rosie snapped.

Any other day, possibly even if it were as hot as it was right now, and even having had the shittiest morning with car trouble, the super uncomfortable encounter at Trevi's and that she wouldn't be able to make her food deliveries, she might have been impressed at her older daughter's ability to be both scathing and sarcastic at the same time. An Olympian with her sport. But right now, Katie Walsh was three things—shocked, angry and nauseated. And she wasn't sure which one was stronger or if they all fed off one another.

Brie and Cece sat in the back, frozen. The car full of girls was never quiet. In fact, at times, Katie found it hard to concentrate on driving. *How ridiculous that my two younger ones can sense when I'm about ready to unleash my temper, but my oldest, super-smart one plays dumb.*

She pulled into their driveway. "Brie, you and Cece go in and get yourself a snack. We'll be in in a minute."

"Okay, Mama." Brie waited patiently for Cece to tumble out and follow her to the front door.

"All right, lady, you want to act like a smartass, I'm not *asking*. Tell me right now what the hell you were thinking."

"Jeez, chill, Mom," Rosie said.

"Don't," Katie said in a sharp voice. "Not only did you and your new friend break about fifty school rules, you committed a crime. What in the hell is going on? Why would you do something so blatantly wrong?"

Rosie had always been smart. But never quiet. Except for this year. The last few months, that quiet had started to worry Katie. She had drawn inward and was hiding things. Recently she'd made a new friend named Sienna and had gotten even more secretive.

Do all teens hide things from their mothers? Katie didn't know where to begin to ask for advice, but it was obvious she needed some. When Rosie did talk, she went out of her way to be as nasty as an overripe dead fish. All of them smelled the stink. Part of it stemmed from Katie not allowing Rosie the same cell phone privileges as other high school freshmen. Also, Katie hadn't let Rosie trade in her glasses for contacts yet. The social media apps on her phone were nonnegotiable, but Katie'd said contacts were a possibility if her daughter could prove she was responsible enough to take care of them. So far, that opportunity had tanked. Today was the last straw.

"It's not a big a deal. It's not even difficult. I showed her a few codes to bypass the firewall so she could get into her *Score Beauty Points* account because her mom's as stingy with you about Wi-Fi access and data." Rosie's tone was angry, short. Anger was her first defense when she was afraid. *Good, she should be scared.*

"Not a big deal? You're suspended for the rest of the week. When you go back, you're on probation for two months. You're grounded, and you lost all your privileges, including all phone ones. I need to think if there are any other punishments. Right now, I'm too angry."

"Great," Rosie spat. "It's not like I have any privileges anyway. What are you going to take away? The free babysitting I do for you once a week?" She slammed the door and stalked across the driveway.

Katie got out of the car, stormed after her daughter and caught her arm right before she hit the stairs to hide in her room.

"We're not finished, Rosie Anne Walsh."

"God, you kept it together at school. I thought you didn't care," Rosie tossed out as if she were chewing gum and blowing bubbles. "Now you're all pissed off?"

"I was trying not to vomit all over your principal." Katie raced into the bathroom where she was violently ill in the toilet.

"Mom?" Rosie said, her snotty voice gone.

"Mama?" From her spot in the downstairs bathroom, Katie looked up the stairs where Brie stood, her clothes covered in vomit. "I think I'm sick."

Chapter Four

"Fuck!" Leo ripped his helmet off his head and tossed it across the garage.

"Whoa, calm, man," Matt said.

Leo turned on his brother. "Your mechanics have your welding equipment screwed up. Several nozzles need to be replaced and this machine isn't even two years old."

"That's why I asked for your help, because I couldn't manage the shop and train new employees at the same time with the way business has increased."

"You're not going to have any business if your equipment is ruined."

Matt took a deep breath as though preparing to speak to a toddler in meltdown. "You knew this coming in. What's irritated your stuck-up ass?"

"I'm not stuck-up." Leo scowled. Disgusted was more like it, ever since gorgeous had blatantly but inexpertly flirted with him when she'd brought her car in earlier.

In the bar entrance on Friday night, she'd appeared aloof but beautiful. A current had buzzed between them. When she'd showed up with her car, he'd witnessed another side of her, not mysterious siren at all but, rather, part goofy, uncoordinated mess. She was cute as hell.

Until he saw the ring on her finger and realized she was married. Married *and* openly flirting with him. And like a moth turned to dust in a split second, all her beauty had disintegrated.

He was surprised Gage's wife, Natalie, would be friends with someone like her. He'd been fooled before by a cheater. Once was enough for it never to happen again. Once had nearly ruined him.

But fuck if he couldn't get the raven-haired woman out of his mind. So he'd gone back to work and tried to turn her image to ashes. He'd experienced a spectrum of emotions in the five minutes she'd stood in the parking lot. Surprise at seeing her again, humor, wonder if she'd recognized him. An instant later, anger had rolled in.

"Right," his brother said. "I'm not sure which is worse, you thinking you're not stuck-up, or your petulant-child tone. *Leo*, *brother*, are you ever gonna get over yourself? I like the other version of you better, the 'laid-back, life's-a-party' attitude you put out. At least that way none of us have to worry about your condescension."

"What the hell, man?" Leo shoved his brother.

"You can't even see your 'I don't give two fucks attitude' covers up your general pissed-off-ness at the world."

"I give a fuck," Leo said, shocked at his brother's words. "Why do you think I agreed to help you?"

"Don't patronize me," his brother ordered. "I didn't even want to ask for help, but I was desperate and you're an expert welder. But it's harsh to be around you."

Matt started to turn away, but at the last minute said in a quieter voice, "It's been ten years, Leo. We've all had shit happen to us. It's like you let a part of yourself get sheared off. And those of us around you have to be cut by your blunt edges. Let it go, man." And with those lovely words, his brother stalked off.

A part of him hadn't been lost or buried. It had been ripped out of his gut. He still felt the void. His family didn't even know the whole truth. And what the fuck was Matt talking about? Harsh to be around? Did the rest of his family agree?

"Hey." His brother turned back and interrupted his thoughts. "I need one more favor today, if it's not too much to ask. I have to get this tire order in, and we got a call to pick up a car for service. It's Mrs. Walsh. She's a good customer, single mom."

Leo nodded, still too angry to talk. Although he wasn't sure who he was mad at. Himself? Life?

"Take the Expedition. She'll need a car with enough room for two or three car seats. Can't remember how old her girls are anymore." He tossed Leo a set of keys and left him there fuming and alone in the garage.

Leo changed out of his welding clothes and showered in the apartment above the shop. He tried to wash as much grime off as he could. *Turns out there isn't enough hot water or soap to wash away self-disgust.*

Am I walking around generally pissed off at the world? He dressed and left his hair down. As hot as it was, he was sick of having it tied up under his welding helmet. He was sick of a lot of things. It didn't happen often anymore, this feeling like he was about to explode, but the last few days, feeling the pull to the mysterious goddess, then realizing her soul was one big mindfuck, had stirred up old demons. Demons he thought he'd shed in his travels all over the country.

He'd returned to Opal because he missed his family, and he thought he truly had excised all his ghosts. They couldn't touch him here in his hometown, in a place Monica had never been. Or so he'd thought. But one glance at a plain gold wedding ring on a beautiful woman and everything surged back up.

He drove with the windows down. The heat dissipated a bit as the sun settled into the horizon and the humidity disappeared. *Finally.* October was behaving like a fickle celebrity, unable to decide what outfit to wear. Summer, fall, no, summer. This evening air calmed him with its promise of cooler nights and more.

And now, *well shit, this day never ends*. He pulled up to the address Matt had texted and parked on the street. In the driveway was the same crappy minivan. The one attached to the very same married woman. He let out a huge sigh and dragged his hands through his hair, trying to chill his temper before he knocked on the door and pretended to be friendly.

The house was gorgeous, set back on a large green lawn. An old, two-story craftsman perfectly maintained or renovated, he couldn't tell. The workmanship was spectacular including all new windows made to replicate old. Pewter-gray shingles covered the house, and a lighter shade of gray adorned the front door. Huge black planters sat on the front porch and red geraniums still poured out of them despite it being autumn. A little girl's neon-pink bike lay on the grass beside the ugliest camo green helmet. Rockers and a swing graced the porch.

Fuck. This woman even has kids. Why is she flirting with me?

A life he once thought he'd have, the wife, a child, bikes forgotten on the lawn on a lazy fall evening. Exactly like this. Leo's anger churned over into pain. *Sneaky son of a bitch.* Would it ever leave him be? The anger seemed so much easier to deal with.

He needed to put thoughts of cheating women and destroyed lives out of his head. *Get in, get her keys, get out.* He barely had to speak to her. Leo dragged his ass up the walkway and rang the doorbell.

"What do you want?"

Damn! Leo didn't realize kids could sound so snobby. The one standing before him, maybe fourteen or fifteen, bristled like a mistress scorned. Her black hair was pulled back in a ponytail and huge blue eyes stared at him through her glasses. Eyes so pissy they felt like ice burning his skin.

"What are you doing answering the door?" he asked before he could remember his intention not to get involved.

"Duh." She rolled her eyes all the way to Hawaii and back. "I *live* here." The kid had snark, he had to admit.

"Yeah, honey, but shouldn't your mom or dad answer the door?"

"Well, honey," she mocked him, drawing out her words. All of a sudden, he had thoughts of Sister Baldrick's scornful words about to inform him of how stupid he was back in second grade when he couldn't read yet. "Since my dad's dead." She put her hand on her hip. "And my mom is helping my sister clean up puke and throwing up herself since..." At that moment a little girl with bright red curly hair and a face plastered with red freckles appeared and vomited all over the older girl's feet. "They all have the flu." Her voice changed to soft, needy. "Oh, Cece," she finished and looked down at the child.

Poor thing. He recognized her real voice then, unhidden, no put-ons, no snarly sarcasm, only pure despair. Oh, yeah, he recognized despair.

"Rosie, who is it?" a tired voice yelled from upstairs.

"Who cares," the girl yelled back. "Some stupid rude guy." Then she slammed the door in his face.

Well, fuck! Not only was his idea for a quick car swap ruined, he'd just gotten served up a landfill-size pile of crow.

'My dad's dead.' Her words had held the weight of past sorrow, something he recognized. And he couldn't imagine one so young without a father. Matt had said Mrs. Walsh was a single mom, but Leo hadn't made the connection. And wasn't he a fucking asshole. *Jesus! Fuck!*

He'd made all kinds of ignorant assumptions about her and, worse, he'd acted on them, been a complete jackass to her. *Definitely one of my worse moments in life.* There were at least three, maybe four ladies inside puking up their intestines and they needed help. He couldn't just walk in himself. Not only because the young lady who'd opened the door would probably stab him with the daggers coming out of her eyes, but no woman needed a strange man in her house "helping" even if his intentions were good.

Leo pulled out his phone and dialed his friend. "Gage, it's Doc. Yeah, I'm at Natalie's friend's place. No, the dark-haired one, Katie Walsh. I came over to swap her van out to take to the shop and it looks like they're all sick as dogs. Yeah, no shit? Thanks, brother. I'll be here."

* * * *

Leo'd planned on waiting until Natalie arrived to make sure the girls had help, then take the van to the shop, hopefully salvage it and figure out how to apologize for being an ass. Too bad Natalie ignored his attempt to leave and dragged him inside to face the destruction.

It was five hours later, and Leo had barely survived the battle. Like a four-star general, Natalie had taken charge. First, she'd stripped all the soiled bedding, manhandled him into helping remake the beds and shoved him into the laundry room with strict instructions. Then she'd gathered Katie and the two youngest in Katie's bedroom, which had an attached bath. Rosie had her own room where she'd holed up after she'd helped Natalie. Leo hadn't heard any hurling from there, but he'd also steered clear of the mini badass.

He'd cleaned up all the puke from downstairs, done two loads of vomit-covered laundry and found buckets and lined them with trash cans to put by Katie's bed in case the girls couldn't make it to the bathroom in time. He'd walked their dog, well, puppy, that they'd ridiculously named Kitten. A beautiful blond Lab who was close to one hundred pounds, but still had all the crazy energy of an animal on steroids. Then he'd found Katie's keys and driven her dying-a-slow-death automobile back to the shop where he'd picked up his truck.

After, he'd gone to the store to pick up all the foods four ladies recovering from the flu would need. Gatorade, ginger ale, apple juice, crackers, broth, bread, English muffins, donuts, lollipops… He even bought flowers. Flowers weren't near enough atonement, but it was a start. He'd texted the list of Katie's clients Natalie had given him about their food deliveries being late, and the reason why. Hopefully they were understanding and not jackasses like him.

Natalie had to leave at one point to pick up her own girls, and she'd forced him to stay by threatening to uninvite him to Thanksgiving. Everyone had stopped puking, which was a good sign, and they were all passed out or asleep with exhaustion. He was worried the girls would wake to find a complete stranger and freak out, but Natalie said she told them all who he was and asked him to stay until Connor came home.

He'd learned a shit ton in one day. Not only was he capable of being a jerk to a single mom with three girls, but that woman was Connor Duggan's sister. A man he'd met a few times since he'd moved back to town. A man whose reconstruction work Leo greatly admired and hoped to learn from. A good man, with a precious family whom he'd insulted.

Apparently, Leo did have a stick up his ass.

Duggan was on the other side of the mountains, picking up a shipment of reclaimed hardwood for one of the buildings he and Jackson Kincaid were redoing in the Corvallis neighborhood. The same neighborhood in which Leo's dream house awaited.

Now Leo had a long night ahead of him…a long, quiet night. After checking on Kitten who was sprawled on her dog bed, snoring on her back, he took off his boots, propped himself up on the oversized sectional and found an old Avengers movie. Everyone needed to believe in superheroes once in a while, even thirty-five-year-old men.

* * * *

"He has the most giganticest head I've ever seen. It won't fit, Brie." There was a trying-to-be-quiet-but-not-succeeding high-pitched voice whisper-yelling next to Leo.

"Hmm?" Another voice hummed across Leo's forehead, tickling his eyes enough to open them. One very surprised lanky girl jumped away but not before he saw she had the same stormy gray-blue eyes as her mother. Strong, like granite but lighter, and full of secret thoughts.

"Hi. You have a big head," the smaller-in-size, but not smaller in personality said. "Are you Leo? We were trying to put my bike helmet on you in case you rolled over and fell off the couch. We didn't want you to hurt your pretty head. I'm Cece. I'm the youngest. I talk. A lot! My mama says so. This is Brie. Did you puke too? How did you get such a humongous head?" Leo sat up and swung his legs to the floor. "Wow!" she whispered. "I want to be super-big like you when I grow up so I can beat up Jamie Michter, because he's always calling me Freckle Face."

"Hush, Cece," the one who resembled an elf queen said. Tall, skinny, black curly hair and her mother's eyes. A lady waiting to happen, studying him like she could see all his faults.

"I *am* Leo," he said and put his hand out first to Brie. "Nice to meet you." She never took her eyes off him and gave him one hard shake before she snuck her hand away.

"Oh, goody. I like your voice a lot. I sure do, Leo, like a lion. It's kinda scratchy like mine." Cece took his hand and dragged him into the kitchen. "Can you make toast? Since I puked everything up I'm awful hungry and Mama doesn't like me using the toaster because she says I like to burn things and stink up the whole house. And nobody likes a house stinking of burned toast."

Leo couldn't help but smile at this sprite. No flu would get her down for long. He imagined nothing did. He motioned to Brie. "Would you like some toast too, darling?"

"I'm my Uncle Connor's darling already." She walked around him to the kitchen. Before she climbed up on one of the stools by the island, she added, "But I suppose I could eat a piece."

Leo smiled. *Okay, one sprite and one honest, practical girl, nearly ready to be queen.* He had a gauge on two of the ladies who lived here, which he would count as a success. The other two were still a mystery. Understanding dawned that getting to know one particular lady who lived in this house came with a package deal. His brain was working on that notion, but first how to get over the hurdle of his giant assholeness so she would actually give him a chance. A puzzle he found he liked imagining.

"I do, you know," the little redhead said. She followed his every move. She climbed up and sat on the counter by the toaster.

"You do what?" Leo asked. He found two plates and the butter dish.

"Like to burn things," she said with her voice and her eyes and her hands she waved in front of him. He found it difficult to hold back his smile. "I mean I don't like to *burn*, burn them, like hurt things, but every time a bagel or piece of toast starts turning brown, I can't help it. I want to see how far it'll go. I mean how does the toaster *do* that? It's fatisnating." Leo didn't tell her he liked to burn things too, seeing as it probably wasn't on the list of ways to endear their mother to him.

"Fascinating," Brie corrected her.

"I like to say it my own way," Cece said to her sister, as snotty as a fairy with a Minnie Mouse voice could.

"Right," Brie said quietly and mumbled something else under her breath.

Leo wasn't sure how in the hell he'd ended up here. In a stranger's kitchen making toast for two little girls at—he glanced at his watch, two o'clock in the morning—after having verbally insulted their mother, cleaned up their puke and fallen asleep to Iron Man doing a free fall from a skyscraper. He was fuzzy about which part of the day was fiction and which was real, but for now he was going with it.

"You don't have to sleep on our couch. If you're homeless or lonely, you could move in." Leo chuckled at her simple honesty. "Uncle Connor has lots of room. He let us move in after my daddy died. We brought all our furniture. We weren't homeless, only heartbroken, Mama says. This house isn't gi-gigantic. But my mama's bed is. You could sleep with her. It might even fit you too."

"Cece!" Brie said.

"Oh, puuuleeease," Cece said. The women in this house were Stanley Cup-worthy eye rollers. "We all know Mama's lonely. How could you not be lonely in such a big, huge-O-mongous bed? And it's super nice to cuddle with someone in bed. Then you don't get nightmares. Right, Leo?"

Before he had a chance to take stock of where in the heck this conversation was going, she was off again, so he winked at her, wisely kept his mouth shut and finished buttering the toast. Although he tucked away the image of cuddling with Katie Walsh to contemplate later. He hadn't cuddled anyone in a long time. *What do you know? I really like the idea of catching up on some cuddling.*

"But you probably shouldn't move in now, 'cause I heard Mama tell Uncle Connor we're looking for our own place because it's time for us to stand on our own and time for him to get unstuck. Although I don't know what Uncle Connor is stuck in. Do you?" She batted her eyelashes at him. And he wondered how many seconds' silence he had before she started talking again.

"Hush," Brie said. "You're not supposed to eavesdrop or share family stuff."

"I wasn't. I was overhearing, not easydropping. It's two different things Miss Know-it-All. Are you a know-it-all too, Leo, my lion? I mean you don't look like a lion, more like a black bear, but your name makes me think of lions."

My lion? Leo winked at this tiny whirlwind of energy and said, "Nope, still learning new stuff, every day." *Boy, am I.*

Her eyes grew wide and shiny like she was about to cry, and she whispered as if she'd discovered the one kindred spirit in the whole world to hers, "Me too." And she threw herself off the counter into his arms which barely caught up with her actions to catch her in time. She wrapped her tiny arms around his neck and hugged him tight. Leo closed his eyes and squeezed back. *What a wonderful child.*

He felt the pain of regrets and grief of a soul like this precious one, sharply for an instant before it disappeared as Cece arranged herself on his hip and started talking again. "I thought it was a bad thing, learning new things every day. 'Cause I want to know everything already like my sisters. But if someone like you is still learning new things, maybe it's not a bourbon."

Leo placed her on a stool by her sister.

"She means burden," Brie said. Leo placed buttered toast before the girls and poured a bit of icy watered-down Gatorade for each of them. He leaned over the counter and watched as they ate. They were both a little pale, but it seemed they'd recovered fast from whatever bug they'd had.

"This is the best toast I've ever had!" Cece practically squealed.

"Things always taste like heaven after you've been sick, darlin'."

"I think it's because you made it, Leo."

Brie was silent, but she polished off her toast too.

"Now come on," Cece said and yawned. She hopped down and dragged Leo back to the living room. She handled the remote like a pro and chose a kids' nature show about turtles off the coast of Ecuador. She fluffed a pillow and curled up at one end of the couch. "Leo, will you tuck me in?" she asked.

He gently gathered a throw blanket around her tiny body. "Wow, you even tuck in really, really good." She gazed at him with awe. Brie had followed them and was curled up at the other end of the sofa, already wrapped in her own blanket. Leo wasn't sure of the protocol of being in a house in the middle of the night with two little girls he hardly knew while their mother was upstairs asleep, but, again, he didn't feel right leaving them alone. He sat down between them, stretched his legs out and settled in to learn about ocean life off the coast of Ecuador.

Chapter Five

Katie heard the television before she saw it. She must be alive, because she was pretty sure the *Octonauts* theme music would not be playing in heaven. Maybe she was near death. Or death warmed over, as her father used to say. Holy hell, her body hurt. Every single part screamed with aches. At least the vomiting had stopped. Talk about Armageddon. All of them sick at the same time. Well, Rosie had waited until it was dark to start throwing up. *Ugh!* The entire night was one ugly blur.

Natalie had taken care of them. Katie owed her friend big time. She peeked into Rosie's room to see her oldest passed out asleep on top of her covers with a bucket sitting beside her bed. Katie studied her daughter. She slept so peaceful and open. Unlike most of her waking hours these days spent glaring and eye rolling and lashing out with her venom. Or quietly seething at all of them. Katie honestly didn't know which was worse. The lashing out sucked, but the quiet unnerved her.

It was morning, early yet. The sky was tinged with the first opaque sunrays. *Maybe everyone else is still asleep.* Another thing to be grateful for. After she checked out the noise coming from the television, she might grab some weak tea and crawl back into bed if she could make it that far. It always amazed her how the flu wiped her body out so completely, and how long it took to recover as she got older.

Even getting to the bottom of the stairs, she had to sit down and catch her breath before her legs gave out beneath her. Well, she confirmed, she wasn't dead or having a nightmare. The Octonauts were busy saving anemones. Brie and Cece were curled up on either ends of the couch, sound asleep, covered in blankets with their legs stretched toward the middle.

And there in the center of her couch, also sound asleep, was a man named Leo. Natalie had told her he was here. Hmm, helping with a bunch of vomiting strangers, when at Trevi's he'd treated her like a rat daring to crawl out of the sewer. It still stung and worried her because she had no idea why he'd been so cold. Natalie had assured her he was a good guy, saying, '*Leo might come across as intimidating, but he's one of the best guys I know deep down in his heart.*'

Huh? How deep? His head was back, eyes closed, legs crossed at the ankles. His arms rested at his sides on the couch with both her girls' tiny feet secure under his hands as if he were holding them there for safekeeping. *Beautiful.* The thought came unbidden to her mind. Not only the man, vulnerable, resting in peace without a scowl on his face. But his enormous arms taking care, protecting her babies.

Heartbreaking hit her next. How much her girls would miss without a father. All those important milestones, and tiny moments like the one here, stretched out into emptiness. Their dad would never get to see them grow. And they would never get to delight in his presence, his love for them. She grieved for her daughters more than she grieved for herself. It was another layer of grief-exhaustion, to carry the weight of her children's loss along with her own.

She was grateful for Connor. But a dad was something altogether different and in this quiet solitude she felt John's absence like a jagged cut to the thumb from a sharp kitchen knife. The girls adored their uncle, but she'd always mourn their loss of a father.

Speak of the devil, or rather think of the devil. Connor walked in the front door.

She shushed him before he could get a word out, then gestured to the couch. He set his keys down and crossed over to sit next to her. "Hey," he whispered. "You're alive."

"Barely," Katie said.

"Did everyone survive or were their casualties?"

"Well, if you mean, did we all survive the flu? As far as I can tell." She leaned her head on his shoulder. "If you're inquiring about the day from hell I, and your special niece-who-shall-not-be-named, had yesterday before the flu crippled us, then the verdict is still out."

"Shit! Should I ask?"

"Nope, but you'll find out anyway. Maybe after I've had twenty-four-hours of uninterrupted-by-vomit sleep." Although she wouldn't tell him anything about her interaction with Leo at the mechanic's. It was too embarrassing to share, especially with her brother.

Plus, as rude as Leo had been to her, she didn't need her brother to get into a fight for her. He was protective about the girls in his life.

"Natalie said Leo got caught in the crossfire," Connor said.

"Mmm-hmm." Although she was pretty certain she was the one who'd been caught in his crossfire.

"He seems like a good guy. Gage and his brothers speak highly of him. Bet most guys would have run screaming from a house full of sick women. I owe him one. Guess I should let him get home. I'll carry the girls up."

Katie made her way to the kitchen and turned on the small light over the range to heat water for tea. She heard talking in the living room, but she kept her back to the voices and pulled a mug down from the cupboard. When the sweet orange scent hit her, suddenly tea equaled nirvana. Tea and honey, exactly what her body wanted right now. She hoped Leo would say goodnight to Connor and walk out of the front door, but he must have seen her.

"Hey," he said.

Katie lifted her mug with both hands and turned around. Yep, still outrageously handsome and intimidating even after a night of taking care of a houseful of sick women, one of whom he absolutely couldn't stand. Except, he was here, talking to her. On purpose. She didn't say anything. She'd already made a complete sweaty, drippy, idiotic fool of herself in front of the man, after which he'd looked at her like she was gum stuck to the bottom of his shoe. She was perfectly fine hiding behind her mug surrounded by an orange honey haze.

His hair was down. Thick, black hair. Eyes, almost as dark as a night with no stars, prodded into hers. He was more myth than man. Or any man she'd ever been with. Ha, that was funny, since she'd only ever been with one man. Only she was too tired to laugh and still delirious from the events of the last two days. It was Tuesday, right? *How many days did we lose to the flu?* God, so many messes to untangle. And she decided right then and there she couldn't do whatever this was with this man in front of her. Ordinary, single mom Katie Walsh was no match for a dark secret of a man who stood before her silent, assessing. And all her energy needed to be focused on her girls and a new start to their life.

She walked around Leo toward the front door. "Natalie said you were a big help. I should thank you."

"Listen." He pulled his sweatshirt over his head and followed her. He rubbed his hands up and down his face before putting them in his back pockets. *There were those gorgeous hands,* she thought. *Rough, and wild, those sculpted bones of his.* "I'm sorry about—"

"It's okay." She interrupted him and closed her eyes at the sound of his voice beating into her heart. She needed to ignore his luscious eyes and the rough timbre of his words, and be pragmatic. "You don't know me," she said. "I think I must have already been sick when I spoke to you yesterday. Apparently, I act like an idiot when I'm dizzy with the flu."

"You gonna let me apologize?" His gravelly voice, low and sweet, caressed her. And she knew she'd made the right decision to close the door on any sort of connection blazing fast and furious between them in a dark entryway. Because even his voice was beautiful, like warm caramel. And to feel that caress and have him treat her like shit again would burn.

She shook her head and opened the door to the early morning. "No, I…" A bit of rain had fallen overnight, and she breathed in the scent of a chilly autumn dew being gently warmed by the sunlight. This was her reality, the rain and the sunshine. Not some mythical man standing before her. "Thank you for your help last night."

For a moment she thought he wasn't going to leave. Then he moved to the doorway and paused. He didn't look at her but *with* her out to the rain-littered yard. It was true — they didn't know each other. But feeling him this close, the pinch of hurt returned, because from the first second their eyes had met at Lachlan's, life had stirred inside her as if they'd belonged to each other. Then he'd treated her like dirt.

He stepped out to the porch, turned briefly and put his hand over hers on the door. Both of them stared at their connected hands. She pulled hers back to the safety of her mug, avoided his eyes and shut the door.

* * * *

Leo was unable to lose himself in work. It sucked. His one true salvation over the years and it wasn't helping for shit right now. He trudged through several repairs at the shop, but tasks he could do practically blindfolded he instead had to pay very specific attention to, simply so he didn't fuck up by mind-wandering. He couldn't concentrate. Well, to be accurate, all he could focus on was Katie Walsh. Katie and her daughters who'd somehow touched a spot in his chest long grown over with weeds.

A wicked sorceress whose eyes carried the myths of ancient battles, but which, during their last encounter, had been shuttered. And he had no right or claim, but he didn't fucking like seeing her closed off. He wanted to go back in time to the bar when their eyes had first met, and start over, speak to her. What would he say that wouldn't sound fucked-up? Maybe he'd put his hand out, introduce himself and see if the touch of her hand in his gave a jolt every time.

Or to the parking lot when she was so obviously cute and flustered and instead of acting like the biggest jerk on the planet...yeah, he wanted to obliterate that encounter. He was so out of practice in anything involving the notion of getting to know other people. Jesus, it was clear as spring water now. He'd been fucking sleeping or hibernating for the past ten years. He'd become a shell of himself, with no substance.

Ironically, the one auto repair he absolutely couldn't complete was Katie's van. She was right to want to never see it again. It was the kind of junk that made people hate cars and car trouble. And, he found, he didn't actually want to fix it. He wanted her to have something better, something badass, something safe for her and her girls. He chuckled. Well, the longer it took him to fix her van, the longer she could use their rental. *Slowest repair ever. There's a first time for everything.*

The last time he'd shown true concern for another's safety, it had gutted him. Not that he treated people like crap, but he excelled at focusing inward. *Selfish.* Which might be worse, someone like him with his advantages in life, a solid background, his loving family, his talents, not giving a flying fuck about what went on around him.

Leo put his tools down. Like after their first encounter, he felt the desire to create. Stepping away from Katie's heap, he walked further into the bay in the back and studied the metal scraps his brother had been saving for him. One more person in his life he'd mostly shut out, but who had still been thinking of him and his art.

For the past ten years, any art he'd done had been commissioned by others, envisioned by them. His own passion and ideas, well, he'd buried those with his heart and his dreams. But now? Inspiration beat inside him, like breathing for the first time in a decade. After years of slumber something was waking up inside him, stirred by a woman, and even with the possibility of pain he wasn't afraid to let it rise. He needed to experience it, let the creativity flow or anything else would be half-assed. And Leo was tired of living halfway. Owing his rebirth to a woman who didn't want anything to do with him was an unexpected tangle.

She'd closed herself off, for self-preservation, out of fear, out of pain. Perhaps all of those. He thought he understood why *he'd* closed up all those years ago, but could he still use his own tragedy to keep himself apart from every worthy experience and relationship in life? Did he want to? No. It was time. Time to climb out of his self-imposed prison and exist with the living again. With all the beauty, warmth, pain and uncertainty that rode alongside.

Leo sat down at the workbench with his sketchbook and pencils and let his mind dream. He might be rusty, but the inspiration felt damn good.

By the time he was finished, he'd filled up pages with ideas. Several of them were a goddess in the making with her arms thrown out, her body bowed back in passion as if the morning sun were made for her, and there she stood receiving the light's caress. It was still a work in progress. Another sketch he loved immediately, oddly enough, was a lion, full mane, roaring into the night. He'd only done animals for the pieces the Native American Society commissioned from him. But this lion roared out his emotions too. Fierce, angry, vulnerable, all at the same time.

He hadn't even welded anything yet, but he felt lighter. Leo stretched. He wiped the sweat from his forehead with his bandana, then wrapped his hair up in a ponytail. It was after five, but he could still hear equipment running in the front of the shop.

"What the hell are you doing?" he asked his brother without any heat in his words.

Matt kept his head under the hood of Katie's van and said, "Jesus, man, did the past ten years deteriorate your brain too? What the hell does it look like I'm doing? Fixing. A. Car." When he finally looked up, though he was smiling, and Leo breathed a sigh of relief. They seemed back to ribbing each other for fun.

"Calling that heap a car is stretching it," Leo fired back.

"Truth." Matt wiped his hands on his rag. "Thought you'd have this new starter installed hours ago, anyway. Saw you sketching so I figured I'd finish it for you before I left."

"Was thinking we wouldn't finish it, ever," Leo said. "Let her keep the Expedition as long as we could."

"Aww, did drawing bring you back in touch with your inner soft spot?" Matt teased.

Leo cuffed him on the back of his head before his brother could dodge out of the way. "I feel bad for anyone even remotely associated with this pile of shit."

"No joke, but we can't just give her a car, as much as putting this disaster out of its misery would be a blessing for mankind. I've been on her case to ditch this mess for two years."

"What can we do for her? She's a beautiful widow with three growing girls, her own business and a car that probably sees more action here than a dealer does in Vegas." Leo noticed his brother's silence. "What, asshole?"

"Beautiful widow?"

Shit.

Matt had a huge grin on his face. "This is awesome."

"What?" Leo snapped his rag against his brother's arm.

"You are so fucked, man. Falling for a woman with three kids. When you come back from the dead, you come crashing back."

"Not what you're thinking, man."

His brother nodded, put his rag down, closed the hood of the car and said, "Right. Whatever you say. Well, I need to be on time for my date. Close up, will you? And some advice, don't dick her around. She's a good woman with a shit past."

Leo crossed his arms over his chest and scowled at his brother. Too late since he'd already been a dick. But he planned on remedying his behavior.

"Hey, so our sister's really going to be a mom, huh?" He wanted to take the topic off him, but he also needed to try harder with his family. He'd never intended to shut them out too.

"Yeah." Matt smiled. "She and Isa will be great. Whoever they adopt will be in good hands. You should call 'em. Better yet, go visit. You'd love their farm."

He laughed. "Can you see our sister, the type-A MIT graduate, feeding chickens and getting stuck in manure?"

"Shocked the hell out of me, but she's happy, Leo. And she deserves happiness. So do you." Matt shoved off the van. "And don't be embarrassed if you need a refresher talk from Mom about the birds and the bees. It has been ten years." His brother took off jogging to his truck, his laughter trailing out behind him.

Fucking idiot. But Leo found himself laughing too. He closed the shop, got cleaned up and decided it really was time. Time to wake up. Time to right some wrongs, not the least of which was being a shitbag to Katie Walsh and scaring her off.

In fact, he had several women on his list of wrongs to right.

It was well past time to make something meaningful out of his life. But how did one find meaningful amidst the rubble?

Even though he wanted to get to know Katie, from the way she'd shuttered her brilliance and vulnerability and closed the door in his face, she wasn't ready. Shit, he didn't feel ready either. Although that didn't mean he couldn't start making things up to her in his own way, quietly, behind the scenes. And it didn't mean he had to let the other ladies on his list sit back and wait.

With the thoughts whirling in his mind, he smiled, especially when he thought of which lady he was going to take care of first. One he'd been studying for months and after a lot of waiting she now belonged to him. A silent, grand, old house that might, if he laid the foundation right, help him figure out the rest of his life. What he wanted, who he wanted, who he *deserved* to have in his life. No more time to contemplate. Time to get his head out of his ass and start putting down roots.

Chapter Six

"Let's talk," Katie said. She gave Rosie a croissant and sipped her herbal tea. The week of flu Armageddon was finally over, but Katie still didn't feel back to normal. The espresso smelled amazing, but she couldn't stomach it. It had taken her girls four-point-two seconds to feel recovered. Rosie wasn't allowed back at school until Monday, so this morning, Friday, Katie had dropped the younger two off and forced her oldest to come to The French Connection with her.

Newly renovated since flooding had damaged the building a few months ago, they'd kept the old charm, rough hardwood floors, tall windowpanes and high ceilings surrounded by gorgeous trim and crown molding. She loved these old buildings with their stories hidden in the walls. The entire bakery was awash in sunlight this morning and Katie basked in the warmth like a cat, because outside it was a chilly forty-five degrees.

"About what?" Rosie said, fidgeting with her plate.

Katie studied her daughter. Along with her silence she'd begun holding herself differently. She'd always had an attitude. Katie and John had joked she was a demanding whirlwind even in the womb, kicking at Katie's stomach to announce her displeasure over many things. If Katie slept a certain way, if she ate a vegetable, if she even thought of a hamburger, kick, kick, kick! And oh, how Katie'd craved hamburgers when she was pregnant with Rosie. She'd been vocal since the minute she was born, and even though she'd been a great baby and kid, if something had bothered her, everyone miles wide was aware of it.

She was smart and unwaveringly forward thinking, but lately her attitude had turned angry and sullen. Katie didn't like it one bit.

"What's going on with you? What in the world made you think it was okay to break the law at school, and why you'd ever think for a minute I wouldn't care?"

"Not everything's about you, Mom," she said, her snarkiness surfacing. She pulled her croissant apart.

"I didn't say it was. I know high school is difficult, but you can talk to me, or your therapist—"

"I don't need therapy anymore. God, Dad died like five years ago."

"I mean to talk about other things. Whatever's so horrible that's brought all these changes in you. You're nasty to all of us, when you even deign to pay attention to us. You quit piano. You don't show interest in food. I haven't seen Charlie in months."

"Charlie's not my friend anymore," Rosie said quietly and pushed her croissant away.

"What? What happened?" The two kids had been inseparable, almost speaking their own language since pre-school.

Rosie scanned the park in the distance. "He said he didn't want to be my friend." Her words were full of vulnerability. "He called me a bitch and said I only cared about being popular, that the other people I wanted to hang out with were nasty and lying to my face."

"What?" Katie said and scooted her chair around to be next to her daughter. Rosie rested her head on the table, but Katie had seen the start of tears. What the heck was high school about these days? When Katie had been her age, she'd had her nose in a book and her biggest concern had been how hard it was to get the chlorine out of her hair after swim team practice.

"But I'm not popular. The only friend I have…is Sienna. She's popular. And I thought she liked me even though I'm awkward and wear these hideous glasses and don't have any cool apps on my phone. I was…I was only trying to help her in the lab. I wasn't deliberately trying to break the law."

"I believe you weren't trying to break the law, but as smart as you are, you had to know what you were doing wasn't allowed?"

"I thought it was a dumb school rule no one would even find out we broke. Kids break other rules all the time and they don't get suspended."

"You realize what you did was way more serious, right?"

Rosie picked her head up and used the sleeves of her sweatshirt to wipe her tears and nodded.

"What got into Charlie? That doesn't sound like him at all, honey."

"No idea. At the end of the summer we were still friends, then school started, and after the first few weeks, he started avoiding me. I didn't think anything because we don't have every class together and he had joined newspaper, but he stopped eating with me at lunch and he changed seats in English, so we weren't sitting together anymore. I followed him out one afternoon and he was so different, like he hated me. I asked him what was wrong. That's when he yelled at me and took off before I could even respond."

"Oh, honey, I bet that hurt." Katie was shocked. Charlie was one of the nicest, most unpretentious kids she'd ever known. Polite, smart, easygoing. His parents were divorced, and he lived with his dad, who worked all the time, so he spent a lot of time hanging out at their house. She realized now she hadn't seen him at all since school started two months ago.

"Yeah," Rosie said, her voice small. "More because I don't have a clue what I did." Ugh, raising kids through the teenage years might be the death of her. Her child could be so smart and mature and yet still so young and vulnerable at the same time. *So damn difficult to parent a changeling.*

"Hey, ladies." Katie turned and saw Ellie, her huge black rottweiler, Buffy, and Kitten's Labrador brother, Chewie, walk up to their table.

"Ellie, you look—"

"Pregnant, I know. It's like my belly popped out overnight," Ellie said, her entire face lit up, as though she couldn't be happier or prouder of the fact she'd finally sprouted a belly. She'd been dying to show off a baby bump since she'd found out she was pregnant at about eight weeks, almost three months ago.

"I was going to say, beautiful," Katie said. Ellie glowed. She was in deep love with Jackson Kincaid, Connor's best friend. They both had tragic pasts and now they had each other. Theirs was a love story for swoony hearts everywhere.

"Oh, my gosh," Ellie said. Buffy had her head on Rosie's lap, her eyes closed and was preening under Rosie's touch. "Wow. I mean, Buffy's pretty laid back, but she outright adores you. Hey, I have a litter of kittens at the clinic right now if you want to come see them?"

"Yes!" Rosie said, lighting up. "Can I, Mom?" Katie couldn't remember the last time she'd seen her daughter full of joy. Even though she wanted to keep talking, she'd do almost anything to keep that smile on Rosie's face for a little while longer.

"It's like a neighborhood gathering." Connor strolled up to their table. And he wasn't alone. Leo Treversini's face relaxed into a gorgeous smile when he saw her.

* * * *

There it was again, a punch to her heart. How could a man dressed in a ratty old sweatshirt and cargo pants, both covered in sawdust and dirt, be so gorgeous? Like he'd rolled in a dusty attic while painting and barely taken a break for coffee before he headed back into the fray. And it wasn't fair this intensely beautiful man was a jerk. There should be laws about that. Mean people shouldn't be allowed to be so handsome. Although, she had to admit, even though she hadn't seen him since she'd shut the door in his face on Tuesday morning, he'd been like a secret Santa doing nice things for her and her girls.

First there were all the groceries he'd stocked their house with and the puked-on laundry he'd done. He'd taken her van to fix and left her with a huge, new Expedition to use, with all the upgrades. The upgrades were fun, but the sweetest part was that he'd installed Cece's booster seat, so when Katie had gone to take the girls to school yesterday, expecting her broken-down heap, she'd not only had a pristine car with heated seats, but her baby had been safe.

Yesterday he'd left a basket full of goodies on their front porch. New colored pencils, markers, sketch pads and pretty new journals for each of her girls. A card for her with a huge gift card to Spa La La, her absolute favorite spa in town.

"Katie?" Ellie's voice brought her focus back. "Is it okay if she comes down to the clinic with me and the dogs? You could sit and enjoy your quiet morning?"

"Sure," she answered as Connor's phone rang. He stepped away to answer it. "I expect you to be on your best behavior, young lady. And we are finishing this conversation later." Katie pulled Rosie in for a hug before she took off with Ellie, the happy Rottweiler prancing between them, Chewie straining to lead the way.

When she turned back, Leo was still standing there, and her brother was gone.

"He had a drywall emergency." Leo gestured toward Connor who'd exited the café.

"Oh," she said, casting her glance anywhere but into his eyes.

"Mind if I sit?" Leo asked.

"You *want* to?" Katie blurted. His expression went from happy to pained.

"I do." He waited for her to make the decision. "I know we got off on the wrong foot."

That's putting it mildly. But she did need to thank him again for everything he'd done the last few days. She nodded toward the vacated seat and scooted hers back around the other side. No way could she handle being right next to him. She might combust from his hotness.

"Your girl seemed happy. She likes animals?"

"Yes," Katie said and sighed. "They to gravitate toward her. They're not swayed by her snarky attitude."

Leo laughed and the warmth filled her entire body. She couldn't help but smile.

"I got to experience her snarkiness the other day. When I came to pick up your car, she was the one who answered the door."

"Uh oh." Katie closed her eyes. "What did she say?"

He laughed again and took a sip of his coffee. God, she could get lost in his sexy lips, full and gorgeous, highlighted perfectly by his beard and mustache. "I think I offended her when I suggested she not answer the door alone without her mom or dad. She very succinctly explained about her dad. A few seconds later Cece puked all over her shoes. Then she slammed the door in my face."

Now it was Katie's turn to laugh. "Oh, my gosh, I am so sorry. I—"

"No, I'm the only one who should be apologizing. If you'll let me. Apparently I have a stick up my a...behind," he said and wiggled his eyes at her.

"So, it's not only me who noticed?" Katie said. She was nearly floored by the humor in his eyes. Humor was the last thing she expected from him. Every time she'd seen him so far, the intensity of his gaze had branded her. Intense curious and intense angry. Now his eyes were warm, but different. Hot coals simmering like she wanted to climb in and get cozy. Everything about this man was hot.

Leo shook his head. "No, ma'am."

"Oh, God, not ma'am!" Katie covered her eyes. "I already feel old and outdated especially after recovering from the flu."

Leo chuckled. "Leftover manners from my very Southern, very Italian grandmother who would be appalled at the way I treated you the other day when you needed help with your van. When I said we got off on the wrong foot, I meant me. I really would like to start over. Leo Treversini," he said, serious now, and put his hand out.

Katie remembered how his touch felt. Fiery and rugged, soft and risky all at the same time. Would she feel all that again? Was it worth the risk? She blamed her defenses being down after the exhausting week and the hidden ways of kindness he'd sprinkled them with, like sparks from the fire lighting up the night, and carefully put her hand in his. "Katie Walsh."

He never took his warm eyes away from hers, seeking connection as much, maybe *more* than she did. And this time, maybe the combination of his eyes searching her soul while his hand held hers she felt so much more. *Holy cow!* She pulled her fingers away and scrambled to put her things back in her purse.

"Rushing off?"

His voice was low, and he wasn't laughing now. It sounded like he was challenging her not to leave. She paused. What was she doing? Should she stay or leave?

"Katie, I was a jerk the other day, worse. I thought I had good reason, but that doesn't excuse my behavior. I'll say it as many times as it takes for you to give me a chance."

"A chance for what?" Katie said, more confused than ever.

He smiled again, and that smile thrilled all the way to her toes. "To talk. To be friends, maybe even, if you're feeling the same thing I am, to let me take you on a date."

"A what?" *I must still be feverish.* His smile never left his face and she could swear he found her shock and confusion amusing.

"You do know what a date is?" he teased.

"Technically, yes." She nodded like she was dealing with a three-year-old. Except she was the ignorant one in this situation. And how had she gotten herself into this conversation anyway?

He cocked his head to the side like Connor's puppy did when she was uncertain. "Technically?"

"Oh, my God, I'm sorry. This...I can't. I have to go. Gaah! I'm completely out of my league." She shrugged into her coat, nearly knocking her tea over. "I'm...you and me. And a date? Do I admit I haven't actually been on a date, ever? This is so embarrassing. I'm thirty-seven. I have three daughters. I was married and have no clue what a date would be like or what sex toys I like. Or how my daughter got to a point where she was suspended. I have so much work to catch up on, I... Oh! Shit!" She covered her mouth and her cheeks heated all the way to her eyebrows.

"You could hear every word, couldn't you?" she said in a muffled voice with her hand over her mouth. Katie grabbed her purse and walked as fast as she could out of the door without running like a crazy woman. Even though she was apparently full-blown acting insane right now. "Oh my God! Oh my crap!"

"Katie, wait." He gently cupped her elbow and stopped her mad getaway.

"Go away, save yourself from the crazy lady," she said with her eyes closed.

"Hey, I like it."

She looked up in surprise. "You like crazy women?" And there it was. She got to watch him laugh again, this time closer. His large, powerful body shook with it. "I am losing it," she whispered.

"I like your *honesty*. The other day, by your car you were being authentic too and I was an asshole." She stiffened and he dropped his arm. "Worse, I hurt you," he said quietly.

"Why?" she said in the same quiet voice. "I don't even know you, but it did hurt. How is that possible?"

"Because, you were walking around the world, being you, open, funny, kind, sexy, real. And I made you feel horrible about yourself. And no one should ever make a person feel bad about themselves."

"I… Why then? You… Ever since then you've been nothing but kind to me, to my kids. I don't understand."

He moved a few inches closer. "Saw you at the bar Friday night," he said as if that explained anything, but she listened, because while he spoke, he searched her eyes. She'd never had someone peer so deeply into her soul. The connection simmered hot between them.

"I remember. I saw you too." How ridiculous. Duh, they'd seen each other.

He shook his head. "It felt like I recognized you. Didn't get it. Not till I saw you again at the shop. I don't believe in coincidences. Heard you talking to your van, being goofy even though you were stressed out. You turned and I thought you were scared of me—"

"Scared?"

"People aren't always kind in their judgments, especially based on appearances. I'm not exactly small or clean-cut."

"No," she said and grinned. This was a serious moment, but she couldn't help it. He wasn't either of those things. She imagined he never had been. "Your looks didn't bother me." *Unless he means hot and bothered.*

"I get that now. I was too caught up in my own stupid shit. Then you were cute as hell, but before I could realize I mistook your shock over one soul recognizing another for fear, I saw your ring." He paused. "I thought you were married. Married and flirting with me."

His words sent her jarring back a step, but he caught her before she fell on her butt.

"Katie?" He took a step closer.

"I, uhm, there's so much...you, your words. Married?" She nodded, then shook her head. *What is happening? And why can't I form a coherent sentence?* "I am, *was*. I mean. Huh?" *One soul recognizing another. Cute as hell.* "Could you repeat everything you just said?"

His face lit up and he intertwined her fingers with his. God, it was like she'd known how her hand would feel to be tangled with his, as intense as his stare, strong, rough, safe, exciting. His heart beat through his calluses to her own skin, warming her. She stared at their hands, wanting to know his touch, then traced back up his body to his face.

"You said a lot."

"Yep." He squeezed her hand, let go and took a step back. "Meant every word. I think you feel it too. Like I said, it took me a bit to understand it for what it is."

"Understand it? What *it*?"

"The gift of you coming into my life. Your light. The connection we have. Especially since I untangled my head from my ass. Think about whether you'll give me a chance. 'Cause, gorgeous, I'm thinking it's not something either one of us can afford to miss out on." He leaned in and touched his lips, his gorgeous life-changing lips, to her temple. "Don't want to miss out on really kissing you either. Think on it." And he was gone again, strolling up the hill, occasionally glancing back in her direction to smile.

Only this time his exit was so different, it wasn't even laughable. Cryable maybe. *Life-changing indeed.* Katie stood there in the middle of the sidewalk on a bright, chilly fall day surrounded by ruby red leaves from the young maples, imagining kissing Leo Treversini, and thought, *come back*. She never wanted him to walk away again. Which meant she was in fact certifiably insane. He was a complete stranger. She needed help, immediately.

Chapter Seven

Even though he'd only planned to say a quick hello, Leo couldn't help but smile. *Take things slow and easy.* Nope. Shit, he'd tossed that thought right out of the window as soon as he saw her open like a flower again. Vulnerable, gorgeous and he'd taken advantage and gone full steam ahead.

At least she'd let him explain. It was a start. And it felt like a hell of a lot more because she hadn't shut the door, literally or figuratively, in his face. Instead she'd shown her silliness again. Not dizzy with the heat and the flu, but he'd caught her off guard with everything he said. Those open depths when she afforded him the view into her soul. This time she hadn't been sad or sick, just totally beautifully surprised, and smiling. Boy, did he like that smile. In fact he *liked* how she let every emotion show.

He'd blame her eyes. It was definitely those smoky, crystal beauties that had him admitting he wanted a chance with her, admitting he wanted to kiss her.

He walked back to the building Duggan and Kincaid were working on today. Leo's knowledge about old home renovations was extensive, but Connor Duggan was the king when it came to restoration. He was like *This Old House* crew all rolled into one, minus the New England accent.

When Leo had shown up earlier this morning and peppered him with questions about the drum sander, Duggan had stepped back and let Leo take the lead. He'd never had so much fun getting dirty as he had using the large sander to strip the wood floors. Making them shine with a new coat of stain would probably feel phenomenal. Although there was something to be said for peeling off all the old stains and paint layers, discovering one owner's story under another, like setting ghosts free.

Directly after having become intimate with a drum sander and all the dust it spit up was not how he would have liked his next meeting with Katie to proceed, but he couldn't say he was sorry now. And even though he wanted to learn more about restoring old homes, he had a different intention for seeking Katie's brother out again.

When he arrived at the work site, Connor was out front checking off notes.

"Duggan, got a minute?" Leo asked.

"Hey, thanks for the coffee and the hard work this morning. We're drowning in projects so please say you need a full-time construction job? I can use more good men or women."

Leo smiled. "Too many jobs on my plate already, but I appreciate you letting me geek out with the sander this morning. My darling is going to need all her floors stripped as soon as I clear out the rest of the garbage and knock down a few walls."

"That's right, you bought the massive Victorian on the hill with the two street-front retail spaces. Gorgeous."

"Yeah, too bad she's a disaster. It's like they destroyed her on purpose so no one else could appreciate her. I'm up for the project." Leo rubbed his hands together.

"I hate it when people destroy beauty on purpose. Let me know if you have any questions. She's my favorite style to renovate. And her foundation looks good. Can't go wrong there."

"I'll be bugging the heck out of you, but I actually have another beauty in mind I want to talk about…your sister." *May as well put it out there.* They were both grown men.

"Excuse me?" Duggan stopped his notes and faced Leo with his full attention.

"I asked her out on a date. Wanted to give you a heads-up. Man to man."

He faced the silent stare, wondered what the other man was thinking. Leo might have been perfecting the selfish asshole bit for the last ten years, but unlike the common belief, a man *could* change. Especially with the right motivation. In his case it meant shedding his disguise, his cavalier *I don't give a shit* attitude, or as his brother put it, the stick up his ass. He wanted to be the kind of man his family and hopefully someone as beautiful as Katie could be proud of.

"You're not asking permission, are you?"

Leo smiled and held out his hand. "Nope."

"Hmm, you already know she comes as a package deal. Most men would run as fast as they could right out of town."

"I like the whole package." He could also admit he was completely intimidated, but he didn't need to say that out loud. "And I've spent a lot of years running. I'm ready to let some beauty in." Still he waited. Jesus, he was bearing his soul. Did he need to shed tears? Maybe offer a blood oath?

Finally, Duggan smiled and shook his hand. "I guess taking care of all of them while they had the flu is as good initiation as any. And Gage and Nat love you." His face grew serious when he finished. "Those girls aren't merely 'some beauty.' They're *everything*. Tread carefully."

No, they absolutely weren't common. The threat or warning didn't scare him. Any brother worth his weight would have his sister's back the way Connor Duggan had Katie's. "You have my promise," he said.

Before he walked away, Duggan slapped him on the shoulder. "One teenager, and two more diving headfirst in that direction. Good luck, man."

Connor's laughter followed Leo all the way down the block, and it did not do one thing to dim his smile. In fact, he started whistling.

Guess I'm not dicking around anymore. He thought he'd have to work harder to get Katie to talk to him. Of all the ladies in his life, he'd planned on approaching Katie last, but unexpectedly meeting her today had not sucked. She'd let the connection zing between them again, and he was a goner. Of the many beautiful qualities he was coming to discover about Katie Walsh, the fact that she was so genuinely herself was his favorite. Unabashedly open without any airs. *Fucking refreshing.*

Not a bad day's work, he thought, *not bad at all.*

He winked to his Victorian before he got in his truck to head to Trevi's. *Papers signed, money exchanged, keys in hand.* Things seemed to be snapping into place. Or maybe it was due to many things, his heart being lonely and finally coming the fuck home, his brother calling him out on his bullshit, a goddess's eyes stirring up his emotions. The combination was heady, exciting. It thrilled through his blood. Making connections, the way he wanted, on his own terms. Now all he had to do was count the minutes until he could convince Katie to go out with him. And he had a feeling one date wouldn't be nearly enough.

* * * *

"Hey, girl, you okay?" Natalie took one look at Katie when she rushed into Ellie's vet clinic and came around the counter toward her.

"I think Leo Treversini just asked me on a date," she blurted out in a whisper. There was no way she wanted to have this conversation in front of Rosie.

"What?" Natalie screeched. "Here." She grabbed her coat and ushered Katie outside to sit on the bench in the sunshine.

"Don't you have to be at your desk in case the phone rings or anything?" Katie ran a tight ship of her own, three girls, meals, schools, after-school schedules, art camps, sports, music, bedtime, along with her own responsibilities for her clients, and yet she was always in awe of how other people handled their busy jobs and lives.

Natalie tapped her ear where her tiny earbud rested. "Got it covered. Now sit down and repeat everything, because I don't think I heard you right."

"It's ridiculous, right? I'm simply Katie Walsh, but I think he did, or at least he said he wanted a chance. Is he reserving the right to change his mind? I would. I mean a date with me? Feel my head—am I still feverish?"

"Okay," Natalie said. "Calm down, focus, and listen real hard because while I might be good at this kind of pep talk, I am so over having to give it. First Ellie, now you? Why in the heck wouldn't Doc want to ask you out? You're fabulous! There's no 'simply Katie Walsh' anything!"

Katie stared at Natalie and tried to calm down. "Who's Doc? And why did you sound so surprised when I said he asked me out? Because of his gorgeousness?"

"He *is* gorgeous and so are *you*! How can you people not see this? And Leo is Doc."

"I don't mean I'm not good or pretty enough, I meant I haven't focused on myself in so long. I'm simply Mom. I haven't thought about men or sex or dates since John died. Not until recently. To be honest"—she lowered her voice—"I don't think I've ever been on a date before. And...wait, he's a doctor? I'm so confused, Natalie."

Natalie giggled and started over. "Okay, Leo Treversini is also called Doc by some of his friends because he has a PhD and the guys like to tease him. It started years ago, and it stuck. I was—correction, *I am* shocked he asked you out because Leo does not date. Ever. He keeps relationships as far away from himself as he possibly can ever since...well, ever since something happened a long time ago. I shouldn't tell you because it's his business. Well, shit!" She threw her hands up. "How do I get myself in these situations? I should be a matchmaker but with the ability to set everyone straight from the beginning, so they don't have to go through all the drama. Although the drama is kinda fun to watch."

"Usually your amazingness soothes me, Natalie, but I have to admit I have no clue what is going on right now."

"I know." Natalie smiled. She stood up and opened the door. "I have to get back to work but call me if you need help picking out an outfit for your date. I rock at date-style too!" And like the badass she was, she strutted back into work and left Katie sitting by herself with no better understanding of the past half-hour.

"Picking out an outfit for what?" Katie asked herself and tried to wade through the tangle of vines Natalie had twisted around her. Before Katie could make sense of anything, Natalie stormed back out. "What the heck do you mean you've never been on a date? You were married and, newsflash, you have three daughters!"

"Uh, I thought you had to get back to work?"

"Do not change the subject on me." Natalie stood in the open doorway, waiting.

"Well, I was with John since high school. We didn't exactly date, unless you call sneaking around, hiding in my treehouse, making out in the back of his truck and jumping headfirst into marriage when we were barely nineteen. I mean twenty. God, my brain is tired!" She threw her hands up in the air. "Then babies came. There were boatloads of diapers and both of us were busy. I mean we did everything together, but we just never *dated*."

Natalie stared at her in shock. "So, you're telling me you've never been taken out on a real live date?"

"No? I mean, I don't think so. Does ice cream count?" Natalie could be fierce when things were important, and Katie definitely wasn't sure how to answer.

Natalie's face went from her thinking pose to wide-eyed, to one huge smile forming over her entire face. "Oh. My. God! Your first date is going to be with Leo Treversini! This is epic!" she screamed with her hands in the air like she was at a rock concert. And, leaving Katie sitting alone, she went back to work again without any further explanation.

* * * *

Katie left Rosie to play with Ellie and the animals and took a walk. This neighborhood, she'd played here as a child, running through the long, stretched-out park. Her parents had often brought them down for music on Sunday nights. She remembered the feeling of relaxing on a blanket in the summer evenings, surrounded by people, food, laughter. She'd thought she wouldn't like the music, but surprisingly it felt almost as good as being lost in a good book.

And of course, she remembered the fresh hot sopaipillas from one of the market stands, puffy warm pillows of deep-fried dough served with honey. Other kids went for the ice cream, but she always craved the hot, honied delights. It was her first memory of something that truly made her drool. And always late on those nights when she climbed into bed, she could still smell the sweetness on her hands.

Even though she didn't recognize it at the time, now she could see clearly that that bite was what had cemented in her a love of great food, of spectacular treats and how food made her feel.

At first, she'd started learning to cook for herself, for the discovery of new tastes and scents. It had brought, shy, quiet, book-nerd Katie so much pleasure to take ingredients and magically turn them into something else. When she and John moved in together, not only had it been a matter of necessity to stick to a very small budget, but she'd secretly loved making meals for him.

John had teased her, calling her Julia Child, but he'd inhaled everything she made, even the flop meals. The man didn't have a picky bone in his body. She probably could have fed him oatmeal and he would have been fine.

After his death, food had saved her, but not because of creativity or taste. No, for the better part of the first year after he died, she hadn't been able to taste a thing. Buried with his body on that frozen December day, the frigid air and pain obliterated desire to eat among other things. Cooking helped pick her up and get to work to support her family. Sending her creations off to others, she'd felt like an *other* too. Outside herself, disconnected. Rosie had helped too, packing up meals, labeling them. She'd wanted to be near Katie and Katie had forgotten all about those moments with her oldest daughter until now.

Regrets. Too many to count for any parent, she imagined. Mothers harbored so many. But she didn't want to linger in them, and having recognized this one, this oh-so-important one, all she could do was face it head on and fix it.

Like shedding skin, or more than one skin at the same time, it seemed as if she was on the precipice of many changes. The old homes and buildings along Corvallis were sturdy, waiting. She felt a kinship here, as if they too were ready to shed one life and become something new again. It was both strange and beautiful to her to be in her late thirties and feel a rebirth of her soul. Walking uphill, she breathed in the scent of wet leaves, burnt orange stuck to the sidewalk and a pile of yellow ones glittering as the sunlight danced in the leftover raindrops.

She found herself a few blocks past Lachlan's pub, higher up on the hill, gazing down into town. Old buildings followed the long graceful curve of the park. The river sparkled like a mirror in the bright morning light. A new florist was coming into the corner down from the pub into one of the shops her brother's company had recently restored. There were still a few empty shopfronts and several old homes in foreclosure. But one couldn't help but feel the energy exploding here, with Jackson and Connor redoing so many of the buildings. A mix of homes, restaurants, shops, community spaces. A constant hum of life, strong, resilient.

She turned away from the view and her gaze landed on a behemoth of an old Victorian on the corner. Imposing but gorgeous, even in its rundown state. And unique, the corner showcasing a curved front with a wraparound porch and, leading down from there, a gorgeous staircase spilt down the middle of two shopfronts on the street level. Ah, she loved this home. As a child, the grand dame had intimidated her, as if only the extremely wealthy and sophisticated were allowed inside. Katie had never been wealthy or sophisticated.

Now it appeared to have been through something similar to her — a tragedy leaving her in rags. Perhaps it too had been without love for many years. Rusty wrought iron handrails, missing gutters...so many details lost in the too-old paint job. The old lady was still standing, but it felt as if she were searching, begging for help.

As unrealistic as it seemed, Katie wanted her. She hadn't even seen the inside, but she could imagine. A large great room with gorgeous views. Sitting in the curved window with her coffee. Hardwood floors throughout, high ceilings, dramatic crown moldings. Shimmery chandeliers in every room. History. Ghosts. Along one block, towards the back she could see through the fence to a huge backyard and double garage set against the alley.

The storefronts at street level caught her imagination. Neither had anything spectacular about them, except for the gorgeous old windows and frames. They'd been transformed over the years too many times. One had several of the windowpanes painted. *Shame.* The other one was piled with junk and old wood boards, probably a few hidden rodents. Both had potential and dreams written all over them. One would make a perfect market-type place with fresh foods to go. Put a kitchen in the back and she could do personal chef and catering out of it.

My dream space.

Yes, she was on the precipice. *I want a home for me and the girls. I want my own commercial kitchen space. I want to cook with my daughters again. I want to not be lonely anymore.* Oh, Lordy, did her dreams have to be so enormous?

Even with foreclosure prices, this gem was out of her league.

Desires. Longing. Shedding of skin. All these powerful emotions she'd been feeling lately.

Leo's face came back to her mind, the electricity when their eyes had first met so exposed and beautiful. How some invisible power had punched her in the gut. *A recognition.* All the pretty words he'd said to her not half an hour ago.

She could admit now that from the first moment, she'd wanted him too, or at least had been drawn to him. She craved love and intimacy and sex again, but talking about it with Penny or her girlfriends was one dimensional. It was as if she hadn't fully understood desire again until she saw him, just like with this house.

She *yearned.* That was what it came down to. It felt exhilarating because she couldn't remember the last time she'd been motivated by anything other than grief and regrets or the need to mother, to simply get things done.

Craving and getting were two separate things, though. And she was seasoned enough in life to know one's dreams didn't always come true, and that one didn't always need what one wanted. An expensive new home needing a complete historic renovation, an evolving career, a *man.* Katie laughed and shook her thoughts away.

No, she absolutely didn't need a man. What in the heck was she thinking even considering a date with *anyone*, let alone with Leo Treversini? The last thing she needed right now was a relationship. After all she had three girls to get through puberty. Good grief. What she needed was a vacation!

The Victorian and Leo, both lovely warm dreams she tucked into the back of her heart. Her business was one dream she could focus on currently. And reconnecting with her daughters was at the top of her list. Two out of a handful of dreams wasn't bad to start with, not bad at all. And with a smile and her mind drawing plans, she went to find her teenager, hoping Rosie hadn't gotten into any trouble in the hour Katie had been away from her.

Chapter Eight

"I still can't believe you bought that enormous house, Leo," his mom, Mary, said. She stood in the kitchen of his childhood home and chopped garlic while his dad rolled out fresh pasta and Leo got to work on the sauce, one of his dad's specialties he'd passed down to his kids. "But I can see why you did. The charm of that old place. Oh, it's enough to seduce even the most hardened bachelors."

Leo burst out laughing. "Is that how you see me, a hardened bachelor?" He thought he'd mostly tried to stay under the radar...of everything. Apparently his family saw things differently.

"It's the nicest way I could think of phrasing it," she said, giving him the sass she'd always tossed around their family. When his mother sugar-coated things in her own unique way, it was serious.

"That bad, huh?"

She stopped chopping. "Leo, I've been worried about you since the day you were born. It's what mothers do. But since Monica died, I understand you had to deal with things your own way. But it has not been easy watching you wear a mask and keep your beautiful heart locked up, when you have so much to share with the world."

"Hmm." He leaned over, kissed her on the cheek and took the cutting board from her to toss the garlic into the hot oil. He'd really had no clue how his attitude had affected his family all these years. "I'm working on changing some things." He wanted to tell her about Katie, but he didn't really know how to explain things since he'd barely met the woman, and he figured he'd better get Katie to agree to go out on a date first before he told his mom he was potentially in love with a complete stranger. Then she'd really have cause to worry about him.

She poured more wine. "Good, because I missed you." Her voice caught.

Leo turned down the heat and pulled her into a hug.

"I'm back for good. I'm sorry I've been a pain in the ass. Missed you guys too."

"All right," his dad, Alberto, said. "Pasta's ready to go in the water, so break up the reunion and let's eat."

His mom pulled away and used her apron to wipe her tears. "Okay, while we eat, you can share the designs you have for your gorgeous house and how I can help. I want to decorate the little nook off the kitchen, with all the light coming in. It's perfect for a tiny art studio or a breakfast spot. Lots of ideas, honey, if you want my help."

"Absolutely," Leo said.

They enjoyed the spicy red sauce and garlic bread on the patio with candles and porch lights, trying to eke out the last few alfresco meals before it got too cold.

"You know the other reason I bought that house?" *Aside from wanting to fill it with family.* "The two small storefronts out front came with it." He waited till the end of the meal to mention it because he suspected his mom's reaction.

"One used to be a pawn shop?"

"It was a butcher first, a German sausage shop and butcher. The other was a small repair shop, and then too many stupid things to acknowledge."

Leave it to my father, the history professor, to have memorized all the history of that neighborhood.

"Yep. They're both empty now and not too run down. Updated wiring and plumbing. With a few finishing touches. I thought one side might make a great studio for kids' art classes."

His mom put her wine down, stared at him. Her expression blossomed into excitement. "You talked to Matt?"

He nodded.

"I want to see it right now." She stood, grabbed their pasta bowls and turned toward the house. "I'm making coffee for us to take. Then we can go."

* * * *

"I couldn't have picked a better spot myself," Leo's mom said. She strolled around the soon to be kids' art studio.

"Well good, because I wasn't sure what I was going to do with it."

"I'll need your help," she said. "Look at those windows. We'll get so much wonderful light in here."

Leo nodded. "Whatever you need. In between all my jobs and working on the house, I'm all yours. Shouldn't take much to get her polished up."

"You know she means helping with teaching too, don't you, son?" His dad was taking measurements and notes to see how many long art tables would fit.

"What?" Leo said.

"Duh, honey," his mom said, linking her arm with his. "You're the real artist in the family."

"The real artist?" Leo roared with laughter. "You're good, Mom. I'd almost forgotten. You haven't lost your touch at all."

She gave him her smile of success. "Nope. In fact I'm still perfecting my butter-you-up skills." She rubbed her hands together. "Thought I'd gone all rusty, but apparently not."

"Not rusty at all. But *you're* the real artist."

"The PhD behind your name begs to differ. Besides, I'm no welder or metal artist and think of what the kids in this neighborhood would discover with those kinds of classes." She raised her eyebrows that came with an attitude of their own. "I could do the painting and sculpture and you could do metal welding. We could help each other. Maybe put some feelers out for what other kinds of classes kids would be interested in. Come on." She shook him. "Think of how much fun we could have together. Plus, we could entice more boys with you as one of the teachers, I have a feeling."

"Anybody home?" Connor Duggan knocked on the glass door and poked his head in. Before he could say anything else, a flurry of red curls ran past Connor and threw herself at Leo, who again considered himself lucky he caught her.

"Leo, my lion," Cece said and put her tiny hands on his cheeks. Hers were covered in chocolate like she'd decorated her face with war paint before a battle. "I never thought I'd see you again! Where did you go? When I woke up you were gone."

"Whoa, sorry, Leo." Duggan tried to contain his laughter. He turned to Leo's parents. "Connor Duggan. My niece, Cece Walsh, otherwise known as Leo's long-lost best friend," he said by way of introduction.

"I've heard all about you, Connor, and the work you're doing here in this neighborhood. It's wonderful." Leo's mom shook his hand. "I'm Mary, Leo's mom, and this is his father, Alberto."

"Hi," Cece said. "Leo took care of us when we were all puking. Do you like my new boots? They're for riding horses, but my mama can't afford to buy me a horse. After I was done puking Leo made me the best toast *ever*! He even watched Kwazi rescue hammerhead sharks in the open ocean with us. And he tucks in real good."

"You're very lucky," his mom said seriously. "Leo takes good care of the people in his life. Did he make you his special honey tea?"

"No," Cece whispered. Her beautiful eyes grew huge and they all chuckled.

"Forgot about that," Leo said, thinking back to when he was a child and his grandmother had taught him how to make honey tea, sometimes with a splash of whiskey, when he was sick.

His mom winked at Cece and offered her hand. "Want to see my new studio where Leo and I are going to teach kids' art classes?"

"Art classes?" Cece whispered with the reverence of someone witnessing a miracle. Scrambling down from

Leo's arms, she took his mother's hand immediately. "I love art classes."

Mary showed Cece the space and described exactly how she envisioned it looking.

"Huh? Two minutes in your mom's company and my niece is the quietest I've ever heard her. Mary's like genius-level super parent, isn't she?" Connor said.

"She has a way with kids," Alberto said. "She's missed teaching since she retired, but she is going to love this space and being with kids again, Leo. You just made up for ten years of worry. Well done, son."

"Ten years, huh?" Connor asked. "I bet there's a story there."

"Not any kind of good one," Leo said. He didn't know if he ever wanted to tell his story, but now was definitely not the time.

"Better told with whiskey on a dark night kind a story?" Duggan said.

Or maybe never. "Exactly. Where are the rest of the ladies?" Leo asked, to change the subject but also because he was curious about Katie. After their talk the other morning, she'd looked confused in a cute way, as if she had no idea what to make of everything he said. It was way better than the hurt he'd put there last week. He'd give her time to settle into the idea and hoped she'd grant him that chance he asked for. Not too much time though—he had a life to make with her and her girls. He smiled at the thought because it didn't scare him in the least.

Connor smirked at him. "Rosie's grounded, shut herself in her room. Brie is working on a writing project and Katie's cooking up a storm for her clients. Cece was feeling neglected so I brought her to get hot chocolate and see how the neighborhood's changing. She likes to see the work on the old homes and buildings. I swear she's going to be a general contractor someday. She's got the bossy voice down pat and she likes to tear things apart and put them back together." Duggan smiled, proud of his family.

"Uncle Connor, we have to go home right now." Cece dragged Mary back with her. "I'm going to take every class here and they cost *money*, so I need to talk to Mama about how to make more money. I wonder if art classes are more expensive than horses?"

Cece made them smile with her pixie voice and more hot chocolate on her face than she probably had in her body. And those red boots, they appeared two sizes too big, but she didn't seem to mind. Leo'd make sure she got to take as many art classes as she wanted, if it was okay with Katie. He had a feeling he was going to enjoy this ride and that it was going to be unlike any he'd been on in his life. He couldn't wait to plan one magnificent first date.

Chapter Nine

There were days, many in fact, when Katie accepted her true career — a revolving door chauffeur. Drop Cece off at elementary school, take Rosie to the connected middle-high school on the days she missed the bus, which seemed to be frequent. Mondays she dropped off her clients' food she'd made over the weekend, followed by a trip to the grocery store. Some days she tossed in a visit to Ellie's clinic because Connor's dog insisted on getting into trouble at least weekly. Then round two to pick everyone up or drop them off at lessons of some sort or another. The zombie life. Today she had the added pleasure of, after running errands, going back to the high school to talk to the guidance counselor.

Rosie had mandatory meetings scheduled for the time of her probation, but Katie had made her own appointment. She didn't mind all the running around in this behemoth Leo Treversini had loaned while her junk heap was being surgically repaired. Maybe he'd make a mistake and burn her van down. *Would car insurance pay for that?*

This gorgeousness was huge and comfortable. It had heated seats and smelled like new car. *Mmm*, Katie sipped her coffee in the parking lot. Maybe she'd sit here all day. Then she wouldn't have to deal with anything. Not her teenage daughter drama. And definitely not hot, amazing Leo Treversini. She was trying really, really hard not to think about him.

She'd mostly succeeded. Okay, she'd completely failed. Then Cece had come home last night, her hot-chocolate-covered face screaming about art classes with Leo and Mary.

An artist? How many pieces to the Leo Treversini puzzle were there? First a shrouded mystery in a moody bar. A mechanic with a chip on his shoulder, who, until he opened his mouth, had appeared out of smoke like a gladiator fighter pilot from a different dimension. A helpful stranger who took care of her and her girls and not because he had to, it appeared, but because he wanted to. A secret Santa, leaving them gifts on their doorstep. A dusty, steaming hot mess who'd followed her from the bakery to the vet to apologize, get super close then make her insides feel like triple flavors of ice cream swirled together in all their goodness. Piece by piece, she was learning about him.

In the end a gentle gladiator who kissed her forehead, left the ball in her court and walked away. She could have sworn he'd whistled down the sidewalk.

And of course he had a PhD. Nope, the man wasn't the teensiest bit intimidating at all. Regardless, she couldn't deny the smile blooming on her face when she thought about his words.

John had been wonderful, but he'd never made her entire body practically vibrate with the need to be closer to him. And she never once would have used the word fierce to describe her late husband.

Everything about Leo screamed it. Fierce in size. Fierce in intensity. Fierce in beauty. *I mean that body.* Katie fanned her face. And those lips, *eyes*, she meant to think eyes, but as compelling as they were in their inky dark depths open to her and exploring hers, it was those lips so close to hers and the feel of them on her skin that thrilled her.

He wanted more with her? A single mom of three crazy girls who didn't even have her own address.

With his gorgeous looks and talents and passion, she couldn't help but wonder what a date with Leo Treversini would be like. He sure was fun to daydream about.

* * * *

"Katie, so good to see you," Mariam Ahmed, the district guidance counselor, said. Tall, thin, dark clothes to match her dark skin. Black hair piled on top of her head in a large bun. The first time they'd met, she'd struck Katie as more of a fashion model than a real person. It only took mutual tragedies shared in a grief group to see Mariam was as real as the rest of them.

Today, her arms overflowed with files and paperwork and her mug barely hung off one thumb.

Katie took the mug to help and smiled at her old friend. They'd met in group counseling after they'd both lost their spouses and had quickly become friends. Mariam was the kind of friend Katie valued deeply.

There was none better to watch over middle and high schoolers.

"Why has it been so long since we've seen each other?" Katie said when they embraced. For a few seconds she closed her eyes and soothed an old ache. Even in grief, Mariam's dark brown eyes always shone with such gladness, welcoming. It was the first thing that had drawn Katie to her while they'd stood drinking horrible coffee all those seasons ago.

"Life is always moving us along isn't it? And while I know you're concerned about your girl, I'm so glad you came in. Please, sit."

"Mariam, I'm about to sound like one of those ignorant parents who doesn't have a clue about what is going on with their child After last week, I...we need help. I feel like hacking is only the tip of something. I don't have a clue who this Sienna is. Her best friend dropped her. My girl has become so withdrawn. I thought maybe it was teenage angst, but things are starting to scare me."

"I was shocked to hear Rosie was involved. After learning more from Principal Oscar, I'm probably going to add more stress to your life, but I'm here to help. It turns out, Rosie actually did the hacking, not Sienna."

"God." Katie covered her eyes with her hands. "How? Why? What?"

"Now." Mariam started with a small smile. "This might not make you happy this instant, but for a fifteen-year-old to have the knowledge to do what she did? Well, let's just say her programming and math skills surpass those of most college graduates today."

Katie gave a wry smile in return. "She's always been academically smart, but hacking? I had no idea her street smarts were abysmal."

"Honey, I haven't met a freshman with street smarts! Apparently, the girls were trying to get into their Score accounts."

"Which is what, exactly?

"Score Beauty Points. The straight answer is it's a social media app for girls to learn about beauty. My screaming bitch answer is it's where girls learn to use physical appearances to bully, shame and manipulate others. Like the worst type of clique online. You post photos and other people score your appearance and leave comments.

"There's almost no safety or protocols for who can use it, what photos can actually be used for. It could be grown men behind the accounts too. Basically a parent's worst nightmare and internet safety shit storm."

"Whew, don't sugar-coat it for me."

Mariam rubbed her forehead. "I definitely do not envy parents right now, Katie, but as a damn good counselor and your friend, we are going to get through this and help Rosie, and hopefully a bunch of other kids struggling too."

"I'm so glad these kids have such a kickass counselor like you," Katie said and made her friend smile.

"Now, let's talk about her friend dropping her."

Chapter Ten

Katie wasn't sure if talking to Mariam had eased her worries or not. One thing was certain, she was a supreme idiot and horrible parent for having no clue about so much of Rosie's life and influences right now. Social media was absolutely going to give her a heart attack. She had three girls to get through to adulthood and days like today made her seriously question her abilities to get them safely through to *tomorrow*. Regular cliques were bad enough, but online bullying?

It turned out that the morning was a lot more than speaking with Mariam about Rosie's school life. It was an entire education for Katie about teens, internet safety and a bunch of crap she had to look forward to for the next decade at least. If her youngest didn't already have her own social media accounts. Hah! She wouldn't put it past Cece.

Adding to her already fabulous day, she had to return the beautiful comfortable car and pick up her demented psycho van today. She definitely didn't want to give up this luxury she was currently driving, but she could admit she was both giddy and nervous to see Leo—like a schoolgirl—and a tiny bit nervous to see him back at the scene of their horrible interaction, Trevi's.

Since then he'd been nothing but kind and generous and *hot*. The man was so insanely gorgeous, he made her shimmer. But even with his apology and grace like a wolf, his long legs and huge muscles— *Gah! Get a grip, girl. Don't forget what a jerk he was last week, all angry and jumping to conclusions and insulting*. It was a fact. His words could singe both in good and painful ways, she needed to remind herself.

Lusting after a hot body was one thing. Being without for so many years, she could give herself that, but swooning when he was near was not playing it cool, and she intended to be composed. *Right*, she sighed, and pulled the comfy Expedition into the lot, because she'd been perfectly calm and breezy every time she'd interacted with him so far. Yep, Cool was her middle name.

"Hey, Katie," Matt called. She walked into the office and tried to hide her disappointment that it wasn't Leo who greeted her. "You sure you want your van back? We replaced the starter. Again. But a new starter is only part of the problem."

She closed her eyes and sighed out all her stress from the morning so far. "I know, I know, Matt. The real solution would be to toss it over a cliff and put it out of its misery, but I'm trying to hang on a bit longer." All her dreams from the other day filtered through her mind like late-afternoon rays, casting long, flickering lights. Too bad the dollar signs behind them snuffed out the pretty glow. "Having no car payment is really helpful right now."

"Honey," Matt started, and she knew what was coming.

"Oh, Lord, don't *honey* me. It's a money pit and I pay more than it's worth each time it needs a new starter, and I'd be better off with a new car, but—"

"Hey."

She and Matt both turned toward the door as Leo, dressed in a suit—*Good heavens, he's lethal!*—walked in. *I might faint*. Talk about singeing, the man burned a path of gorgeousness on a boring day, but in a charcoal suit with a shimmery granite tie! What was he thinking? One silk tie would take away from his intense edge? Was the man mad? All it did was make him sexier.

She was too busy lusting over the way his suit fit him perfectly, over the contrast of the pale gray dress shirt against the skin of his neck and black beard, that she almost didn't see him motion to Matt to leave them alone, nor did she realize how close he'd gotten until she could smell that wonderful, hidden woodsy cologne and heat. A combination full of more potency than any one man should be allowed to own. She closed her eyes, took a deep breath and smiled. *I'd like to uncover each and every mystery he possesses under that gorgeous suit.*

"Gorgeous? You okay?" Katie blinked her eyes open to see him grinning down at her. *Yep, cool as a cucumber, all right.* But what was a girl to do? She huffed out another sigh and he chuckled at her.

"Stop laughing at me," she said. "There's something about you. You come near and I...I feel all wobbly inside." *Welp, super smooth. The epitome of chill.* "No!"

She put one hand over her eyes. "Stop. Be quiet, you I mean, me. Me…I mean my mouth says the stupidest things around you. You are not supposed to be in a suit." She peeked through her fingers at him. His goofy smile said she was officially losing it. Which she was. Officially. Every. Single. Time. Around. Him. Except for when she closed the door after he'd helped them through the flu.

She realized her other hand was sitting nice and pretty pressed up against that dark pearly tie and Leo Treversini's warm chest. She tried to pull it away, but he was faster. He placed his large hand over hers and held it there. And, as much as she probably should listen to her own pep talk from earlier this week about not getting involved with anyone right now, she really, really liked how her hand felt warm and tight between his chest and his rough hand.

"Katie Walsh," Leo said, and she looked from his chest and where he held her hand to his face. Eyes to eyes. Pretty much the best feeling he'd had in ten long years when he got to drown in those ancient wise pools of hers. Dangerous and heady and so, so open. He had the deep pleasure of watching her face light up. Her smile, the way it warmed her entire being, was a sight to behold. Aimed at him, it was a treasure. One he intended to take good care of.

"Hi," she said, and ever so slightly leaned closer to him, as if she were finally giving herself permission to be close. And that he liked even more than her smile.

"You're all dressed up," she said, still not taking her eyes off his.

"Had an interview. It's just a suit," he said. Her eyes grew wide and her smile, if possible, got even wider.

She shook her head, which teased his nose with her scent, flowers, dried lavender, musky like his own wild garden. *Sexy as hell on her.*

"There's no *just* anything about you," she said quieter now, contemplative. "What are you doing here?"

"I work here." He grinned at her. Her warmth swirled around him. She still seemed dizzy, out of sorts, her body responding to his. He liked how she didn't or couldn't hide it. *I feel the same.*

"Not looking like *that* you don't." She gave him some sass.

"Like what?" he asked, quietly.

"Stunning," she whispered. "Intimidating."

"Exactly how I feel about you." He pulled her closer. "You feel that?" She nodded. The connection between them was a warmth he'd been without for too long. *And those full lips of hers.* Those did not say silly and uncoordinated at all. Nope, they spelled siren. And he wanted. "Wanna know something?" He lowered his voice.

"Yes," she said.

"I really want to kiss you right now." He leaned in one fraction more. "But I'm not going to."

She huffed in a breath, giving him her beautiful confused grin. "You're not?"

"Nope. Don't want our first kiss to be in the front office of our greasy garage."

"Oh." She nodded like she understood, but couldn't hide the disappointment on her face and he held back his grin. "We're going to have a first kiss?"

"Unless you don't want to." Damn, he hoped she wanted, but he tossed the decision back in her court.

"I think I do," she whispered.

"I'll let you think on it."

"All right. Our garage?" She looked around and stepped back. He let her go, let her hand fall and ached at the absence of her soft skin immediately.

"Matt and I own it together. I've been silent for years. Our grandfather left it to all three of us, me, Matt and our sister, but it was always Matt's dream. I've been helping out since I've been back."

"Oh, so you own part of a garage, you teach kids' art classes, take care of sick strangers when they have the flu and you have a PhD."

He closed his eyes and sighed. "Heard about that did you?"

"Wait, and you said you had an interview. How many sides to you are there, Leo Treversini?"

"A lot of those are simply labels, Katie Walsh."

"Right. But a lot of those labels say an awful lot about you. Are we going to keep calling each other by our first *and* last names?" She grinned. And as much as her disarray around him was adorable, her warming up to him enough to tease him was hot.

"I like your first and last names, Katie Walsh. Like the way they sound on my tongue. Feels like I discovered something amazing and precious every time they roll off my tongue. And I really, really like seeing you blush when I say them—"

"I don't blush," she protested, still using her sexy hushed voice, as though she couldn't believe it herself.

"Mmm-hmm," he answered, tucking his hands in his pockets to keep from grabbing her back to him. He was practically bouncing on his heels with energy for her. This day kept getting better and better. Every side she showed him—confused, shy, demanding, strong, wanting—combined to form his goddess. *His.* No question. A thought he'd definitely have to contemplate later. He wanted her to be his, like he wanted to be hers.

"I feel like you and yourself"—she swirled her fingers around his face—"are having an entire conversation about me in your head you're not sharing." *Smart too.* His sexy, smart goddess. Yep, he officially liked this day.

"Stop." She covered her eyes.

"Stop what?"

"Grinning like you've uncovered all my desires and you want to devour me."

"I don't know all your desires, Katie Walsh." Her cheeks flamed when he left the most important part of her sentence out for them both to contemplate. Because he did, want to eat her up, savor every inch of her. "You think about a date with me yet? Did I give you enough time to consider?"

"A weekend could not ever be enough time to consider a date with you, Leo Treversini. Besides, I'm too busy to date. You're too busy."

"We could be busy together," he said and winked. Then he had the pleasure of watching her roll her eyes at his cheesiness. Her face was so damn expressive. "Come with me, Friday night. There's something I want to show you. It doesn't even have to be a date. It could be us having another interesting conversation together. Casual. Two adults, out with each other, some awesome kisses."

"You're pretty sure they're going to be awesome?"

"Absolutely. Those lips of yours, warm and soft against mine."

She didn't just blush. He swore she leaned in closer to him again, lured by the pull that twined around them. And those eyes of hers got smoky every time he mentioned kissing. He couldn't wait to see her face transform when he pressed those lips against his...and when he explored the rest of her body.

"Picking up your albatross?" He changed the subject before either of them melted into a blushing puddle on the cement floor.

"You fixed it," she said accusingly, with a hint of a pout on her face which went right to his dick.

"Believe me, I didn't want to." He took a step closer, caging her in against the counter. Fuck, but the only thing he wanted to do right this instant *was* kiss her. *Liar*. He wanted to a whole lot more than kiss. He was having a hard time carrying on a conversation with her standing so close to him. And yet she wasn't close enough, not to his liking. Naked closer, under him, on him, wrapped all the way around him—that might assuage his hunger for her.

"Oh?" She leaned back and met his gaze.

"You're right about it being a piece of shit, but what worries me is how unsafe it is."

She bristled. "It's been me and crappy-van for years now. I can handle it."

"I'm not trying to insult you or be snotty about it. But if it keeps breaking down, it could happen somewhere at night, you delivering your food, all alone, or with one of your precious daughters. Before you get even more angry with me, from what I've seen so far, you are one hell of an awesome mother and woman. If you've been driving that piece of shit for as long as you have, then you also know I'm right.

"And I'd bet you've been having the same worries as I described. So, while I'm certain you can handle it, it would ease my mind if you didn't have to. We have some used vehicles in great condition we could talk about. The Expedition you've been driving, for one." Leo didn't like how the cute had wiped away from their conversation, but all fired up and defensive were just as attractive qualities. She was one strong woman, and that added to her sexiness.

She relaxed her shoulders and sighed. "Sorry. I get defensive. I know I need to replace the demon, I...it's..." She looked down and swallowed. Focused on his chest, she said so quietly he almost didn't hear her, "I bought it with my husband."

Instinct had him bringing his arms around her in a hug. An instinct so dusty and unused he almost didn't act on it. But when she melted into him, he was glad he did. And even gladder when she started shaking. *Shit.* He mentally slapped himself upside the head. She wasn't over her dead husband yet. Inwardly he sighed because he couldn't make a play on a woman who was still mourning her first love, fanfuckingtastic kisses in store or not.

But then she pushed away from him, leaving her hands on his chest and she wasn't crying, she was laughing. "And isn't that the stupidest reason to hang onto a car giving me more stress than all three daughters combined. I mean I was trying to kick the crap out of it the last time I was here. What am I thinking?"

He held on to her and gauged her mood. Was she still mourning her husband?

"I've hated that car for years, but buying it with him is one of the last memories I have of us being happy before he got sick. It's not one of—it is *the last.* And sometimes, Leo, when that pain lances through me, I think how dare I toss away our last happy memory.

Then I realize, it's only hollow echoes of grief toying with me. Echoes which will probably always be a part of me. Whether I keep the menace van or not, I'll still have the memory, right?"

Right then and there, Leo made a place inside himself for all the special parts she trusted him with. Precious glances into her heart, flirting and calling him *Leo* in her soft, sexy voice. Intimate, warm, open. In their few encounters, she'd shared more about her character than any woman he'd ever been with, including his wife, which both humbled him and reminded him he needed to tread carefully here. "Yeah, darlin'," he said, wrapping her back in his arms. "Sacred memories are yours. You can hang on, keep them safe, new car or not."

"You want to know the truth?" She searched his eyes.

"Always. I always want the truth," he said. How deeply he meant those words after his past.

"I don't want a car payment," she whispered, like it was a state secret she was confessing.

"Right." He smiled at her. "But think about how much that heap is costing you. Probably makes more sense to trade it in and when I say trade it in, I mean burn it to the ground, so no one ever has to come in contact with it, and get something safe and reliable." He couldn't figure she had much in the way of a mortgage, seeing as she lived with her brother, but he really had no idea about her finances. "Matt and I would give you a good deal." He squeezed her gently and loved the feeling of her pushed up against his chest when she spoke.

"I bet you would."

"I like it when you tease me." He leaned in and folded her backward a bit.

"Hmm." Her hum vibrated through his chest and her smile changed from flirting to hot in an instant. He wondered if she was aware of the change or what she was capable of. "Here's another truth. I want my own house. I mean one for my girls and me. I feel like the college drop-out who still lives in her parents' basement. I've been saving, but I may never be able to afford my dream. Maybe I'm afraid to try. I don't know. I want to expand my business, start catering and add to the personal chef part. Those are all details. What it comes down to is, I feel selfish."

Leo laughed. The warm smile filled her face again.

"I do. All the sudden I feel like I'm waking up, and I *want* things, Leo Treversini." *Is she reprimanding me for laughing at her?* She gripped his shirt. She could reprimand him all she wanted if this was her way.

"It's okay to want things, Katie. And a new house, your *own* house and expanding your business aren't necessarily selfish. And if they are, that's okay. They would also benefit your girls. Double points," he said. "What else do you want?"

She paused and stared at him. "A date with you." And her eyes grew huge, as if she couldn't believe what she'd said.

Chapter Eleven

The only good thing about this class, Rosie thought, as she walked into art, *is neither Sienna nor Charlie is in it with me.* So, neither her new friend, who was overpowering and — Rosie was learning — super manipulative, nor her old friend could share this space with her. It was a relief of sorts, to be in a space where she didn't have to feel stressed out the entire time, worrying about what one or the other was thinking, or even worse, not thinking about her. She could breathe easier.

The annoying thing was, they had a new art teacher, so they'd have to do the *let's get to know one another* crap. She barely knew herself these days, let alone how to explain who she was to others. Every art teacher was the same. All of them ordering them to copy what they did, line for line so all their art turned out exactly the same and the teacher could hang all the perfectly pretty pieces on the school walls. She was tired of pretty copies, because it was all a lie. Life wasn't perfect, and neither was art.

Great. She walked into the classroom on Friday morning and saw Mr. Treversini leaning against the teacher's desk welcoming each student. *Really? He's our new teacher?* All she'd been hearing at home was Leo Treversini this and Leo Treversini that. If it wasn't Cece singing his praises and proclaiming she was going to take painting classes with him, it was Uncle Connor crushing on his renovation skills. The worst was that he'd asked her mom out on a date. Rosie sure hoped no one in school found out. Her year was going swimmingly already. She wasn't sure she could take much more loveliness.

Can't wait to see what kind of art this clown has in store for us. She found a seat at the back table and buried her nose in her latest graphic novel. Maybe he wouldn't even notice her.

"All right," he yelled and clapped his hands together, once loudly. It startled her enough to glance up. He had on a black flannel shirt, dark jeans and old motorcycle boots. "We're here for art. If you're not supposed to be in this class, leave now and we promise not to laugh at you." A few people laughed. Most stayed silent. This used to be one of her favorite subjects. When they'd gotten to play and create, when it had felt good.

Last year they hadn't even had art, as their teacher had had a baby during the first week of school and no one had been able to find a replacement. But before that, Rosie had begun to lose interest. She didn't see how copying was learning anything, and she'd found out the hard way that whenever she deviated from the instructions, she got in trouble.

"Since I'm late to the game and we have a lot to accomplish, we aren't wasting any time," he said and passed out two pieces of paper to everyone, a blue permission slip and a blank lined piece of paper. "Get these blue slips signed and return them to me ASAP, please. We are going to UsedUp. To explore and pick out pieces for our year-long exploration on self-discovery."

More than one student groaned or sighed, and Rosie felt their pain. *Self-discovery, great.* Exactly what high schoolers wanted to do, study themselves. Worse, Leo chuckled at their obvious pain. *This is going to be awesome.* She rolled her eyes. *Please don't act like you know me.* She stared at him. He only paused for a second and must have heard her silent plea, because he kept going. *Whew!* She could give him points for not being a *total* loser.

"Now, tuck your permission slips away somewhere safe and take out a pen, because before we create, we talk. Then we write."

More groans filled the room, but the students did what he asked.

"Now, because I know how much you all love to volunteer, I'm going to make each of you talk for a few minutes, out loud, to the entire class. I promise you won't melt into a puddle of embarrassment and the pain will be over soon. You," he said and pointed to the table at the front of the room where two juniors sat. "You two start. Then we'll move on to each table.

"Tell me two things, your name, and what art means to you. I'll start to give everyone an example." He leaned back against his desk. "I'm Leo. Mr. Treversini, if you feel like being formal. To me, art is beauty and pain, regret and anger, forgiveness, exploration, protest, carnage, creativity. It's emotion exploded through whatever medium you choose. It's a journey, a way of connecting to others, a savior." He smiled and scanned the room. "To me, it's the bravest form of self-expression. My goal this year is to help you become great artists, and to do that, you need to learn about yourselves."

The entire class was stunned into quiet. He pointed to the first table and said, "Gentlemen, begin." Even though she still wore her mask of indifference, Rosie listened to each student. Some joked, a few spoke softly. Corey Bluementhal said art was for tortured old men who couldn't find a date and Mr. Treversini chuckled. "I see I have my work cut out for me."

Then it was her turn. And she didn't know what to say. Her norm lately, which she hated. She had all these huge feelings and she couldn't figure them out or understand them. She certainly didn't feel comfortable talking about them. Especially not with a teacher who looked more like an action figure, *and* who was wiggling his way into her family.

"You're up, kid," Leo said, nodding at her.

She quickly glanced around the classroom. "I'm Rosie." She wished she could be outside under the riot of leaves changing colors, waiting to be cast off their branches, hidden, quiet. "And, I don't know anymore what art is to me," she said in her harsh tone. *Shit*, she thought, she hadn't meant to be so honest or sound so stupid.

But Leo nodded and said, "I'm sure many of us feel that way at times. Which is why I hope to help you all figure it out for now, as I believe its meaning to each of us can change as we grow. This class, this journey is going to be awesome. Now take a few minutes and tell me what you'd like to learn this year. No names on your papers. Free expression. No one will judge. Help a new teacher out and put all your crazy down for me to see."

Chapter Twelve

"I can't think of a better way to end my day, Katie Walsh," Leo said into the phone when he answered, which immediately made her smile.

This man. How am I going to tell him we can't date? Even his phone voice stole into her body like lava and awakened a path throughout. *And his words. A woman could get used to this.* Too bad she'd have to save it all for her dream life. She could take all these delicious memories to her solitary island vacation and they could keep her company.

"Are you driving?" she asked. Normally she hated talking to people when they drove, because even if they were hands-free, she stressed for them. And they always sounded tinny and staticky, but not Leo. Of course his low smoky voice would power through even the car sounds.

"Yeah, darlin'," he said. *Darlin'?* Had she ever been anyone's darling, let alone someone as hot as Leo? "Coming home from a visit with my parents'."

"Oh," she said and sank down into the chaise lounge on the front porch. She had a blanket wrapped around her to ward off the chilly air, and a glass of red wine beside her. All the girls, including their rapscallion, Kitten, were asleep. It was late, and she should have been in bed, but unfortunately, she needed to get this call out of the way. However, now she wanted to savor the sound of his voice. "Was it a good visit?"

"Yeah, always is with them. We grilled out. Trying to soak up every last warm-ish night on their patio before the cold sinks her claws into town. Had my mom's cider doughnuts for dessert which means I might need a gazillion extra hours at the gym, but it was worth it. What are you doing?"

She didn't know which image she liked more, him eating cider donuts or him in workout clothes, sweaty, at the gym. Good Lord, she was a goner.

"Katie?" he prompted.

"You work out?" came her stupid reply. His chuckle shook her out of her Leo-induced sex haze. She blurted, "We can't date."

"Come again? How did me saying I work out take us to not dating?"

"You're my daughters' art teacher," she whispered, as if worried someone would hear her. Not that it mattered because everyone in her house knew before she did. Mr. Leo Treversini, PhD, was the new art teacher for the middle and high school. Her girls had shared this information with her in their very different ways. Brie had announced it as soon as she'd gotten home. And when Katie had asked Rosie's retreating back if it was true, her oldest had said, '*Yep*,' before she'd escaped to her bedroom.

The icing, however, had been Cece's meltdown to rival all meltdowns because it wasn't fair, Leo was going to be *her* art teacher and her baby hadn't decided whether or not she was going to share Leo, my lion.

When had Cece decided Leo was hers? Another great parenting moment for Katie. Gold stars all around. Her youngest had already formed a serious attachment to the man which included calling him her lion, talking about him, his toast-making skills, his beautiful mother and his art classes. It would have been kind of cute if Katie hadn't decided she couldn't date one of her daughters' teachers.

"Thank you for the congratulations on my new job. Please keep your praise to a minimum," he said, full of humor. And dang, she couldn't help it—the man made her smile like no one ever had. "I am in fact. Accepted the position this week. Thought art teachers were genuinely liked?"

"I can't date my daughters' teacher."

"All right, then I'll put in my notice tomorrow." This time *she* laughed.

"Leo," she admonished.

"Katie." He mocked her in his charming fun way. It was as though witnessing her crazy life made her more likable in his eyes. "Technically I wasn't employed with the district yet when I asked you out and you said, 'Yes'. Although I *had* just come from the interview."

"Wait, what's a man with a PhD doing teaching kids?"

"Not to toot my own horn, but shouldn't we want highly educated people teaching our kids?"

"Absolutely," she said. It was one more thing to like about Leo. People should demand the best of the best instructing their kids. "It... I... Is it a step down for you? I mean, most people in our country don't get a PhD with the intent to teach middle school, or, all the guardian angels help you, high school."

"It is not a step down," he said. "But you're right, I never thought I would teach, even at a higher level. I was one hundred percent focused on making art. It turns out life had other plans. But now I get to create and influence young minds and I couldn't be prouder to work with those kids."

What other plans did life have for you, Leo? "Maybe you're crazy. Most of us want to run screaming from middle schoolers, me included," Katie said.

"Nah, I get 'em. And I was kind of a shit when I was their age. You meet my mom—she'll be happy to tell you some doozies." He laughed after he said it.

"Leo," she sighed.

"Where are you?" he asked, serious now.

"On my front porch."

"You by yourself?"

"Yes."

"Good."

"Why?"

"Mmm, I have my reasons."

"Are you going to come spirit me away to my newly imagined dreamland where I don't have any responsibilities?"

"Sounds good, but no."

"I do want to go on a date with you, Leo. I haven't wanted something for me in a long time, but it feels like the world keeps giving me signs I *shouldn't* go out with you. And I feel like I need to listen. Too many complications to think about."

"Hold that thought," he said, and she heard the click of him hanging up.

"Leo? Leo?"

"Right here." He stepped out of his truck now parked in her driveway.

"What?" She was too shocked to move. She spoke into her phone, even though he wasn't on the other end anymore. His strong, lean body climbed the porch steps, stopping shy of the last one. *Dazed again, by Leo Treversini.* Until Kitten started barking.

"Oh shit." She jumped to open the door, before their crazy dog woke all her other babies. Of course, having good taste ran in the family and Kitten lunged herself right at Leo and put her paws up on his shoulders shaking like mad, tongue lolling out of the side of her mouth as Leo rubbed her down and made her purr. Yes, they had an enormous blond lab named Kitten who purred if anyone rubbed the special spot right above her left hip. Everyone giggled or rolled their eyes at the name Connor had given the dog, but it was more apropos than it first appeared. She acted more like a cat than a dog, chasing the sun for naps, purring. And when she slept deeply, her tail swished back and forth, reminding Katie of a lazy feline with no worries.

"Come here, you crazy mutt." Her brother came through the door to grab Kitten. "Leo, Katie," he said, smiling when he saw them both. "Hands to yourselves now. No funny business." He smirked and dragged the dog back inside before he shut the door to thankfully give them privacy.

"Never a dull moment in our relationship," Leo said, chuckling.

"Leo, we can't have a relationship." Katie sighed and wrapped her sweater tighter around her.

"Beautiful, come here," Leo said, and she went because the man had superpowers over her. Since he stayed a step down, they stood almost eye to eye. He was still an inch or two taller, but she didn't feel quite so intimidated.

"What are you doing here?" she asked, and instead of answering, he pulled her into him. And all rational and responsible thought disappeared, because she couldn't deny how good it felt to be held by him. Katie sucked in a breath. All the shedding of skin and wanting she'd been experiencing smoothed away in his arms. No more wandering and searching—instead it was like being home. How could that be wrong? Not to mention the way his touch sent her blood thrilling.

"There's nothing inappropriate about you dating me and me teaching your girls. It's two separate things, Katie." The man could read her mind.

"It feels irresponsible."

"It feels like you're searching for excuses. Which I can appreciate—you have three girls to raise. I absolutely respect that. If anything, it makes you sexier in my mind, the way you are with them. How you've taken care of them by yourself. You put them first."

"Crazy man," she whispered and inched closer.

"What are you afraid of?"

"Everything," she blurted out and got to watch him smile up close. That didn't feel bad either.

"We had this conversation before, a few times. You get worried. I talk you down. If it helps, I'm afraid too, but being with you makes me feel the best I've felt in a long time, Katie. If you don't feel the same, then us going out might be irresponsible, me being your daughters' teacher. Because you don't seem like a casual-fling kind of person to me. But this connection we have—and please tell me again you feel it too—it's a once-in-a-lifetime feeling. I promise to take care of your emotions. You don't have to worry about me hurting you again."

Snuggled up against his warm body, she could smell him, after a long day's work, engine oil, a hint of charcoal from his dinner. She leaned her face right into his chest. "You smell good," she said, her voice muffled.

"Mmm." His voice rumbled through her.

She raised up on her toes and wrapped her arms around his neck. He was like a boulder anchoring her. One hot, solid rock she wanted to roll around on, naked. *Oh!* The thoughts he stirred up in her suddenly very active imagination. And his eyes this close... midnight swirls of desire. The evening wrapped around them in their own special cocoon.

Complicated? Maybe. Irresponsible? No, she thought. There were plenty of adults with kids who handled dating without freaking. And she wanted to date Leo. Every new thing she learned about him, every new way he sought to make her feel comfortable were gifts to enhance her life.

She didn't want to wait. Instead, she went for it, slowly to surprise him, studying his rugged face. She moved closer. Thick lashes hovered over his obsidian eyes. His expression intensified and a small whitish scar became visible within the laugh lines around his lips. The curve of his mouth enticed her, and she leaned in, closer and closer, until eventually she hit her aim and touched her lips to his. *Softness, warmth... electrifying.*

She froze, suspended in time, and tried not to sigh into a puddle of lust as she savored each sensation. His body locked around her, sending hot sparks through her body. "You have the prettiest eyes I've ever seen,

Leo Treversini," she said quietly against his mouth and expected him to smile, but he didn't. He didn't smile at all.

In an instant, his life transformed. Leo locked his arms around her, securing their connection. Her lips were lush, and his entire body went hard. *Jesus!* One brush of contact scored through him like a lance, burning, intense, mystical. She rested there, utterly still, until she spoke, not in a whisper, but quiet, smoky. His entire body vibrated with the desire to take control and skyrocket their kiss. Instead he closed his eyes and treasured the extraordinary.

Her soft, warm lips, resting on his, their bodies tucked together in the darkness. No kiss had ever been so perfect. One instant of sublime pleasure, a soul-opening flight into the graceful curve of the earth.

Slowly she let her lips roam, exploring his. They didn't delve deeper. It could hardly even be called a kiss, and yet, maybe this was how it was supposed to feel. Surreal, each nerve ending on his lips hummed alive with her light movements. Her gentle breath on his skin as if she were an invisible feather mapping his features. Her lips getting to know his.

"Leo?" she said, and he savored that too, her voice rippling through his body, the way her hands tentatively caressed his neck under his hair. He was breathing for the first time after a grief so deep and painful, no one but him knew it existed. An underwater hidden rope no longer held him. Her caress set him free and put him back together after a decade of brokenness.

Without breaking the connection, he nudged her nose with his. "Yeah?" he said and had the pleasure of feeling the current pass through her body. Time flowed in slow motion. Her heart beat in sync with his. Leo breathed in the scent of her skin like warm bread and lemon. He wanted to drown in the red wine lacing her lips, her secret hint luring him to take, to discover all of her.

Sin and salvation mixed together. Every cell in his body surged, akin to the moment after he lit his welding torch, a second before he set the fire to metal and sparks flew. They breathed each other in. Slowly, softly she moved. He left his eyes closed so his skin could focus the warm brush of her lips on one cheek, then the other. She used his body for support, pulling herself up, and he moaned at the feel of her. Trusting in him, so she could reach higher to place her lips softly on each eyelid. No one had ever touched him so carefully. Now he was the blind one, memorizing each gift she gave him. *Reverence.* She paid his skin reverence. And he basked in it.

Her soft palm on his cheek added to the sensations rippling through him. She carefully snuck her fingertips under his black beanie and he nearly stumbled at the delicious contrast of her cold fingers on his warm scalp, as her small but strong fingers tangled in his hair. As if she were trying now to climb inside him. His entire being rumbled with barely controlled vibration.

It wasn't until her chest shifted against his, gentle curves against hard muscle, and her mouth mapped a path to his ear, and with those sinful sainted lips whispered, "Leo, you make me *feel*," when he lost it.

He grumbled out her name, "Katie," and lifted her away from him, digging his hands into her hips. Hands that wanted to play with her skin, to reciprocate, to tease, to suggest, then to ravage. *I make her feel?* Sweet

Jesus, it took all his strength not to devour her right there on her front porch for the entire neighborhood to witness. "Damn, woman," he ground out.

And there she was before him, his goddess, her hair whipping out behind her. Eyes on fire with lust, with power. Even the dim porch light flittering across her face gave her blush a sensual quality. Nearly hidden was the uncertainty on her face, and he wanted to wipe it away. "Do you have a clue what you do to me?" He gently squeezed her waist. "I need to say goodnight and head home before I give your neighbors a show." Leo turned and made his way to his truck. "Oh, and Katie." He opened his door and before he climbed in, said, "Best kiss ever."

Their best kiss ever might have electrocuted his nerves, but it was the last glow of excitement on her face that gave him a restless night's sleep. And, damn, but he'd never enjoyed a lack of sleep better.

Chapter Thirteen

"The pink ones!" Cece screeched and bounced on Katie's bed.

"My princess," Ruby said to Katie's youngest daughter. "You have got to calm down a smidgen if we are going to paint your nails tonight."

"I know what a smidgen is," she said, throwing herself at Ruby who caught her. Cece clung with her tiny body like a koala to a tree.

"I'll bet you do," Ruby said, twirling her around. "Now, let me take care of your mama. Then we'll have a nail-painting party."

"Can we paint fire-breathing dragons on my nails, Miss Ruby?"

Katie giggled at her daughter and at Ruby's expression. "Ruby's pretty talented, honey, I bet she can paint dragons on your toes."

"Funny," Ruby said, dropping Cece down in a backward somersault. "Your mama is absolutely hilarious." She used her fake British accent which had Cece turning over into giggles.

"Honey, go ask Uncle Connor to order your pizza before he leaves." Katie and Ruby watched the little girl race out of the bedroom.

"Now, Ms. Walsh," Ruby continued with her fake accent. "Tell me what the dress code is. It's a good thing I'm here early or we would be in disaster land right now, young lady."

Katie mock glared at her. "First of all, you're here early because you're babysitting my minions tonight. Second, disaster land? I haven't even gotten dressed yet. And third, I have at least ten years on you, missy."

"Eight, in actual years. Fashion years are an entirely different form of measurement." Ruby dramatically fake swished her jet-black hair, cut in a new sleek bob, over her shoulder. "Oh, the young lasses who don't know how to dress for a date." Ruby fanned her face. "Because you've never. Been. On. A. Date!" she whisper-yelled. "How, in all that is spectacular in the world, you — gorgeous hot mama — have never been on a date? Did your baby girls magically appear out of thin air?" Ruby spoke as much with her hands as she did with her words, all expression, all the time, and was swirling them now through the room.

"Ugh." Katie tossed more clothes on the pile and sat down next to them. "Long story short, John and I dated since high school. We were attached at the hip, but never really went on dates. We were young and in serious puppy love. I went from ignorant, shy girl with her nose stuck in old mystery novels to one half of another person. John and I spent every second we could together. Then we got married and made babies. I barely blinked, and he got sick and I had a funeral to plan as a widow. Now here we are!" She flopped back on the bed and closed her eyes. "Oh, Lord! I can't believe I actually said yes to Leo. What the hell was I thinking, Ruby?"

Ruby sighed and sat down next to her. Then she poked Katie until she opened her eyes. "I bet you were thinking saying no to a date with that magnificent specimen would have been a sin, amiright? And good Catholic girls like us don't sin."

"Partly." Katie giggled. "He is gorgeous, isn't he?"

"Uh, duh! But Natalie also said he has a heart of gold and what a beautiful combination, smoldering good looks and love inside."

"Yeah," Katie sighed.

"Now, where's he taking you? Some fancy restaurant? A boat ride along the river? Candlelit terrace dinner?"

"Uh, no," Katie said. "His exact words were, 'Dress casual, comfy shoes, nothing you'd want to get dirty.'"

"What?" Ruby's screech was reminiscent of Cece's. And watching Ruby's face contort in horror was so awesome Katie burst out laughing.

"An epic first date of all first dates and he tells you to 'wear nothing you'd want to get dirty'? Is the man clueless? His one fault. There had to be one somewhere." Ruby shuddered.

Katie was so grateful Ellie, Natalie, Sasha and Ruby, a small group of silly, intelligent, kind, brave women now considered her part of their circle, and wanted her to experience an epic dating life.

But she sure had the jitters, ever since Monday at the auto shop when her frail barrier had been whisked away and she'd stood wrapped in Leo Treversini's strong embrace, her body against his. First his cheeky flirting, then his tenderness in listening to her expose a bit of her heart and she'd…she'd, God, she'd split open in the best way. Free, her body turned on again, humming.

And not just turned on in a sexual chemistry way, although Holy Mother she had been! She had been a walking zombie, going through the motions as a mom, a chef, a sister. Leo's attention, and the physical way their bodies fit together, felt like *belonging*.

Their almost kiss last night on her front porch…*talk about epic.*

I haven't wanted a man the way I want Leo in ever. No, wait. That can't be right.

"Am I doing the right thing?" she said softly to Ruby as the doubts crept in. Her age, her responsibilities — which came before everything — her duty to honor her late husband…

"What? You're not chickening out on this gold ticket chance. No way. This is the dream we all wish for, and you're living it."

"It's just…Ruby, I feel…" She put her hands on her stomach. "Shaky, guilty in a way, like I had my chance at…love, life? Am I ridiculous or what?"

Ruby leaned over. "Honey, I don't know what to say about losing your husband. But I do believe you should take the chances you have in life to grab onto something beautiful. You deserve to give this a chance, without any guilt. And a man like Leo deserves to grab on to something beautiful too, you."

"Is it really so simple?"

Ruby stood. "Simple, amazing or both, I think you should try. And," she said and winked at Katie, "maybe you're feeling butterflies because you're hoping for a spectacular kiss *or more* on your date to end all dates!"

"If it's going to be as incredible as you imagine, I sure hope it's not the last date ever," Katie said and they laughed.

"Come on." Ruby shook her hands out like she was getting ready for a fight in the ring. "We can do this."

She rifled through Katie's clothes, went in and out of the closet talking to herself the whole time and finally said, "Okay, these cute skinny jeans make your butt look awesome. This floral top with the capped sleeves. A bit flirty, a bit sexy, gives flare at the hips and Leo won't be able to keep his eyes off your cleavage. I think your mini goddess was right—the sparkly pink tennis shoes and that gorgeous fuchsia bomber-type jacket with the fake fuzzy collar. You know, to keep you warm in the cold autumn night. Although for the sake of women's dreams everywhere, I hope there will be other things keeping you warm tonight." Ruby fell back on the bed, fanning her face.

* * * *

Katie neared the landing and the murmur of voices from downstairs reached her. Even Rosie's voice was noticeable and surprisingly not snarky. *Small miracles.* Her brother had left. Thank goodness, because he'd been giving her shit all week about her date when he informed her Leo had asked Connor's permission. She was definitely going to have a word with Leo. She didn't need anyone's permission. She was her own woman, although she had found it kind of cute he respected Connor. Leo Treversini was full of surprises.

And speak of the man himself. She had the pleasure of watching him unannounced. He was grinning down at Cece, who had her hands on her hips, huffing and puffing at him. When Katie got to the bottom of the stairs, as if sensing her, Leo turned his head up and he didn't just glance. No, she was right about there being no *just* anything about him.

His eyes flared into desire. But his mouth, those gorgeous lips of his, almost smirked as if he remembered the way hers teased his and was now ready to do some of his own teasing. *Paybacks. Yes, please.* He didn't hide his perusal and his expression smoldered as if he loved what he saw, like he'd won the lottery. One flash from his gorgeous eyes and he had her practically fainting. She was the winner, here. She didn't even have her coat on yet and the temperature soared through the roof while he delivered silent messages of desire.

"Leo, catch." Ruby tossed Katie's jacket to him. Katie nearly started giggling at the glare Ruby gave Leo. It said so much but mostly it silently and boldly yelled, *'Don't fuck with my friend. You feel me?'* Ruby might appear glamourous, but she also had a police detective father who'd insisted on Ruby taking self-defense classes for years. Katie was pretty sure she could be a bruiser when she needed to be.

"Mama! You didn't tell me I didn't get to go on your date with Leo," Cece demanded as if Katie had stolen the man out from under her tiny toes. "You *said,* 'we' have a date tonight."

Katie lifted her daughter's chin up. "*You* have a date with Ruby and your sisters. I have a date with Leo." A twinge of guilt tugged at her heart. This wasn't only the first real date she'd ever been on. It was the first man she'd even been interested in since John had died. They'd all seemed fine with it when she told them. Well, everyone except Rosie who'd sighed with annoyance, loudly enough for the entire universe to hear. Katie's reservations shot into her heart.

With the poutiest lips Katie had ever seen, her precious babe said, "You be nice to him, Mama. He makes the best toast I've ever had."

Toast isn't what I expected to come out of your mouth. Katie found it extremely difficult not to laugh at her daughter's Shirley Temple-like drama, but with heapings of practice she was able to keep it together. It was also a relief to know at least one daughter liked Leo enough to care about his well-being. She nodded solemnly. "I promise to be nice to him, and you promise to behave tonight."

"K," Cece said, smiling up at her. And she nearly had Katie in tears when she marched back to Leo. "Leo, you take care of my mama, okay? She's the best mama I have. She loves me through all the cookie factories in the entire world, *and* back! I can't afford to lose her too."

Then Katie really had to keep her shit together when Leo put his hand on his heart, knelt down and said, "I promise, firelight."

"Firelight?" Cece whispered and swayed into Leo.

"Yeah, sweetheart. You're as pretty and powerful and bold as the light from a fire."

Cece wrapped her arms as far around his huge frame as they would fit. "I sure do like you, Leo, my lion."

Leo pierced Katie with his eyes, then smiled at her daughter. "Good, because I like you too."

Brie and Rosie huddled over Ruby's makeup and nail polish organizer. Kitten sat between them, her tail and tongue wagging, as if waiting to choose her polish color too.

"Everybody be good tonight," Katie said.

Brie smiled at her. Rosie pretended not to notice them although she did make room for Cece to push her way onto her lap, which was huge, because Cece loved her big sister, but Rosie had made herself extremely unavailable lately.

Leo held her coat up, his secret grin of appreciation lingering.

"You be good too," Ruby said and winked before she shut them outside.

C h a p t e r   F o u r t e e n

Pink Converse. This woman kept surprising him. He hadn't been sure what to expect when he'd told her to dress casual, but he hadn't imagined her walking down those stairs so amazingly cute and sexy. And damn, the warm scent of her hair he'd gotten when she stepped into her jacket — spicy, sexy, floral. He wanted to wrap his arms around her, pull her to him and breathe in every inch of her. If they hadn't had a full-house audience of her daughters and Ruby, he might have. Of course, he might have also turned her around, pushed her up against the door and kissed her while stripping her sexy outfit off her. She was all he could think of after last night. He'd been in a lust fog all day.

Instead, he took her hand, led her to his truck and right before he helped her up said, "Hey."

"Hey," she breathed back, staring into his eyes.

"You look beautiful," he said, hustling her up against the door, and he took his time studying her, like a new piece of intriguing art. "I like the shoes."

"You said I should wear something comfortable." Damn he liked her voice, especially mixed with the feel of her fingers on his neck.

"Mmm- hmm." Suddenly casual and comfortable took on a whole new image in his head. Her naked on his bed, waiting for him. He closed his eyes and leaned in. "Smell good too."

"Leo?"

"Yeah," he said, lost in her.

"Are you going to kiss me again?"

He stayed close, but opened his eyes and smiled, surprised at her honesty and the hope in her voice, when he'd thought her nervous as she'd come down the stairs a few minutes ago. "Oh yeah."

"Oh yeah?" she said and if possible, her voice got sexier.

"But not right here in front of your brother's house." And he watched the disappointment take over her face. It was going to be a *fucking* long night. He smiled, but it was also going to be fun and sexy as hell building up this tension with her.

He helped her up, rounded the hood and climbed in. As soon as they were driving, she said, "Speaking of my brother, I have a bone to pick with you, Leo Treversini."

"Using both names when you're mad at me? And we haven't even had our date yet," he teased and took hold of her hand. He was going to take every chance he had to touch her tonight.

"Not mad." She softened her tone and took in their joined hands. Her thumb caressed his skin as if this were the first time she'd ever touched him. The woman could convey awe and discovery simply with her quiet presence. With each moment, she healed more of him.

"Katie," he prompted when she didn't continue. "You're mad I talked to Connor?"

"Not mad. I just don't need anyone's permission to go on a date."

"Hmm." He pulled his hand away so he could park. After helping her down from the truck, he leaned in close. "I'm liking this spot a lot."

"The car door?" She batted her eyelashes at him. "I had no idea how romantic you were."

He wrapped his arms around her. Their bodies were flush together — his favorite place to be. "This okay?" he asked.

"Mmm-hmm." That fucking gorgeous smile of hers could make a man forget more than where he was, could make him forget all his past sins and regrets, all his future goals. *Caught perfectly in the present.*

"I like it when you tease me," he said and brushed her hair off her shoulder. He had to touch her hair, soft, mesmerizing. Jesus, he'd never been so lost in a woman before. *Ever.* Maybe ten years of fooling around and never connecting with people had left him so wanting when he finally found someone worthy, he dove in headfirst. None of this easing-in-slow bullshit. Yet, at the same time, for this woman, he'd go at whatever pace she wanted. He had a feeling every step would be worth it. "I like this spot because I get to be close to you, Katie Walsh. I like leaning into you, or…" He switched them around, so he stood against the truck and she was resting against him. "Feeling you against me."

Her laughter rumbled through him. "I'll admit," she said, holding on, "this is a pretty nice place to be."

"Yeah," he agreed and fuck, but they were both like two teenagers in lust. He liked this feeling a lot. "I didn't ask anyone's permission to take you out."

Clarifying this point was important to him, because it mattered to her.

"Connor and his ego have been teasing me all week about you asking him." She searched his eyes.

"I didn't *ask*," Leo said. "I informed him I wanted to date you. From one guy who wants to be an important part of your life, to the one who already is. Respect. I've been working with him. Didn't want him to think I was a dick. But to be honest, if he'd gotten his feathers ruffled, I would still be taking you out tonight. Now, as much as I really like being wrapped around you like this, we have a reservation. Are you ready to have some fun?" He turned Katie around in his arms to face the bar.

"What is this place?" Katie asked. *'Are you ready to have some fun?'* he'd asked and she thought, *Finally! He's going to kiss me*, because a meeting of their lips had *fun* written all over it. Fun and hot and wild and dangerous and *oh boy* he made her senseless. Ever since the other day at the auto shop when he'd mentioned all the kissing, and on her porch when she'd caressed his skin with her lips, lip dancing with Leo had been all she could think about. So far there had been nothing more than a very few intense moments in the dark last night. One of the most profound experiences of her life. But she wanted more.

Calm down, honey, she told herself. *You've never been one to be whiny and selfish. Not selfish*, her other self said, *needy*. Good lord she needed to quit talking to herself in multiple personalities.

She was trying not to show her disappointment at their lip distance, but her confusion was another thing. "Where are we?"

"Giocare," Leo said and tucked her hand in his. "Come on." Before she could question, he'd opened a towering wooden behemoth of a door and led her into a noisy bar. Only it was so much more than a bar. Once inside, the entire place extended up with enormous ceilings. Tiny white lights streamed across the dark ceiling beams. Down the left side was a long bar with high shelves displaying what looked like every liquor bottle in the world. She'd never seen so many bourbons and amaros at one time. How she'd love to get her hands on some of those for cooking.

In the back, toward the end of the bar, sat small tables with low booths in dark purple velvet. Stretched out to the right, also with seriously high ceilings with more pretty twinkling lights, were long stretches of super-fine fake green grass, like carpet. People stood playing a game with heavy balls. She turned to Leo and found him watching, not the action in the bar, but her.

"Bocce," he said. "Thought we could work up an appetite before I feed you." And he wiggled his eyebrows. "I reserved a court for us. Tried to think of what we could do on a first date that didn't include me taking you right back to my bed and having my way with you." He'd leaned in to whisper in her ear and tingles zipped through her body. *Whew!* She couldn't tell if he was teasing or not, but she could picture it in hot vivid detail. "But it is our first official date and that didn't seem quite appropriate for someone like you."

"It didn't? Why?" And she knew he could see the pout in her lips when he chuckled. *Again, with the blurting things out loud!*

"I want that," he said.

Phew. I do too. Could she, Katie Walsh, widow, single mom of three girls, really be allowed a man like Leo to have his way with her? She wanted to have her way with him, too.

"But I want a whole lot more with you. I want to know everything about you."

"I want to get to know you too." And goodness she couldn't take her eyes off him. "We better get something to drink, Mr. Treversini. I need to cool down." She took off her jacket. *Two can play at this game.* If he was going to tease her silky red panties right off her, then she could make him feel the pain of waiting too.

"Hmm," he grunted and motioned for the bartender. "This might be a lot harder than I thought." And Katie burst out laughing. "What'll cool you down?"

You, she thought, *but only after you engulfed me in flames first.* Then she'd come down from this flaming high he'd put her on. "A cold beer, something not too hoppy would be great," she said.

"Two," he said to the bartender. "And we have a reservation for six o'clock under Treversini." He leaned close to her ear. "Ever played bocce before?"

"Leo, I haven't even heard of bocce, but if involves you standing close to me and showing me how to move, I have a feeling I'm going to like it."

"Killing me," Leo said, cozied up against her back and caging her in gently to the bar. "Killing me, woman." His nose nudged her ear and sent sparks all over her skin.

"You started it." Katie faced the bar but felt each spot on her body where Leo's touched her. "This place is beautiful," she said, scanning the shelves behind the bar with all the bottles, lined up and sparkling.

"Mmm-hmm," he said directly in her ear.

She placed her hands on the wooden bar top and caressed the surface. Lordy how she wanted to do the same to Leo's skin. Good thing their beers arrived because she was about three seconds away from turning around and letting Leo have his way with her.

"Number four," the bartender said, setting their beers down.

Letting out a ragged breath, Leo took her jacket and his beer while she grabbed her drink. Then he wrapped her hand in his and led her to one of the open bocce courts. *Court? Arena? Field? What did one call a place to play bocce? And can we play holding hands? Because I really like my hand in his.*

The place buzzed. People drank and laughed. Once in a while cheers soared from one of the games. She and Leo were at the last court against the wall. Behind them was a tall round table and a few stools where Leo set their drinks and hung their jackets.

Scattered near her feet sat four red balls, four blue balls and one small white one. Balls! Of course, because her mind had been permanently stuck under the heading of *Hot & Bothered* since Leo had first wrapped his large hot body around hers at his shop. His *hard* body. And she'd imagined him ravishing her on his workbench with all his tools scattered around. Last night, her dreams had been of kissing him like she'd done on her porch. Only when she'd felt his control slip, he hadn't set her back and walked away, but instead unleashed their want for each other right on her front yard. Why did she have to live in a calm, neighborly neighborhood and not the middle of nowhere, some remote mountain cabin with a huge fireplace and an even bigger bed?

"Katie." Leo nudged her. She'd zoned out for a minute. Hmm, that seemed to keep happening around him. She couldn't say she disliked it. Nope, not at all.

"I'm not very good at ball games," she said and watched his wicked smile take shape. A long sip of cold beer helped cool her off, a smidgen. She pulled the glass away and fanned her hand in front of her face to help bank the coals. Nope, it wasn't working, especially as Leo put his hand on her lower back and pulled her close. She had to twist her head up to see his eyes and the mirth in them, but there was more. Unhidden want shimmered. She didn't mind seeing that at all, and she certainly didn't mind being pressed this close to him.

"Katie," he said quietly. "You are making this night more exciting than I could have imagined." He leaned in. "And I fucking imagined."

Chapter Fifteen

Leo wasn't kidding. He'd always had an excellent imagination and he'd used all his powers dreaming of an endless night with Katie. Vivid dreams, well, more like wide-awake scenes had flashed into his mind late last night after her soft seduction on her porch. Instead of trying to sleep, he'd sketched more ideas of his metal goddess sculpture, welded together with the fire from his torch and kissed by love from the goddess herself. The result was an entire series of a powerful woman, vulnerable, sexy as hell, intoxicating.

And he'd certainly imagined a first date with her. After all, it was her first, as she'd mentioned in the bakery. Leo had taken that knowledge and wanted to cherish it, like he wanted to cherish her. From their interaction so far, he knew she was cute and goofy, strong and sexy. She was cautious, but full of longing for more in life, for herself, for her daughters, for her heart. He didn't want to overwhelm her, but he had put thought into how to make their first date special, because he wanted a million more with her.

In the end he'd decided to go with fun, because she made him laugh with her quirky honesty, and also because he sensed she was still nervous, and he wanted the night to ease her mind, not give her more reasons to doubt a relationship between them. The fact that he might have to get close to her to help her toss the bocce balls had entered his mind, but he'd definitely underestimated the heat between them surrounded by people in a busy, loud bar. Wildly underestimated.

They'd had fun. She was a riot to watch learn a new game, like a kid with a new kite, cheering as it soared and pouting when it got tangled in a tree in equal measure. She jumped up and down and clapped when either of them did well and chatted and encouraged the group next to them like they were old friends.

But it had also been a sweet kind of torture.

Watching her lick her fingers after a bite of cheesy fries had him harder than he'd ever been in his life. That and listening to her laugh. He'd expected it to be deep and powerful, like the goddess she was in his mind. Instead it was lighter, musical notes caressing every inch of his skin the way her touch did last night in the lamplight.

It didn't matter that they were surrounded by other people and the scents of beer and fried food permeated the air — what he'd come to think of as her scent, a hint of spicy mixed with a bit of lavender, snaked its way through all the others in the bar and drew him to her. It was more layered tonight with a musky perfume she'd snuck behind her ears. He'd breathed it in when they'd waited at the bar for their drinks.

And her hips. *God.* She sauntered up to take her turn and he had to close his eyes for a moment to get himself under control. The woman had hips and used them with swagger. Her confidence was hot.

The first few times he'd stood behind her, he'd wanted to put his hands on those hips, pull her back to him and not let go. The full bar both kept his control and frustrated the hell out of him. He wanted privacy. And the way her entire face lit up when she won a round, the surprise, the glee, the hint of a smirk... Damn, he wanted to kiss the smirk off her face.

Beginners' luck was all over her tonight and Leo didn't give a fuck about losing. Winning didn't matter when he got to watch her play. When he got to see the way her neck and chest flushed with the fun she was having. When she flirted with him. *Sexy as hell.*

He might have made a mistake thinking he could handle playing bocce with her. A game involving bodies in motion, sweat, tossing balls and flirty competition. Everything out of her mouth was sexy already and he'd gone and added hard balls to the equation. *Dumbass.*

"Oh, they're heavier than they appear," she said and flitted her eyelashes at him and lifted her red ball into her hand. "I want to get close to the pallino, like a caress? Correct?"

Jesus, fuck! What had he been thinking?

"Are you sure I'm supposed to knock your blue balls out of the way? I don't want to hurt them." That time she full on smirked at him, intentionally. The woman caught on quick to this game they were playing. And it had nothing to do with bocce.

His creative imagination took her flirting and innuendoes and fueled his cravings. He imagined them naked, in his bed, on the floor, in the backseat of his truck, in the shower. *Fuck imagination sometimes.*

Blue balls indeed. Someone had had a grand sense of humor when they'd picked the colors.

"Is it hard to lose to a newbie?" she teased him. Katie cocked her hip and put her hand on it. Leo followed the path of her hands. Oh, my goodness, she'd beat Leo Treversini at a game he'd been playing since boyhood. Never in her life would she have guessed she would enjoy tossing heavy balls down a soft court. Had she been wrong! Of course, add Leo to any equation and suddenly she loved sports.

She also never would have guessed walking into such a crowded place with the high ceilings, noise flowing, that a game could feel so intimate. An intimacy which could have been because she and Leo had only played against each other while the other courts had teams, but she was pretty sure it simply had to do with Leo. His voice when he leaned in close to instruct. Such a contradiction, his dark, formidable frame mixed with the cute, sexy grin he gave her.

And he'd touched her while they played, his fingers on her hand, his arm brushing hers, his thumb gently rubbing her neck. She felt on fire, heady with round after round of seduction.

Leo finished his beer in one swallow. *Oh, Lordy, the man's body, the way his throat moves. How can a throat be sexy?* Then he grinned the sexiest grin she'd ever seen and wrapped her jacket around her so she was forced to put her arms through. The whole time she could feel his heavy breathing the caress of his eyes, the intent on his lips. "Leo?"

"I didn't lose," he said in a grumbly voice. And he grabbed her hand and walked them both out of the humid, noisy bar.

"Uh…" She looked back at the court. "You didn't?" They were out through the door. The cold night air whipped through her hair and for a second she mourned the too-warm bar and the way Leo had wrapped around her from behind to show her how to throw the ball. His low voice murmuring tips to her. The innuendoes they'd tossed at each other. His calm patience at her lack of skill. Watching his sexy body move every time he took a turn.

He was beautiful. She wanted his radiance, and all that ease and concentration focused on her. She wanted him to play her body like he knew her, surprise her with his sexy skill.

"Nope," he answered as they walked up the hill, away from the bar, away from his truck into the neighborhood of old Victorians.

"I thought you said…" She tried to puzzle it out, but then suddenly she was spun into Leo's body. He snuck them against an old storefront window, gathered her close and finally, finally kissed the beejezus out of her.

His lips back on hers? *Sizzling. Homecoming.* It was all she wanted after last night, after her slow roaming. It was the same and yet, so much more. He burned for her. She felt it in his strength, the way he tasted, nipped, possessed. This was no gentle, soft exploration. And it was so worth the wait.

She gripped his head tried to pull him closer. One of his hands held her against him. The other snaked up under her shirt and the feel of his hot skin on her bare back was everything. She wanted to climb him, tear their clothes away, get to the essence of him. "Leo," she panted.

"I didn't lose," he growled and ripped his lips from hers. *No, no, don't stop.* "Not when I got to watch you all night, sexy, hot, strutting your stuff." He kneaded her hip. "Not when I got to tease this spot right here." The skin where her neck met her shoulder had never tingled before the way it did under his thumb's caress. "Not when I get to do this." And he was back devouring her mouth with his. He gripped her head with both hands and arched her body to meet his while kissed her and…she was boneless in his arms. His lips, hot and soft and demanding. He snaked his tongue in and had her moaning with one taste.

He spun them around, lifting her so effortlessly in his strong arms. He rested her against the window, cradling her head so it wouldn't hit. *Am I dizzy from the spinning or the kissing?* She couldn't tell if it was one long kiss or a series. It didn't matter. What mattered was how close he got each time. Hungry skin against hungry skin, as if she were his endless pleasure. Her body echoed his need. As close as they were, each inch of his hard body pressed up against hers, setting her on fire, and still it wasn't enough. "Leo." She barely pulled away to moan his name before she dove right back in for more.

"Never," he said in between a kiss and a breath. "Felt." He nipped her bottom lip. "Anything like…" He soothed with his tongue. "This." He stopped kissing, talking, stopped everything except smiling at her as if he were a lost universe and she the sun come to awaken him "Before."

Her breath came as fast as his, their chests rising and falling together. She wiggled in closer so every single inch of him was pressed up against her, except for their heads, separated now. She nearly whimpered with want. *Bring your mouth back here.*

"*Jesus.* Come here," he said and pulled her away from the wall, the window, whatever it was she'd been up against. "I almost completely lost control out in the open. Again with you, gorgeous. You taste so fucking incredible." His whispered words sang through her and she closed her eyes to focus on his voice. "Can't wait to taste more."

More? Such a benign word, but when he kissed it into her ear and sent shivers through her on this quiet momentous night while her heart nearly beat through her ribs, it was the entire encyclopedia of meaning. A sexy, erotic encyclopedia.

He curved her back to his front now and she could feel him trying to catch his breath too. "That wasn't completely?" she teased. She put her arms on his, took a deep bracing breath and focused on her surroundings.

"God, woman, I was a few seconds away from ripping your clothes off," he growled into her neck.

"I know." She didn't hide the disappointment in her voice. He chuckled against her skin.

She tried to still her breathing and bring herself back to some sort of awareness of what planet they were on. "Leo, why are we standing here? I love this old Queen Anne."

It was the corner Victorian with the matching storefronts along the street. It loomed heavy and sad with only the streetlights to cast their shrouded gaze upon her. On one hand, the low light left a lot of flaws hidden. On the other, with only the small, nearly broken porch light on, its loneliness was palpable. And loneliness at night always seemed heavier to Katie than the hustle and bustle busyness of the day. At nighttime, there wasn't anything to hide behind.

He braced and rose to his full height behind her, removing his chin from her shoulder, but he kept his arms around her. "It's mine," he said.

"What?" she whispered.

"I closed on it last week. Paid cash, not worth much in her current state, which is why I was able to get a super deal and a quick closing. I'm going to restore her. Haven't shown anyone the inside yet. Thought you might like to see it with me?"

The open desire and question in his voice was so raw. "I...you," Katie stuttered and glanced between Leo and the Victorian. She had the odd fleeting feeling that both man and house were like long-abandoned puppies pleading to be rescued. *Is it me they're asking for help?*

She had always wanted to be the one to rescue this house. The man added a new twist to her dreams. There was a tiny prick of pain at the loss of the house. *Can you lose something you never had?* At times she believed so. Did she want to see it as Leo's? All these emotions swirled around inside her, from the worry over dating a man, to the fun and laughter and hot and heavy flirting at bocce, to the hottest kiss she'd ever in her life experienced, to Leo's last spoken words. *'Thought you might like to see it with me?'*

"Katie?" Leo nudged her shoulder. "You okay?"

"I do...want to." Answers rushed out of her as emotions funneled into her desires. She *did* want to see it with him. She wanted to do as Ruby urged and capture every chance she could at happiness. She'd been merely *getting by* for too long now. Maybe this house couldn't be hers, but seeing it restored by a man she was growing intense feelings for, this artist standing with her, his own feelings so blatantly exposed? Suddenly it seemed perfectly right he should own it. "Show me your house, Leo." She wrapped her arm around his waist, and he tucked her close in the same motion.

"It's a hot mess," he said, brushing her forehead with his lips.

* * * *

"Holy crap, what did they do to her?" Katie gasped as Leo opened the front door. He let her go to turn on a few huge shop lights rising like angry ghosts in the pitiful living room and what must have been a kitchen at one point, but which now resembled an abandoned drug lab.

"A lot of fucked-up damage," Leo said.

"It's worse than I imagined. I thought she'd merely been left forgotten to wear and tear on her own, but this?" Katie took in the connecting living rooms and kitchen. Carpet still stuck to some of the floors. "Who would put carpet over these glorious floors?" Walls were yellowed. *Age or nicotine?* A grand staircase stood sentinel among the rubble. And the place smelled like food left to rot in a fridge without power, for decades.

"Whoever owned it last strung out the foreclosure and took their wrath out on this house. Drug parties, floods, a fire gone too far. Garbage piled up. The upstairs isn't nearly as bad and the foundation is still good. I've been cleaning up all week, so I wouldn't completely disgust you. But…" He paused. "She's mine now. I haven't had my own place in ten years.

She's a wreck, but can you picture what she could become?"

Oh, Leo. So tough and vulnerable at the same time. "Why haven't you had your own place?" she asked. "Not judging, just curious." She wasn't one to hide things in her own life or when getting to know others. And if their tongue tango of a few minutes ago was any indication, they were definitely getting to know each other.

He stopped fiddling with debris and pinned her with his intense gaze, a look she'd first assumed was all brooding, possibly angry man. She'd misinterpreted. It was intense and direct, and it was all trained on her.

"Feels like I've been asleep for a while. Way too long. Matt needed my help to train his employees and I owed him. I finally decided to come home, to be closer to my family…well, some of them. My sister and her wife quit their jobs in NYC and bought a farm in Nebraska. I'm due for a visit there."

Asleep for a while. Everyone had a story, even if it couldn't be read initially. He held out his hand to her, turned on a flashlight and led them upstairs. She followed. Something in her softened, melded together. She was made to follow him. *Maybe he feels the same.* He had made it an issue the last few weeks to be present in her life, to wear her worries down. During the daytime that thought might scare her, but tonight she let the dim lights and shadows and her feelings be her guide.

"I also met a woman I want more than an empty one-night stand with." He gripped her hand. "Come see something special with me."

Up two flights of stairs, Leo led her to the rooftop. And it was glorious. An entire extra room for living. Only it was outdoors. She could picture a container garden up here, a patio set, lights like the bar tonight strung across beams. But what made her gasp now was the stars.

"Wow!" she whispered.

"Pretty spectacular, isn't it?"

"I'd forgotten how many there were."

Leo pulled her close fitting her back to his front. She loved how her body felt snuggled up against his, warm, tingly. They stood mesmerized under a shimmery sky.

"Leo, this is so beautiful. Thank you."

"Hoped you'd like it. I've been up here every night to remind myself how something so spectacular can shine through the darkness."

They stood in silence, and yet so much passed between them. She turned in his arms so she was nestled facing him. "You're full of surprises."

"Got one more for you. Hungry?"

"Starving," she said.

"C'mere." He led her to a corner where he'd placed a double chaise-longue full of blankets and a small table with a cooler. "Climb under and get warm and I'll feed you."

'I'll feed you.' Did he know how sexy those words sounded to a woman who spent so much of her time feeding other people? And she loved it, providing delicious meals, but someone doing the same for her? Giddiness rippled through her, stretching out her smile. Katie sat down on the chaise and pulled a blanket over her. Leo put a tray over her lap and proceeded to fill it with an amazing array of food.

"Took a chance on some of these things. I know you're a foodie. I made the bread, but the crackers, cheeses, olives and fig jam are from the store. Wine or beer?" Leo asked, holding up a bottle of each.

"Wine sounds perfect. This is wonderful, Leo. No one ever feeds me. My mom made dinners when we were growing up, but she's a horrible cook. It was more like, get through each meal with no real enjoyment. I..." She faltered because all of a sudden tears threatened. "You made me bread? It feels like I've been wanting someone to feed me my whole life and I never realized it until this moment."

Leo sat down next to her and carefully pulled the tray and blanket over them both. Then he reached out a brushed his thumb across her cheek, taking with it her tear. "Even beautiful when she cries," he whispered.

"I can't believe you made me cry on our first date." She teased him and laughed out a breath.

"Can't say I've ever made a woman cry on a date before." He nudged her. "But I love being your first. And if you like maybe I could feed you again." He wiggled his eyebrows at her and handed her a hunk of bread slathered with goat cheese and fig jam. "Now, eat."

"Mmm," she said, sending her own silent message back to his eyes. "I think I'll let you feed me again." She loved this teasing flirting they did. It was hot and sexy, but comfortable at the same time as if he sensed she needed the lightness of things to balance the heavy current running between them, as if with each move closer they might go up in flames. She wanted the flames, more and more. Every time she was around him, she wanted to know what it would be like to burn with him, but there were parts of her silently unsure.

The fact that she wasn't a single woman looking out for herself, that she had three girls to be responsible for. For the rest of the evening, she tried to tuck away her concerns and just enjoy the wave of her feelings for Leo. Spectacular, breathtaking, unique.

Which means I never felt them with John. She nearly choked on her cracker. God, so many issues with her these days. Was she merely trying to find excuses, to put up walls? Was she afraid? Or should she pull back from this relationship before it burned too hot and left only ashes in its wake?

Chapter Sixteen

Rosie wouldn't admit it out loud but she'd never been to UsedUp and she was impressed. At first, she saw only endless shelves of junk. Old metal hinges, antique light fixtures and doorknobs. Who needed eighty thousand doorknobs? But once they were allowed to roam the aisles and peer deeper into the shelves and crates by themselves, her view expanded. She began to see differently and imagine the history of the old items.

It was like a large antique mall, but mostly with the ugly throwaways, not the fancy chandeliers and wine glasses and expensive linens. Instead, rusty, dirty and gloomy were the prevailing words she'd use. Like one big orphanage of tossed-aside things.

She was fascinated by the old stone garden pots, covered in pale green mossy remains. their carvings partly worn away with time, as they'd been forgotten. Bins of keys, some still shiny. Yellowed sheet music sat in boxes next to instruments with broken strings. Glass bottles, some for perfume, others for liquor with their metal tags dangling from the necks, whiskey, Scotch, gin.

And here was where they got to collect things for their self-expression project. They could begin with a canvas or box or piece of wood — Mr. Treversini had let them choose how to mount or showcase their project. And they could select anything from UsedUp within a twenty-dollar budget for each student.

She found herself drawn to the metal pieces, some of which she had no idea what they were for. Even the old hinges surprised her. She'd always been fascinated by how things fit together, patterns, numbers, electronics. Charlie too. Something they'd had in common, and he'd never made her feel stupid or like it was a thing that boys should like, not girls.

Rosie walked farther down the dusty aisles so no one could see the tears suddenly burning her eyes. Memories caught in her throat. The last time she and Charlie had hung out was July when they'd been creating their own video game. She was writing the code and he was designing the animation. She'd finished her part. But no one knew that, because the only person she wanted to tell was Charlie and he'd basically erased her from his life. And she still had no idea what had happened.

It was choking to have someone she cared about just disappear from her life. The difference between losing her father and Charlie? Simple, Charlie was still alive. She still saw him every day. Only he stared right through her. It almost hurt more than losing her dad, which was silly. Another thing she couldn't admit to *anyone*, because how on earth could she ever think a friend ghosting her was worse than her dad dying? No way in hell she could understand it or explain it. People would call her crazy, selfish, stupid.

It was all so painful and it made her confused and angry.

"Ah, Ms. Walsh, you found my favorite section." Leo stood at the other end of the aisle, holding an enormous old gear or wheel, she wasn't certain. "What do you like about the metal?" He didn't come close, but stayed at his end rifling through a bin, keeping his eyes on the other students as well.

She quickly wiped her face. "It's resilient," she said, clearing the dregs of hurtful memories from her voice. "But also not perfect. It can be damaged if it's not well cared for."

"True." He nodded. "And what about the damaged or scarred pieces—do you think they can be turned into something beautiful? Or are they useless now?"

Rosie fingered the antique doorknob plates in one of the boxes, gorgeous iron, or maybe brass, painted over too many times to see even the finest detail of the scroll work. "I don't know," she said quietly.

He tucked the gear and another large one under his arm. "Sometimes I think it's the scars that make the most beautiful art."

Huh. Me too. I think.

"Ten more minutes today. We'll be back in a few weeks." And he walked away.

She snuck a glance then took in the entire aisle of damaged metal. She wasn't one hundred percent certain how she felt about Leo yet. Most of the kids thought he was cool because he was honest and didn't seem to care what people thought of him. *I wonder what that's like.*

He'd brought in some of his welded art to the classroom to show them, and even she had to admit it was impressive. Her mom seemed happier since she'd met Leo, since their date, since they spoke on the phone and saw each other all the time. And she did want her mom to be happy again. Brie and Cece liked him and loved his art classes. Uncle Connor was practically in a bromance with him. It was just…would he stay in their lives? And if he did, would he really see her, or be one more person who looked right through her as if she were invisible?

On the way back to school, she picked a window seat. Dark empty branches stood out against the gray sky and Rosie's thoughts felt less like a tangled mess. She contemplated what to make for her project, and wondered if she agreed with Leo about scars and beauty. Until Zachary Wilder sat down next to her. She thought he might have tried to smile at her but she was too embarrassed by his entire cool presence and she whipped her gaze away. No scars there, but definitely beauty. He was so handsome he made her blush. Plus, he was just, ugh, super talented, laid back. Nothing bothered him. Maybe when she was a junior, she'd be that cool too, or could at least act cool. *Seems eons away.* She wished she were brave enough to turn back and speak to him, see if he really did smile her way.

As the bus pulled up to school, Rosie saw Sienna in the side entrance by the sports' fields, staring at her with a scowl on her face. Rosie halted on the stairs. All thoughts of art projects and cute boys fled her mind. She and Sienna were no longer friends, if they'd ever been. Being Sienna's ally *or* her enemy — both frightened Rosie. Leo was checking everyone's name off as they exited.

"You okay?" he asked. He followed her gaze and no way in hell did she want the complication of Leo prying into her connection with the scariest girl at school.

"Fine, gotta go," she said before she ran to the girls' bathroom to escape Sienna's stalking and Leo's interrogation.

Chapter Seventeen

"Can you believe this is really your place?" Katie said wistfully as she, Leo and the girls pulled up to his house.

"Ha, with how much work she's going to be, there are days I'm kicking myself."

"That kitchen, *whew!* I do not envy you." The empty house waited at the top of the cement stairs and her face softened. Again, she had the feeling this house spoke to her. "You're not really kicking yourself?"

Never taking his eyes of Katie, he said, "No. I'm one hundred percent in love with her. Fell the first time I saw her."

"Get out of the car!" Cece yelled from her car seat and kicked the back of Katie's seat with her cowgirl boots, which had probably grown into her daughter's skin she'd worn them so much. "We have to see Leo and Mary's art studio!"

Everything was ten decibels at least with her baby girl, but it did nothing to shake the emotion in Leo's eyes with those words he'd tossed out. *'Fell the first time I saw her.' Is he talking about the grand Queen Anne?* He had been gazing into her eyes. His words mirrored the thoughts in her own soul.

The girls climbed out, Cece like a spider clamoring over a pile, Brie tentative, assessing, and Rosie with her built-in scowl. *Oh well, at least she came along. And I didn't even have to force her.* Leo followed them all with a smile on his face, his dark smile full of secrets. And Katie tried to piece together the last few weeks, each special moment with Leo locking into place to form a new view, a new emotion, a new fluttering inside her heart she hadn't dreamed she'd ever be privy to again.

"Come on." Leo held open the door to the art studio. Each time she'd had these heavy feelings beating in her chest over the last few weeks, the worried part of her had searched for excuses to pull back, but something about the all-encompassing warmth of Leo soothed her. His hand grasped hers as they jumped off the relationship cliff together into the water below. He wanted to be with her, three girls and all.

They were here to help him unpack supplies and organize his new studio. The girls had jumped at the idea. Okay, so Rosie hadn't reacted at all. But Katie saw not complaining as an enormous plus. Leo had promised pizza from Martinelli's afterward, which made them all agree whether they really wanted to organize supplies or not. Katie wanted to see his art studio, help him unpack, eat dinner with him and more. She had never in her life felt so comfortable and alive at the same time around someone. She craved him, his presence. *Is so much lust a healthy thing?*

It was oddly quiet when she entered. Cece rode piggyback on Leo and he handed her paint brushes to put in jars on shelves near the back. Brie stacked canvases according to size along one wall. Rosie stood beside crates full of metal scraps and tools, dragging her fingers over the items. Katie wished she could see her daughter's face. Was Rosie interested? She hadn't complained about Leo being her art teacher again. In fact, she was oddly quiet when Katie asked her how it was going, but not teenager angsty quiet, more thoughtful-like.

There were some machines Katie didn't recognize but guessed were for the welding classes. The front door was all the way to one side and next to it were two new garage doors full of windows which could open to extend the classroom to the outdoors.

So cool! I wonder what the other space is like? The two retail spaces had been an aspect of the house that really inspired Katie. *I want my own commercial kitchen, my own kind of studio.* She could picture it, bright white, lots of stainless steel, women working and laughing together. Feeding people and watching their faces light up in pleasure. Someday.

Her dreams were interrupted by Cece screaming, "Mary!"

"I was hoping I'd get to see you today." A gorgeous tall, willowy woman in jeans and high black boots, her long shirt and jet-black hair flowing out behind her, strolled into the studio with more boxes of supplies. *So that's where Leo gets his beauty.*

Mary could be a model with her soft skin and dark eyes set off by the prettiest smile Katie had ever seen. "And who are these other lovely ladies you brought with you today?"

Leo helped Cece down and, taking her responsibilities seriously, Cece took Mary's hand and first introduced her sisters. "And this is my mama," Cece said in her hushed voice she saved for the most amazing announcements. "Isn't she the prettiest? I want to grow up to look like her, but I have red curls like my daddy. Which isn't bad, except I don't get to see him anymore, ever."

"I don't get to see my daddy anymore either," Mary said. "One more thing you and I have in common."

Katie watched her tiniest daughter's smile get bigger, if a thing was possible, before Mary turned to her. "I'm Leo's mom. I know who you are. You catered my friend's retirement party last Christmas and I have been dreaming about those stuffed dates with bacon you made, ever since." She put both hands on her heart in a food swoon then pulled Katie in for a hug. Katie closed her eyes and lingered for a second in the warmth. Even as a grown woman there was something healing about a hug. Her parents were not huggers. Katie's kids had taught her the beauty of cozy embraces, how precious they were. Thank goodness her babies loved affection.

"I'll make them for you any time," Katie said. "And I love your studio." She drew her hand out.

"Isn't it fabulous! Leo surprised the heck out of me. Have you seen the house yet?"

Before Katie could answer, Cece interrupted, "I haven't seen the house! We're having Martinelli's. Leo said so." She had her hands on her hips like a little old lady demanding her way.

"I did." Leo chuckled and that sound shot right to Katie's blood. *Jeesh! The man is sexy even when he's not trying.* Or maybe he was trying, huh? She shrugged her jacket off. His deep laugh made her hot in a way she could barely ignore. Barely only because her daughters were present. "Why don't you go up with my mom and show your sisters the house? It's ugly, but it's safe." His beautiful dark eyes pierced hers, as if he could read her thoughts.

"Sounds perfect," Mary said. "Did you know…" She bent down to Cece's level and fake whispered, "It's a huge house with lots of fabulous nooks and crannies."

"What are nooks and crannies?" It was the last thing Katie heard as Mary took her daughters outside and up the cement steps to the house. It was quickly drowned out by the racing of her heart as Leo stalked her.

Yes, *stalked her*, took her hand and gently guided her back to the storage room where he shut the door then lifted her onto the work bench and commenced kissing her immediately. Good gracious he took her from hot coals to an inferno as he feasted on her. His touch seared right through her, leaving sparks in its wake, and she thought she might combust from his lips alone. The man excelled at kissing. Then he added his fingers to the mix as they trailed a path down her sides.

"Been thinking about you all week," he growled. "Dying to lose control with you again."

"Don't stop kissing me." She angled closer, hoping to convey her message.

Leo roamed his hands over her body, setting her to flame everywhere he touched. Even fully clothed he had the power to ignite her.

She fused their lips back together while tugging on his jacket so he fit right between her thighs. *Not close enough.* Racing her hands under his shirt, she wrapped her legs around him at the same time. *Finally!* His skin burned under her hands.

"So fucking soft," he said and kissed down her neck. "How you feel in my hands. I can't get enough of your body. I want to see it all, naked, wrapped around me."

Yes! Great idea. Katie shoved his jacket off and had his shirt unbuttoned so fast she even impressed herself. "Oh my, Leo!" His chest was strong and magnificent, all those muscles for her to explore, but he only let her gape at him for a second before he bent her backward and ate at her neck, kissing and licking and breathing her in.

"You undo me, woman. Your scent pulls me in and I lose my mind." He lifted her shirt over her head, so slowly, trailing his fingers along her sensitive body, and sharp sparks lit as if he'd scorched her. Impatient, she urged her shirt off quicker and paused only because his eyes blazed in a blue-black flame, as though she was a masterpiece before him.

She had no time to feel self-conscious before he stroked her bra straps down then fit her tightly to him — *oh Lordy, he's hard* — and reached around to undo the clasp. Then his hands, those glorious, rough huge hands stroked over her. She was certain to be burned where he touched. And when he handled one breast and kissed right in the middle of her chest, she arched toward him.

He lingered first, then devoured, but he tasted her everywhere, a soft peck on her chin, exploring her collarbone, the glorious underside of one breast. Thank goodness he focused there. "More, Leo. Please more." Heat burned through her, pulsed at her core. She rubbed her hips against him to feel that wonderful friction of his hardness, unfortunately covered in jeans. *Why are we clothed? Where is the naked time?*

He must have read her mind, or maybe their minds were one. Leo tugged her leggings down and placed his lips right over her silk underwear. The combination of his hands digging into her hips and his hot mouth on her core made her explode in an instant, shaking under him and chanting his name, "Leo, Leo, Leo."

"And fu…" He ripped himself away, all but his gaze which stayed locked on her, seeing her through her orgasm until she found her breath and came back down to earth. His muscles coiled tight, ready to spring. *Please, spring,* she wanted to scream and demand to get what she wanted. And what she wanted was more Leo, more of his erotic mouth, his blazing eyes, his scorching, magical fingertips. More everything except clothes. He needed to get naked, now.

"Losing control with you is fantastic."

"Why do you still have clothes on?"

He placed his head on her belly and laughed. Katie held him there. *Oh, the intimacy.*

Without rising, he met her eyes and grinned. Katie fanned her face and didn't care a hoot that he saw. The man was a lit flame to her hormones.

"Time for pizza." Leo gently tugged her leggings back up and helped her with her bra before he grabbed their shirts. She was so dazed she could barely sit upright.

"No," she pouted when he buttoned his flannel. "It is not time for pizza. It's time for more of all that." He placed her shirt over her head and she face-planted into him. "Why is there never enough time? That was magnificent." At least she got to feel him laugh again.

Finally, he ripped his body from hers as if it were torture and threw open the door to stalk out. *How can he be sexy even stalking away from me?* Then he stomped right back in, gave her the softest most lingering kiss she'd ever had and said, "I want you, when the time is right. You've bewitched me, gorgeous Katie Walsh." He helped her down, wrapped her up from behind and walked them both out into the dusky evening. *Guess he knows how to pout too.*

"Did that just happen?" she whispered as they walked up to the house hand in hand. She couldn't hold back her giggle.

"Oh, it's funny, is it?" He tickled her side and stole one more kiss.

"It's amazing." She leaned in to whisper in his ear. "How much I want you, how much you want me, Leo."

He held her head close, before they opened the door to the chaos of three excited, hungry girls. "Want is too mild a word for how I feel about you, how I think about you, what I aim to do with you."

She was done dreaming up reasons to overthink it. He obviously wanted her body, but he also took care with her and, if she were being honest, she wished he hadn't put the brakes on. Especially because her time without kids was few and far between.

But he also took care with her girls and that was a gift like none she could imagine.

She sighed as Cece pushed the door open and tugged them inside.

"Leo, this house is enormous, huge! Come see this closet. I could fit my whole bed inside!"

The spell was broken as Leo got dragged away. But it streamed into a beautiful image of her babies getting to know a good man who enjoyed them as well. And another, as the pizza delivery guy showed up and Mary beat her to the door to pay. And *another* as she heard all three girls upstairs laughing. *Laughing.* Katie closed her eyes and savored it all.

* * * *

"Gonna walk my mom out, then I'll take you ladies home." Leo kissed Katie's temple before he headed into the overcast night.

"I like that family," his mom said.

"Good." Leo smiled. He'd hoped she would adore Katie and her girls but he never put money on anything these days. It was a pleasant relief to know his mom's feelings were positive.

Although it was all she said until they made it to her truck. Unlike little Miss Cece, his mother—a natural observer and listener—held her words inside unless she felt absolutely necessary to give voice to them. Silence was a perfectly comfortable place for her to reside. *Ha.* He chuckled. That cute little sprite was exactly the opposite, but she and his mother seemed to have bonded immediately.

"Something funny?" she asked.

"Thinking of how Cece could learn a thing or two from you."

"Precious girl." She sighed. "How so?"

"Well, I can tell you have more to say, but you manage to contain your thoughts in your head much of the time."

"Yes, she is a talkative one. Makes up for her sisters. Lovely, all of them. I assume you know what you're doing?"

And often, it was the words his mother didn't speak that resonated. Tonight he was one hundred percent confident in his answer. "Yep."

"Special ladies. Special family."

"I agree." There was no wavering for Leo on this. He recognized their brilliance and wanted to live in their glow, to belong to them.

"Anyone could see the way they adore you." His mom glanced back up at his house while she gathered one last comment. "It's a good house, Leo, a family house."

Leo faced the dilapidated behemoth and crossed his arms. And again, his mother saw things before he ever did. Was that merely a parent thing? The ability to see into the future? Too bad she'd never met Monica before they'd married. She might have voodooed her out of Leo's life faster than smashing an ant hill.

He bought the house before he'd even laid eyes on Katie or had his heart restarted by her aura. Had he known she would be in his life? Hell no. Had he somehow decided it was time to not only stop living a life solo with no connections, but to make space for more? To start anew? It was worth considering. And his mother was correct. It was a family house, a great big beautiful home to fill with kids and their noise and shenanigans. To host parties and great feasts, to cuddle by the fire on a cold December night with an enormous tree lit up, presents spilling out from underneath. To love. His heart sped then settled. *Yep*, he thought. Living a life full of dreams was a hell of a lot better than the dank hole he'd been in.

She squeezed his arm before she went to climb up into her truck, but Leo enveloped her in a huge hug. "Love you, Mom. Thanks for putting up with me." He let her go and shut her door.

"So glad you're home, honey," she said, rolling down her window. Her voice was rough, then she wiped her tears and before she left him standing in the crisp night, she said, "I bet she'll design a great kitchen nook."

Jesus, she could see what Katie already meant to Leo. He jogged the steps to meet his girls. *His girls.* The thought settled in right. After so long getting things wrong in his life, he was indeed on the right path.

* * * *

Leo was unnaturally quiet on the drive home, Katie thought. Or maybe she noticed because her girls were so quiet too, probably because Cece was crashed out asleep in her booster seat. But Leo held her hand in his the entire way home and his warmth was its own sort of special language, as though he were made for her.

When they got home, he gave her a knowing smile. Knowing for him and mysterious for her, but she liked it all the same because the secrets he held felt meant for her. He carried Cece to bed while Katie made sure her other two were settled.

Even on the unlit porch shrouded in darkness, his presence called to her. As soon as she stepped out, he grabbed her and spun her body into his. Spinning was the perfect description. Her head and her heart whirled. Still he didn't speak. Instead he held her with such careful intensity and kissed his hot amazingness into her, as if he never wanted to let her go. As if she were the most precious gift. Those lips of his were a spell. Soft then insistent. She was his last meal and he was hell bent on enjoying it.

Katie had no idea how empty she'd been, how lonely, how much she'd longed to feel connected to another human being until Leo touched her. His presence filled every lonely crack inside her. His kiss ignited each of those long-empty chambers of her heart, her soul, her desire. She'd buried desire when she buried John. But now Leo wrapped around her, tossed the match into her and she was on fire, coals set to flame. She roamed her hands over his back under his jacket, wanting to be closer, wanting to match his heat

He walked her back slowly till she stood against the porch railing. How could he go slow? Her senses reeled with need for every part of her to touch every part of him, bare, with nothing between them. She kicked off her short boots, wrapped her arms around his neck and climbed on. Oh, yes, she fit perfectly around him. Leo tugged her jacket off and dragged his luscious lips down her neck to her collarbone, leisurely tracing the strong curve, making her feel delicate under his attentions as he discovered the skin around the column of her neck with his lips, a graze of his teeth, sucking, teasing, caressing.

She found the waist of his jeans and tugged at his belt. God, was she even breathing? The skin under his shirt was so hot when she touched it that she practically melted. He hissed, then chuckled. Mmm, she loved his sounds. His deep, gravelly voice shot straight to her core, to her heart. It was a special language written just for her on the stars in a dark night sky.

"Your hands are icicles, love." He took them and moved them farther up his chest and hugged her to him which was exquisite, except for the whole no-more-kissing thing.

"Leo," she said on a ragged breath and tried to steal his mouth with hers again. "Don't stop."

He hummed into her mouth. Then he whispered, a husky deep Leo breath in her ear, "I hear giggling. My guess, at least two girls. Right inside the front door. My Spidey senses tell me. Or maybe peeking through the front window at us."

"Oh!" She nuzzled into him and grabbed on to his jacket to hide her face in his body. "Why, why, why?"

She gently beat her head against his strong chest while he laughed at her. "So not funny, mister." She pinched his side and made him flinch, and this time his laugh was big and deep and filled his entire body.

Katie rested her ear against his chest and sighed. She was never going to get laid. She was never going to see him naked, never going to have enough time to savor him. How could each kiss, each handholding, each touch have her dissolving into a puddle of aching need? Thank goodness *he'd* heard the giggles. She'd been consumed with tearing off clothing and she wasn't sure *that* would have made her girls giggle. "How on earth did you hear them? You should be their mother." He barked out another laugh and wrapped her jacket around her.

"Well, first I heard singing and I thought it was in my head, but the letters *K I S S I N G* followed by teasing and giggles jarred me out of my lust-induced fog."

She peeked her head around him and her girls weren't stealthy at all as they scrambled to close the curtains and hide their heads. *Hmm, my two oldest getting along and laughing together. Even if it is at my expense.*

"Thank you for tonight," Katie said on a huge sigh.

"It was a great night, wasn't it?" Leo grinned at her, put his hands on her butt and gave her a squeeze before he lifted her off the railing and set her down.

"Too short for my taste," she grumbled. "You keep moving me into positions away from you. I want the opposite." Her pout was epic, but she felt the right to it. Leo took her hand and walked her the few steps to her front door. Her girls were watching again. Leo made an exaggerated wink at her daughters, swooped Katie back over his arm and gave her the softest kiss. And before he leaned her back up, he whispered, "We'll have time. I promise."

Chapter Eighteen

Even covered in layers of gear, Leo felt most alive, in tune with his mind and body when he was welding, as if he could bend and shape the metal with his bare hands, under the caress of heat and flame, to create. It might have been what had kept his soul from completely withering to dust over the years.

But not until he met Katie had he been so driven to create beauty with it. Flowing hair, a stunning face lit with the deep serenity of peaceful loving eyes. Arms outstretched to grasp onto the whole entire world. The body was still taking shape beneath his flame and his imagination. There was so much in him, so much inspiration from one woman that he couldn't possibly capture it all in one form. He had an entire series of her sketched out in his notebook.

His past wasn't all ugly, but his art often represented the madness of the world, explosions caught in midair, human destruction, slaughter — even his abstract works were sometimes freakish. As a younger artist, he'd thought beauty too common, too simple an image to represent and been more compelled to expose anguish, to entice argument, to poke at the narrowmindedness he felt superior too, not realizing then that everyone held biases or walked with blinders on at points in their lives, him included.

But now? He molded his goddess from a place of hope in his heart. When she was finished, she'd stand proud, strong vulnerable, heartbreakingly gorgeous. But not due to the art or the artist, but for who it represented, Katie rising out of the ashes to be reborn. Her essence, which surrounded him now, breathed true life into it.

Leo turned off the torch and the machine. He tugged off his mask and gloves and while he sucked down a bucket of ice water, he let the silence soothe the ringing in his ears. He reveled in the noise, the experience of welding, the full-body adventure. And when he was done, he valued the quiet space around him. *Balance.* His mother had always urged balance in their lives. Another aspect he'd ignored for too long.

When he stared at the beginning of this new piece of art, his imagination ran wild with more images. A goddess rising, perhaps with her daughters surrounding her, each one powerful and beautiful in her own way. Leo rubbed his chest. It ached. Hell, it ached. He was being cracked open by four beauties. There were more images too. His goddess holding a baby. An image of him wrapped around her while she cradled their son, or daughter. *His* child with her. Fuck, the images hurt, but they kept coming and he let them. He let them ride over his heart and shock him back to life.

He might have kept working, because now his art was his passion again. His emotions, positive and heartbreaking, were his healing. It had been more than a decade since he'd been so caught up in his art that time slipped away. *Rejuvenation.* But tonight he had a date and his date was infinitely more important than his work. His true salvation. Or, he realized like the slow learner he often was, both supported each other.

Balance is a good thing. Leo put his tools away and imagined where to take his goddess for dinner. Maybe a little balance would mean his hands got to mold her body to his tonight, if she was ready. If the time was right. If they could carve out some secret hiding space impenetrable from the people in their lives for a few hours. The thought of his hands on her naked skin had him hotter than any welding torch ever did. *Fuck!* He felt like he was seventeen again, having discovered sex and all the amazing thing two bodies in lust could do to one another.

Only now, he knew it wasn't simply lust. Although plenty of that on both sides, they were like an inferno every time they kissed, but his feelings for Katie Walsh went way deeper. Which had the potential to make their moments, when they finally came together fully, explosive.

* * * *

"Drop it, you ragamuffin!" The front door was wide open when Leo arrived at Katie's. Muddy paw prints streamed over otherwise shiny hardwood floors throughout the entire living room and into the kitchen, where Katie was crouched down before a cornered Kitten. The ridiculous mutt—blond everywhere except for her paws which looked dipped in brown—shivered in full downward dog play-with-me glee, one of Cece's cowgirl boots, also covered in dirt, gripped in her teeth.

"Need some help?" He closed the front door.

Kitten dropped the boot, launched over Katie and slid across the floor to Leo who commanded, "Sit!" and grabbed the dog by the collar and scruff of her neck.

"You are a genius," Katie said. "She's buried that boot and dug it up three times now. And look at the mess she made. Oh, my clean house." Out of breath, cheeks flushed, mass of curls gone haywire around her face, she sat against the kitchen counter.

Well fuck! She'd never looked prettier.

Grabbing the cowgirl boot, she pulled herself up and glowered at the dog. "It's a close race, who's going to be the death of me, my teenager or you, you menace."

Katie stood before him like she'd come from the sky. *Calm down, man.* Covered in stardust, she stunned him nearly speechless. A shimmery silver blouse showed off the sensual curves of her chest and fell off one shoulder, revealing one of his favorite spots on her, her fucking gorgeous neck. A black skirt flowed over her hips and down her legs, but really all he could think was how easy it'd be to drag off her.

He shot his gaze up to her face before his out-of-control libido took over and he jumped her. She combed her fingers through her hair to tame it. Her cheeks and eyes sparkled with hints of makeup.

"I wanted tonight to be special," she whispered. A mixture of vulnerabilities, desires and her hopeful smile skittered across her face.

"You're fucking brilliant." He tried to tone down the harsh needy sound to his voice. He held the dog steady, so he didn't grab Katie and ravish her right in the kitchen.

"What can I do to help?"

"Ugh," she sighed. "That brat can go outside. I'll get the mop."

Leo tugged Kitten outside and came back to help Katie. "Here." He took the mop from her hands and she melted into him.

"Hi, beautiful," he said.

"I intended to surprise you."

"You're the surprise, woman. Every single time I see you, you jolt my heart with how stunning you are." *Keep it in check. Keep yourself together. Do not shred those clothes and take her right here.*

"I cooked for you." She seduced him with her soft voice. She was going to bring him to his knees. "And, aside from destruction dog…" She nuzzled into his neck and breathed in. "We have the house to ourselves… Oh, hell," she said and tugged his mouth down and met his lips with her own needy touch, a starving woman taking what she wanted. "Forget about cleaning up. Forget about dinner."

Katie grazed her hands down his chest and scanned his entire frame with those silver-blue eyes of hers. "I wanted to woo you," she murmured. She started to unbutton his shirt. "But I couldn't care less about dinner or how long it took Ruby to do my makeup or this crazy mess."

Leo wanted to rip his shirt off along with the rest of their clothes. Her words, her sensuality had his desire shooting through the roof, but he let her set the pace, sighed with the whisper-light touch of her fingers toying with each button, discovering his skin beneath. Gently placing his hands around her, he studied her eyes. It wasn't fear or indecision he saw, but a hint of something she held back, held close to her.

"Talk to me." He kissed just below her ear and smiled when she sucked in a breath. Katie Walsh, breathless under his kisses, in his arms. Sexiest thing ever.

"I. Want. You." She pushed his shirt off, leaned in and placed her warm lips on his chest.

Holy fuck, yes!

"But I'm worried." She placed her hand on his heart, over the spot she'd just kissed.

Fuck! "Tell me your worries." He tangled his hand with hers on his chest and gave her a squeeze.

"It's been a really long time." When she smiled up at him, he knew, right then and there, he'd do anything for his goddess. *His.* Not a doubt in his mind she was his. Because this worry that made her question, made her stall, she trusted him enough to hand it right into his heart. "Like past desert into Mars-drought territory long." Leo burst out laughing and hugged her to him while he kissed his laugh down her neck to the spot that made her arch her body into his.

"Don't care how long, darlin'. You're safe with me. Promise." He took her face in his hands when he said these words so she could see the truth, the power of his vow as much as hear it.

"I've been...uhm..." She pursed her lips and brushed her fingers through his hair. Fuck, they'd already locked onto each other's buttons. Her massaging his head was nirvana. "Studying. Practicing...with a few toys." The last came out in a breathy whisper like she was both embarrassed and turned on.

Fuck! Her words and the erotic breathy way she admitted to pleasuring herself were enough to make him come. Good fucking thing he wasn't a randy teenager without much control. The pain of his erection nearly blinded him. It would have been a sweet, tortuous blinding. He cocked his hip into her body so she could feel what her words did to him.

"Do you want me, Leo?" She spread her words out over his chest and kissed him again.

And that was his undoing. "Where is your bedroom?" He ground out the words and grabbed her by the waist. Her eyes lit with a thousand sparks. When he lifted her and urged her legs around him, a stormy desire swirled in her expression, matching his. And he followed where she pointed.

Chapter Nineteen

Sexy stamina! Leo carrying her up the stairs while she kissed him, while she was attached to him, all his hard places rippling over her. She let her hands explore the warm planes of his chest, gorgeous under her fingertips. The pads of her hands had never felt such luxury. Her nails elicited groans from him, drove his kiss deeper. She left the landscape of his body only to drag her fingers through his hair, hold him tightly to her. It was an uncoordinated, wet, hungry ravaging, their kiss.

Who knew when she decided to cook for him, he'd arrive famished? How starved she'd be. And thank the goddesses their hunger had nothing to do with food. His hands caressed her ass, no, not caressing. kneading, *needing*. It seemed forever she was lost in him carrying her while she discovered him, savored his lips. Finally she was on her back on the bed and he followed her down. *Thank God, yes!* She wanted to scream.

He tore his lips from hers and teased her collarbone with his tongue. "This spot drives me fucking insane," he said.

Me too. She writhed and arched under him as sparks shot between them with every connection of skin to skin. Every breath, kiss and sound from him fluttered through her. With each movement he paid reverence to her, like he'd done on the porch under cover of darkness. Now there were no kids watching. No one was going to orgasm block her. The knowledge didn't lessen her need.

"Leo." His name was a wish on her breath. He dragged his body down hers and she wiggled under him. He brought his hands back up under her shirt to take if off and she ripped off her bra to assist him toward nakedness. And he didn't stop. He tugged her skirt and panties down, while she tried to reach for his zipper. "Jeans off."

"Crave you so fucking much," he whispered, scorching her skin with his kisses on her calves, the ticklish skin on her inner thigh, her stomach. Each one a firework, blazing a trail of Leo lust, of unfathomable desire. It looked like her lack of sex life was not a turnoff to him. *At all.* And Katie soared, all her vulnerabilities smudged away by the burning in his eyes for her.

Their bodies raced and tangled together, like they were both in a drought and chasing the oasis. She finally got her wish, and unzipping his pants, pushed at them with her feet. "I need these to go elsewhere." She needed to touch him everywhere, all at once. Wanted their bodies fused. Where would she start? His huge muscled thighs, the strong butt they were attached to, his arms, muscled to forever, arms that carried her. Or…*oh my*.

Leo kicked his jeans the rest of the way off and he didn't stand to let her admire him. She'd have to scold him later, because this man was so insanely gorgeous, tight muscles, dark eyes illuminated in the low lamplight. His perfect erection hard and long and so, so ready for her. He fitted his body back to hers, warm hard planes molding to her soft parts. She was on fire for him. Ravenous, he took her lips and caged one hip in with his leg tangled around her. She liked the feel of his thighs around her. He braced himself up on one arm and Katie took advantage of the position and finally gripped his hard length.

Leo sucked in a breath.

Oh my, *indeed*. Hot, soft skin, hard shaft. Again, she stroked and got to watch him hiss in pleasure. His eyes burned shut and he bowed closer into her touch. He was the beautiful one. A heady drug bewitching her. It was a battle between them, the sweetest battle she'd ever had. He rose to his knees and she strummed her hands up and down his length, mesmerized, loving the guttural sounds he made.

He teased her skin, right under her breasts, circling closer, pulling away then back. Finally, *finally*, without taking his hands from her body, he leaned down and took one of her nipples into his mouth, tasting her. Torturing with his tongue, his lips, his teeth, sucking and biting until she let go of him to grip the sheets. As if torturing her breast wasn't enough, he roamed his strong hands over her hips, caressed her inflamed skin, and she let him. Over and over until her body wept with want. *More!* She had no idea if she spoke aloud or not as the roaring in her blood drowned all sounds.

He gripped her ass the way she loved and lifted her core to his mouth. "Ahh," she cried when his practiced lips met her center. She was shaking before he made contact and when he did, when he took one long stroke of her with his tongue, without any barrier between them this time, then dove his magical tongue inside her, she couldn't help it—she screamed and pushed into him, begging with her body. He rubbed his thumbs against her in an erotic dance so close to her clit, drifting away, then tantalizing his way back. She shivered with his teasing, her body full of need all coiled together in one spot. When it overtook her, she swore she saw stars and, shuddering out her orgasm, came bursting back to life. Breathless, weightless, tremors rolled through her. And through her haze of pleasure she watched him roll on a condom.

"I've wanted you since the first night I saw you and your soul spoke to mine. Tell me you want this too, woman. No pressure. But I need to know. I don't mind at all making you feel good and waiting. Fuck, watching you come is enough to fuel my dreams forever."

She nodded, so lost in desire she could barely speak, but his words were the gift she needed to make this night perfect. "I want you Leo, so much. Come inside me."

And he did.

So hard and tight and powerful, he thrust inside in one gasp. He filled her. It was delicious, so full, his body aligned with hers. Instinct had her pushing back, or rather squeezing him. He pulsed inside her as they lay claim to each other. More need beat in her core. Their bodies found a rhythm together, thrusting and climbing to the top of the ridge, frantic and so wanton for each other. So intent was he on their joining, their pleasure, he rocked their bodies together.

She couldn't quit touching him, his arms, the angled muscles of his back, grabbing at him to pull him closer, deeper. Stealing his warmth and power to feed her own, then giving back in return. With each powerful move of their bodies together, Leo kissed her like he was a sentenced man and she was his salvation. And Katie gave him everything she had, with her body she whispered the story of who she was, laid bare for him to discover as they met each other heart to heart.

It was building in her again, or perhaps never stopped. "Katie, fucking hell," Leo growled and came like a wild animal rutting and staking his claim. "Fuck! Fuck!" His beautiful body surged with power. He buried his head in her neck and kissed her strongly enough to leave a mark. Katie wrapped her legs and arms around him and chased her own orgasm through the most amazing last pulses of him inside her.

"Am I dreaming?" she whispered minutes later, or hours. Could have been eons. Katie came back to earth, back to her home, back to her bedroom. "Was that an out-of-body experience? I've never had one before." Her eyes were closed so she could hold on to the spectacular experience. She let her hands roam and softly caress over his shoulders, down his back, imagining its power. *Mmm, I'll need to see his naked back soon. And kiss it and caress it. Yay! So much to discover still.*

"Woman," Leo growled into her neck. "Are you cheering?"

She loved his growl, his inhibitions gone for her, because of her, with her. He snuggled in closer, even though they'd become one, and it fueled her already giddy smile. She, too, wanted to climb all the way deep into this shared cocoon and savor.

The giggle burst out of her. "Cheering seemed like the appropriate response."

"Agreed. That was phenomenal!" He kissed her neck again, so gently she thought she might cry. "I'd move off of you, but I think I'm incapable," he said.

She tightened her hold. "Don't you dare." *Mmm.* They stayed wrapped around each other until the chill from being naked and coming down from the high made them both shiver.

"So much better than the Butter Finger," she whispered into his ear. Leo's body tightened for a second then he leaned his head up and roared with laughter.

"Thank fuck! If I wasn't better than your toy, you know what would happen?" Leo asked with that sexy quirk of his full lips.

"What?" She widened her eyes and couldn't wait to hear what he would say.

"We'd have to practice." He placed a gentle kiss on her chest. "And practice." He teased her collarbone with his sexy tongue. "And practice." He landed that mouth of his on hers.

"Mmm." She smiled against his lips. How had she ever thought practice was a negative thing?

"Although..." He studied her now, grazed his beautiful eyes up and down her naked body. "Playing with your toy together, now that's something we should put on our list." His husky voice sent more shivers that had nothing to do with her being cold through her body and she arched under him.

"Our list?"

"Absolutely. Katie and Leo's sex bucket list. Can't imagine ever getting my fill of this phenomenal body." He rubbed his hand over her hip, but focused on her eyes. *Intent. Serious.* She reveled in the intimacy.

"I promised to feed you," she said.

"You just did," he said and made them both giggle.

Holy crap, giggling with Leo Treversini, naked after lots of orgasms. Best feeling ever!

"I meant dinner." She squeezed his sides.

He nuzzled into her neck one last time, pushed himself up, grabbed the condom with one hand and tugged her up with the other. "When are your darlings coming home?"

Her smile grew. It couldn't be contained, anyway. "Tomorrow evening," she said and got to watch an entire brilliant set of fireworks play out over his face.

He tugged her body flush with his. "And your brother?"

"He's gone all weekend."

"Well, then, you *better* feed me, get my strength back up."

Ha! She doubted Leo needed any help with his strength. The way her eyes lit when she took in his naked body must have betrayed her thoughts because he chuckled.

"But first"—he bent down slightly and kissed her chest and took her hand—"shower."

* * * *

Watching Leo eat was almost as sensual as watching him make love to her body. She lit the fire in the living room and was going to set the table, but Leo had a better idea. He asked her for blankets and pillows and made a cozy spot on the rug for them. He had a thing for them on blankets together and she was loving it.

Together with the flames blazing in front of them, they devoured chicken piccata with noodles and drank a chilled prosecco Katie had selected specially for tonight. Tonight, which had surpassed her imagination by so far she couldn't even remember what she'd imagined sex with Leo would be like. Their real experience smashed all her earlier thoughts to smithereens.

"Best meal ever." He snuck out the words between bites. With each mouthful he closed his eyes and his face melted into a dreamy *I'm in heaven* glow.

Katie could admit, even reheated, their meal was delicious. Every sharp bite of lemon and salty caper burst in her mouth. The bubbly drink to highlight a special occasion. The entire evening since they'd attacked each other, to their slow mutual appreciation society in the shower, to now shimmered in technicolor. Her taste buds, her sense of smell, her eyesight, all super sensitive. And touch. She absolutely could not forget about touch.

When he wasn't devouring her food, he was playing with her fingers, leaning in to kiss her neck. Like at Giocare the other night, when he'd made contact with her the entire evening. Leo made her feel cherished. His expression was so full of glee, like he couldn't believe he could feel her whenever he wanted. It was enough to make her forget about food or hunger or anything else except how she could bottle that emotion and keep it to herself forever.

"Damn good thing you followed your calling and decided to cook for people. Bet you turn your clients' worlds upside down. I want to lick my plate, it's so good."

"You're good for my ego. I only wish my clients were as effusive as you."

"Are they all dead inside? This is amazing."

"No." She laughed. Leo tugged her onto the blankets and played with her hair. His hands felt so amazing. Now *she* was cat-like, basking in the sun. Her own private sunshine. "I never see them, or hardly ever. I have three standing weekly clients I cook for while they're at work. Then I store most meals in their freezers, leaving one thawed and warm, ready for them to eat that night. Only my friend Penny orders different items. The rest is all very rudimentary. Routine is good, but it's become boring.

"I want to feed the people, watch their expressions when they eat, share in their delight. Well, hopefully delight. I miss people. My job has been a lifesaver, but I long for my own café and catering business, like a Barefoot Contessa."

"A who?" Leo asked but before she could answer, he kissed her quick and powerfully.

"The famous TV chef, Ina Garten. She used to have her own gourmet food shop."

"Don't watch much TV, darlin'." Leo was mapping her neck now with those sinful lips. *Oh.* It was so much more than kissing, like everything he did. It was an exploration of her skin, her body. *Mmm.* She closed her eyes and took in his scent and the feel of his mouth on her neck, soft and searching, discovering.

"Unless it's *Octonauts*," he teased and had her giggling. He propped his head on his arm next to her. "Is that what you've been saving for?"

"Yes. My own specialty food shop. Maybe some light catering thrown in. I've been pinning ideas and images for the last year."

"Café and food shop, I understand. You lost me at pinning," Leo said.

"It's like an online bulletin board where you can save pictures and ideas, your own or others you discover online. All your inspiration gathered in one place, visually. Paint colors and fixtures, commercial ovens, even what kind of café tables or silverware, for example."

Leo sat up and for a second, she thought something was wrong. But he moved back against the couch, pulled her along so she was straddling his lap and rested his hands on her hips. So warm and comforting his touch, holding her like she was precious. He had a fascination with her hips and she was not complaining.

"Tell me," he said, "how you imagine it to be. Even down to what kind of café tables."

She didn't hesitate. To her it was like talking about favorite meals. "I want tons of white paint, bright, fresh. A canvas to show off other things. The silver food cases to display pastries and mini pizzas, bright grilled veggies, falafel. Big green plants everywhere, maybe even a botanical printed wallpaper on one wall. A few antiques in pine to hold wine and specialty vinegars, homemade pickles. Silver buckets full of flowers. Some as décor and others to sell. Big copper dome light fixtures."

"You're so pretty when you dream," Leo whispered.

She shook her head. Not to disagree, but… How could she be choked up all of a sudden? She'd been formulating this dream in her mind for the last year, saving her butt off, but to have Leo acknowledge it, value it, opened a place she'd kept secret for a long time, maybe ever. Hope that her dream could come true. And now all the months of saving and thinking and wondering and planning in her head, all her pent-up patience flooded out of her. She wanted it instantly. Didn't want to wait any longer. She wanted so much, including Leo in the dream she pictured.

Was it too much to crave it all at the same time? When Leo kissed the few escaped tears from her cheeks and whispered words of power and beauty to her, explained how amazing she was and how she could do anything, how he couldn't wait to see her fly, Katie smiled through her tears and let them blur her dream because it wasn't a negative at all, rather exactly how she imagined — a messy, blurry, amazing life full of food and laughter and family and love with Leo.

Chapter Twenty

"That girl is trouble," Zachary Wilder said.

Sienna blew by them, glaring daggers and knocking Rosie's project bin from her hands. "Oops. So sorry," Sienna said and breezed her way out of the classroom. Sienna sought Rosie out to mess with her on a constant basis these days, ever since Rosie had refused to help her with any more computer issues. She hated it, hated everything about school now. Except for art.

He bent down to help her pick up her board and the pieces she'd started to pull from her bin. She'd known who Zachary was since middle school, when she was a sixth grader and he'd just moved to town as a new eighth grader, but this was the first class they'd ever had together. Ever since he had sat next to her on the bus ride, she'd been hyper aware of him, trying to sneak glances at him.

He'd shot up way beyond tall this year. It was like someone took the same amount of kid and stretched him out, he was so skinny. He wore thick black glasses, which looked cool with his black afro. Even his clothes were all black. Stark jeans, messy old Converse, black T-shirts. Every day. *Is he making a statement, or trying not to be seen?*

"Yeah," Rosie said. Art was her last class and she could finally breathe easily, knowing her day was almost over and she could leave soon. Not many people spoke to her at school. Of course she didn't talk to anyone, either.

"I'm Zach. You still friends with her?"

"We were never friends." Rosie spit the words like she'd bitten into a too-tart grapefruit. "I don't have any friends," she whispered. She grabbed her bin and hurried to the back of the classroom to the last table to set up her supplies. She was shaking and her face felt bright red and hot. She put her water bottle up to her cheek and closed her eyes. She *didn't* have any friends, but that didn't mean it felt good. Charlie never talked to her anymore. But worse, when she did see him walking through the halls, he seemed miserable. What had happened to her old friend who was always full of jokes and laughter and curiosity about the world?

And Sienna had used her. Rosie had known it was wrong to hack the accounts when she'd done it, but at the time, it was as if she'd been on a high. She was desperate to be liked, to do what the other kids were doing, to have the Score app. *'I can make you pretty and popular too.'* Sienna had lured her.

Once she'd figured out what Sienna and her group were doing with those accounts, Rosie wanted not one thing to do with them. It sounded way worse than bullying. Sienna had guy friends from a different school who'd wanted to see pictures of the girls. *Eww.*

Rosie'd rather never have any friends if it meant having one like Sienna.

Now, with her face flushed and hot, she tried not to notice when Zach made his way to her table and started unloading his art bin next to hers. Usually she had a table to herself. He was quiet, which gave her rapid pulse time to chill out, for her to feel like she wasn't going to die from embarrassment and shame.

When her breath returned to somewhat normal and she started taking in the room around her, she caught him eyeing her project.

"That's really cool," he said while they worked. "Those gears are awesome. I wouldn't have thought of using them."

"Thanks," she mumbled. Her face was warm again but now she didn't know if it was from her run-in with Sienna or Zach's attention. Admiring him from afar was one thing. Him actively engaging her in conversation...muddled her brain. He was an amazing artist. His drawings won competitions every year and he did the comics for the school newspaper.

"Want to tell me about your project?" he asked as they stood side by side and arranged pieces onto their collages. "It's kind of dark."

"Says the boy dressed head to toe in black all the time." Rosie tried to sound teasing but sometimes her sarcasm shoved itself into every word that came out of her mouth.

He laughed. "I didn't say I didn't like it."

Oh!

"Your eyes are really green when you smile," she said what she was thinking and immediately covered her mouth.

"It's good to know you can recognize colors," he teased.

Wow. She snuck glances at him. *Even boys blush.*

"The...uh, school paper could use more artists. Writers too." Zach gave her a quick smile and took the rest of his project out of his bin.

"What?"

"I mean, if you wanted to join us. We do a lot of our stuff after school so the creeps like Sienna don't bug us. It's nice. It's quiet."

She almost laughed. Nice and quiet sounded like the kind of thing her mother would urge her to do. But actually, Rosie kind of liked the idea. Charlie was on the school newspaper too. Hmm, maybe she could find a way to get her old friend back. And Zachary, *Zach* Wilder, cute and kind, had just invited her. She could use some kind in her life.

They worked in silence for a while until she got up the courage. "I'm not really completely sure about my project yet. It...I'm trying to convey...hiding, I think."

"What's Rosie Walsh hiding from?"

Everything. She stared at him open-mouthed. She couldn't tell him. Then he'd really think she'd gone off the deep end.

"I get it." He nodded, but didn't say any more while they worked.

Got what? She hadn't spoken. But apparently her look communicated enough.

"I could be one," he said a few minutes later. His voice was lovely. Not loud and obnoxious, but strong, assured, deeper than some of the other boys whose voices were still caught in-between. *Too many changes to keep up with.* How was she expected to keep up with all her own changes, let alone everyone else around her turning into aliens? Okay, even she could admit, Zach wasn't an alien. He was cute and he didn't seem caught up in any drama. He reminded her of Brie a bit. Content on a path, not to be bothered by all the petty shit the rest of them were trudging through. It took her a moment and she felt like a dork when she realized she'd been staring at him.

"What?"

"A friend. I could be yours. You could be mine. You know, a mutual friends society where members are nice to each other and have conversations and discover things they have in common, like art and cool eyeglasses and darkness. Hang out."

"You want to be friends with me?" *Nobody wants to be friends with me.*

"Well, I mean if you really don't want any friends..."

"No, I...I do want," she said quietly, playing with the hinges in her box.

"Cool," he said and she glanced at him in time to see his mouth curve up in that crooked cute smile.

"Yeah," she said. "Cool."

Chapter Twenty-One

"What are you doing?" Katie set her keys down and sighed.

Leo caught her gaze and *oh boy*, that secret grin he gave her twisted his mustache up a bit and sent tingles through her. *Why do I have children again?* she wondered. *Only sort of.* She loved her girls but right now she wanted to climb Leo and explore his magnificent body she hadn't had nearly enough of when he'd spent the night last weekend. Her face flushed with memories of how thoroughly they'd enjoyed each other when he'd slept over. And still she felt parched.

"Mama," Cece said with a huge sigh and rolled her eyes. "He's making pasta, you know." Her youngest, wearing an apron far too long for her tiny body, took the bag out of Katie's hand, dragged her purse strap down and set it aside, and walked her over to the bar. "Sit here," she instructed. Brie was holding long ribbons of pasta while Rosie cranked the machine.

"Guess what?" Cece yell-whispered. "Leo let me mix the eggs and flour. With my bare hands!"

"He did?" Katie was still a bit stunned with the image in front of her. All three of her girls and a wonderful man making her dinner. No one ever made her dinner. She was the cook. But feeding three busy girls with their different schedules and tastes, plus her brother, sometimes it all became a chore. Leo had offered to take care of dinner, but she had no idea this was what he'd meant.

"Mom used to make fresh pasta," Rosie said. She didn't make eye contact with Katie, her face intent on rolling out fresh sheets of pasta. "Now she hardly makes special meals for us at all."

"I didn't realize you missed this," Katie said. Leo slid a glass of red wine over to her.

Rosie blinked and for a second Katie saw her little girl still there, mixed with a tentative soul on the verge of young-adulthood, and felt as if she were reading an entire novel in one glance. It was all she could do to hold back her tears. All her daughter's emotions, sadness, loneliness, uncertainty, bossiness. God, daily she was reminded how much she had to learn about raising teenagers. Maybe she'd have it all figured out in oh, say, fifty years.

A piece clicked into place. Her oldest didn't always know how to ask for what she wanted, as a teenager, any more than Katie understood how to give it to her.

"Cece, you're up, girl," Leo said and pulled the stool over to the counter. "Ladies." He nodded to Brie and Rosie. "One of you set the table and one of you get the appetizer for your mom." Her girls got to work while Katie sipped her wine and did nothing but watch. She watched while someone else cooked for her, while someone else set the table and while a kind man who kept surprising her showed her curious, funny daughter how to cut long strips of fettucine. Cece wore flour in her hair, on her cheeks and all over her huge smile, and she was cutting the strips unevenly, but Leo laughed and indulged her. Brie set a cutting board full of grilled crostinis with melted cheese and mushrooms in front of her.

"Wow, you ladies and gent are pros at this," she said and bit into the blue cheese mushroom deliciousness.

"Leo learned to cook from his mama too," Cece said. "*And* his dad."

"I like doing this," Brie said. "We haven't all cooked together in a while."

She's right. When John had died and they'd moved into Connor's house, and his open kitchen, the girls had straggled into the kitchen with her, helping her cook and prep for clients, as if they *needed* to be around her. Afraid if they glanced away, she would disappear too.

During the last two years, as her personal chef business had really taken off, and her girls' schedules had gotten crazy, they'd all scattered elsewhere during dinner time. She'd assumed they hadn't missed it. Maybe she hadn't been paying very good attention.

"Mom's too busy," Rosie said, her attitude back in check, as she strolled through the kitchen.

"Hey," Katie said.

"A mother working hard to make a good life for her daughters isn't something to complain about," Leo said at the same time.

Rosie's cheeks turned pink, but she didn't huff away and leave the room. *Progress.* No, *more* than progress. Leo Treversini working his miracles.

"I didn't mean to sound snarky. I only meant she really is busy," Rosie said. Maybe Katie needed to take her at her word more often. Her daughter was learning how to find confidence in the world, and Katie wanted to support her.

"I am busy, you guys. I'm working so hard to save up for a house, a café of some sort, college for you three. Ugh!" She rested her head on her hands and smiled at them.

"We can move in with Leo," Cece said. "But Uncle Connor would be so, so, so lonely."

Leo laughed, but he didn't seem put out or embarrassed by Cece's suggestion at all. *Hmm,* Katie wondered.

* * * *

"You keep feeding me," Katie said. She was snuggled into Leo's arms as they stood on the front porch saying goodnight. "I really like it." She touched her lips to Leo's and sank into his full, soft mouth. Lingering, she closed her eyes and savored. Every time her lips met his, that spark lit her up and calmed her at the same time. With her eyes closed, she roamed the landscape of his face, memorized the feel of his warm skin, could smell a hint of red wine and garlic and Leo, serious, mesmerizing Leo.

His body closed in on hers. "I love cooking for you. I'd do it every night if you let me."

He really is dreamy. She believed him, his promises, his words, his visions that included her.

She caressed with her lips. Showing him her feelings.

"Woman," he grumbled. His rough deep voice vibrated all the way in her veins.

"Hmm?" she said so he could feel her voice the way she felt his.

"You're killing me."

And she smiled against him. "Doesn't feel like death to me," she hummed against his neck.

Chapter Twenty-Two

"What's your schedule like after your event today?" Leo had started calling Katie in the mornings and evenings, even on the days he planned to see her. There was a connection he wanted to nurture. He'd feed it buckets of hope and fertilizer. But this week had been insane for them both, and after he and the girls had made her pasta on Wednesday night, he'd only seen her a few stolen moments during dinners with all her girls or out on their porch. One morning he'd been working on the house and she'd rushed in, delivered homemade donuts and rushed out to make food for a bridal shower she was catering. She had another delivery today.

With the holidays coming, he wondered when he'd ever see her. Not that he'd ever hold her back, and he'd be right there making her dinner every night if she'd let him, the way he'd offered. Hell, he wanted to be around her and her girls on a permanent basis.

"I'm finished at two. And guess what?"

He'd been equally busy with his own jobs. He and his mom had held their first round of classes last week. They'd started slowly, by word of mouth to get a feel for how the neighborhood responded and to see what the families wanted out of an art center. Painting was a huge success, partly, he suspected, due to his mom's talent and enthusiasm, but also because kids loved using color. Boys and girls alike were awed at the welding class and Leo's chest puffed with pride at the light he'd seen click on for many of the kids. Whenever he'd struggled as a student with all the regular academics, the math and especially reading, art had saved him. *More* than saved — it had made him feel powerful and brilliant. That was what he wanted to give these kids.

After Christmas, when things had calmed down, they were going to have a grand opening. If he had anything to say about it, they were going to have more than one grand opening to celebrate in the new year. But he needed Katie's input for the other one.

"Lay it on me, darlin'."

"Connor is taking the girls over to see Jackson and Ellie later. Kitten needs some doggy bonding with their dogs. I thought I'd come see you. Need any help over there?"

God, she was awesome. "Need? Yes, but I'm sure you're exhausted."

"Ha, I think that's a permanent state for moms, but I want to see you. Can I bring food?"

"You can always feed me."

"Can I bust down walls or destroy something?"

The image of his goddess wielding a sledgehammer and using all her power to help him, made him hard instantly. "I'd love your help," he said, but he planned on getting her naked first. There were more important things he needed help with than ruined walls or unfinished floors.

* * * *

He wasn't breaking down walls when she arrived, and he also didn't get her naked right away. When she walked in carrying a cooler, he was on hold on the phone with the cabinet maker and in the middle of painting the kitchen. He paused mid-roll when he saw her. Sexy tight jeans molded to her body, hair up in a high messy ponytail, an old pink T-shirt that bared her belly and he suddenly lost the ability to speak.

Hell!

She walked right by him, drifted her hand across his chest, confident in how she tortured him, took the paint roller from his hand and said, "I see you went with my paint suggestion for the kitchen. Smart man."

He'd taken all of her suggestions. She just didn't know it yet. Maybe he wouldn't get her naked right away. Maybe he'd stand back and ogle her while she painted their kitchen. *Their kitchen.* The voice in the phone asking if he was still there brought him back to some sense of sanity.

"Yeah, two weeks from now is perfect. Then we'll get the counter guys in here. Haven't decided yet. Thanks." Leo hung up and watched her. His chest hurt again — more of the ice chipping off, being burned away by her. By the images of her and her girls here with him. Would he freak her out if he suggested it? Love and marriage and a shared life together. *Is it too soon?* Should he ease her into it, let her have input, help him with the renovations like he'd been doing?

The other project — one he wanted to be all hers — he'd need to talk to her about sooner or later. Later, he decided when Katie finished painting, stepped off the ladder and gave him her sexy fake pout.

"You painted most of this room before I even got here. Please tell me you have more projects for me to help with?"

"Do I count?" he asked. He tore off his T-shirt. Her eyes burned. *Oh yeah*, he thought with some relief. *I'm not the only one.*

She sashayed toward him. *Those fucking hips of hers.* He needed them in his hands again, wanted to mold them, kiss them, worship them. "Are you a project, Leo? Do you need my help?" Fuck, he loved it when her voice got deep. His siren couldn't hide how she felt about him.

Then she stood in front of him, gazing up and down his body. Her eyes alone seared through him, but when she placed her hands on his stomach, he was done. He had no fucking control around this woman. Why the hell weren't the cabinets and the counters done yet, so he could bend her over them and take her right here? Instead, he grabbed her hand and tugged her up the stairs.

"Leo," she panted after him.

"Project's upstairs." His voice sounded different, even to himself. Needy, raspy. He couldn't talk right now.

"Oh, wow, you painted in here too," she said, but he didn't give her time to study the room. Who cared about it, aside from the enormous new mattress he'd gotten, which now rested in the center? He'd get around to furniture later, enlist her help. With hands as shaky as his voice, he peeled her clothes off so he could bring her naked body flush up against him. "Leo—" she started, but he took her mouth over with his own, while he explored her body with his hands.

He lifted her up so he could crawl over the bed with her, devour her skin. She smelled so good, like sugar and chocolate. "What the hell were you baking all day?" he asked, tracing his fingers over her belly. "This fucking body of yours is my undoing. You smell phenomenal!" Leo took her lips, wanting to devour her.

"Cupcakes," she said through his kisses. He tasted the words on her lips. He dove his tongue in to tangle with hers and wove their bodies together. Her soft curves rubbing against his body set him on fire. Every sensation a lit fuse on him—her hands in the back pockets of his jeans tugging him closer, her legs wrapping around to claim him, her breasts pressing into his bare chest. *Fuck.*

He dragged his fingers down her body all the way to her core, wet and ready for him, and stroked her soft wet folds gently, while he kissed her.

"Leo!" She pulled her mouth from his and attacked his chest with her lips. "God, more. I need to taste you too. Closer. I can't get close enough. I still haven't gotten to savor your entire body."

He fucking felt the same. She pulled his wallet out of his back pocket, tore open a condom and pushed against him. "Let me."

Leo shrugged off his jeans and rolled their bodies over before she could beg. Then, *then* he paused to watch her. Straddling him, her skin flushed, breasts heavy, hips lush and her hair half out of her ponytail in a mess. Silver-blue eyes burned a path into his soul like they had from the beginning, like they always did whenever she looked at him.

She took her focus away from his face to concentrate, and *fuck* but she drove him wild. She said she hadn't been with anyone since her husband, but she stroked him and rolled the condom on like she was made to tease and massage only him, all the while soothing him with words of lust of seduction, of want, while she rubbed and rolled her hips against him, chasing after him with her heat. Her concentration on the task, on his body tortured him, had him so fucking hard he thought he might explode before he even got inside her.

"I have been longing to take my time with you, Leo. You're a work of art."

"Don't care what I am," he growled. And she laughed at him. The woman could tease him like no other. He calmed his need. He'd do anything for her.

She swayed over him like a sexy belly dancer while she stroked his arms then his chest and down in a tantalizingly slow dance. "I love your body, Leo."

He closed his eyes, vowing to let her take charge. But he couldn't help surging up, seeking more contact with her, seeking that ultimate connection.

"Leo." Her voice, ragged, seductive. He opened his eyes to see her hands on her breasts, toying, kneading. "You make me feel so sexy. I'm so needy when I'm with you. Feels so good."

"Katie, gorgeous." He grabbed her hips and dragged her over his cock. "So fucking good."

"Yes," she hissed and threw her head back. She teased him once more then sank her luscious body onto him.

They both paused. He was deep, her heat wrapped tight around him, the caress of her inner thighs branding his skin. And when she met his gaze this time, it snapped something inside him, and he lost all control, bucking up, digging his fingers into her hips, fucking her with abandon.

"Yes." Her body went wild riding him until she too lost herself and grabbed his chest, for purchase…for need? He didn't give a fuck. He pulled her down, grabbed her ass and pulsed up into her again and again, her body responding in tune to his. She nipped at his chest, raked her hands over his skin and into his hair where she pulled his head to hers and kissed the ever-loving hell out of him, breaking him. And he came, roaring her name through the kiss. He was still clenched and bucking up when Katie exploded around him, dragging out his orgasm, the very breath from him, blinding him in the most exquisite way possible.

* * * *

Katie woke naked on her stomach with Leo's body half on her, his arm slayed across her waist and his head tucked into her neck. "Mmm." She smiled and snuggled back into him. He was hard. Again, and she felt so needy too, so wanting when she was with him, like she couldn't get enough, but also secure in the knowledge he would take care of her.

She was warm and satisfied and turned on again. Staying on her stomach, she slowly rubbed her backside against him. The friction from their connected bodies as well as the sheets against her hardened nipples was its own erotic dream landscape.

"Oh," she sighed, when Leo's hands came around her and started playing with her breasts, soft and gentle, then twisting her nipples, then soft again. The contrast. Her breaths came shorter. His body responded to hers, moved against her from behind. She closed her eyes and let the sensations wash over her.

"Don't move," he ordered. But he did. He ran his hands over her back. "Fucking gorgeous body."

Mmm, his hands sent more erotic tingles throughout her as they caressed her shoulders, down her back, taking so much time with her ass. He dipped his fingers down her crease and she moaned. She glanced over her shoulder to see him kneeling behind her. His magnificent cock, hard and proud, covered in a new condom. She shivered at what he had planned. Then his hands were back on her sensitive skin, caressing, loving, tormenting. One finger dragged down, then returned to the path from her shoulders to her ass. *Torture. Pure, sweet torture.* She was going to lose her mind. She squirmed against the sheets, her nipples, her pussy on fire for him.

"More, Leo." She was panting again. It was too much.

"This is pretty fantastic right here." She could hear the smile in his voice, the awe, the desire.

"Please, Leo," she begged, as his fingers slid over her wet pussy. "I can't…I need—"

Then he gripped her hips and pulled. He smoothed down her back with one hand to keep her head on the pillow. "Stay." He kissed and licked, down, down. She'd do whatever he asked. She was drunk on lust.

"Leo." He teased her clit, lapped at her with his tongue like she was his nirvana. He didn't let up and she started coming. "Oh God." He moved once more and thrust his cock into her from behind, riding her through her orgasm, until he lost himself in her and shattered apart.

He rocked into her one last time then collapsed over her. Still connected, he dragged them side by side and wrapped his arms around her while they both floated down from the high.

This time she didn't doze off. She was spent but alive. Leo held her tight. "Wish I'd finished the shower in here so I could drag you in there with me right now. The current one barely fits me. Mmm, but I have dreams." He moved the hair off her neck and placed a series of gentle kisses and nips along her shoulder.

"Shower dreams?" She closed her eyes again and melted into his attentions.

"You have no idea, woman. It's going to be big enough for both of us. Want to help me design it?"

She turned in his arms. "You want my help?" She couldn't exactly hide the giddiness in her voice. She wanted to help. She wanted everything with him.

"On one condition," Leo said. He brought her hand to his mouth and kissed it. "You plan on using it with me. Often."

A tiny flutter of confusion swept across her heart. *What does he mean by often? Am I to visit, like I did today, sneaking a few moments out of our busy lives? I want to be here with you as a family, all of us.* She'd begun to see this as their family home, for all of them, Leo, Katie and her girls, without even asking him. Oh no, had she gotten it wrong? They'd all been helping him work on the house, the girls had been over several times. And yet...

What do you want, Leo? Why couldn't she say the words, simple words? Because her careful heart needed him to ask. It was his house and offering herself and her girls to live there with him...God, her vulnerabilities left her uncertain all the sudden. Is that what mind-blowing sex did to her, left her exposed and fragile?

No. Her heart thudded, begging for attention.

Maybe he didn't feel as strongly as she did. After all, falling in love was different when an entire family was involved. Now her heart galloped in celebration. *Oh! Love.* Katie put her hand over his heart.

"Katie?"

She was in love with him. *I'm in love with this beautiful man.* She'd fallen so damn hard, like it hadn't ever been in her control. A second chance on true love.

"You okay?" He searched her face with his knifelike intensity.

"Yeah." She smiled. She was more than okay. *Can you see into my soul?* The words hovered in her mind. But it was so soon. Maybe Leo needed more time. And she wasn't in any hurry. *I'm in love with a gorgeous, sexy, talented man! And it feels fantastic!* Katie was going to bask in her feelings and enjoy every bit of happiness coming her way. "Never been better."

Chapter Twenty-Three

This feeling had been building and she'd been trying to shut it down, to ignore it, but with one phrase from her daughter she was toast. *'It's like you love him more than you loved Dad.'* For weeks, she'd been riding a high around all things Leo, especially since love had entered the picture. But a weird niggling feeling had been beating at the back of her mind. She'd acknowledged her worries over being in a relationship, but she'd shoved her guilt as deep as it would go. She couldn't blame it on Rosie. It was her own fault, but those words slammed it home in a cloud of dust she now sat choking on. *Do I love Leo more than I loved John?* And how did her daughter know she was in love? She hadn't even told Leo yet.

She'd needed her girlfriends. She needed women she trusted to give her perspective on these confusing vines of love and guilt. Her friends had dropped everything and come to Natalie's house for food, margaritas and advice. For an hour they'd done nothing but gorge on spicy chicken tacos and laugh at Ruby's latest dating escapade.

Katie secretly thought Ruby's dates were distractions for Ruby to ignore the cranky, brooding elephant in her life. She sometimes wondered if Ruby chose her dates based on their absurdity, knowing there was absolutely nothing deep and lasting about the connection between her and the men. But Ruby made it clear she was only interested in fun right now. Katie could understand. Ridiculous amusement without attachments was certainly one way to protect the heart. She sure hoped the elephant got his head out of his ass soon and went for what he wanted.

And what do I want? I want Leo. She sucked in a breath and covered her face with her hands. *But do I deserve such an amazing love?* The thought broke her heart. *Is it love or guilt doing the breaking?*

"Katie, what the heck is wrong, lovely?" Ruby stopped telling stories with her hands and instead placed them on Katie's.

"I am…I'm so happy," Katie whispered. Her breath hitched. She could barely get the words out. "I'm so in love it hurts."

"Whoa! Hey, wait." Natalie scooted closer. "Your words and your face say two different things and those don't appear to be happy tears. Trust me, I know the difference."

The tightness in her heart was choking, needing to burst out of her chest. *What in the hell is going on?*

"Hey, honey, breathe and tell us what's wrong," Natalie said.

"I feel horrible. Or I don't, but I should. I should feel like a jerk, right?"

Natalie shoved a box of tissues in her lap. "I'm not easily confused, but, honey, explain. You're happy and in love with an amazing man who cherishes you and your girls, and you think you should feel horrible?" she said in a very kind calm voice as if she were speaking to a child. Katie felt like a child, like a complete nincompoop.

"How can I be this happy? I *had* my one true love. I loved my husband. I watched him die. He gave me three beautiful girls. And now Leo? This can't be. I can't love Leo more than John." She pleaded out the words as if needing her friends to validate her.

"Are you feeling guilty because you can't love Leo as much as John?"

Katie shook her head. "No, I feel guilty because I love Leo more," she whispered. She grabbed some tissues and wiped her face.

"Oh, honey," Natalie said, letting out a huge breath. "Guilt will bite you in the ass every time, I swear. We women shoulder that burden. I am so sick of it."

"You have nothing to feel guilty about," Ruby said.

"I don't?" Katie tried to take deep calming breaths.

"Hell no! Of course you took care of your husband while his body was ravaged with cancer," she yelled. And now Katie wanted to comfort Ruby. "Here you are finding love again and you can't grab on to it because of the big G! Ugh!"

"I feel like I'm betraying my dead husband. What is that?"

"I don't think it's a betrayal," Ellie butted in quietly and serenely. And they all focused on her. It wasn't hard to do—the aura of pregnancy and love happiness surrounded her. "You've lived several lifetimes since then, don't you think? You're not the same person. And even if your feelings are stronger for Leo than they ever were for John, that doesn't make you a bad person or make those feelings untrue. It makes them unique and, more importantly, it makes them real and it makes them yours."

"I love you ladies," Katie said. She closed her eyes and fell back into the sofa. "But I'm so confused."

"What do you mean? You tell Leo he's your dream man. That you're so in love with him it hurts, in a good way. And you try not to faint when he tells you the same." Natalie patted her hand.

"What?" Katie's eyes shot open and she pinned Natalie with them.

"Don't act like you don't, feel it in the way he gazes at you, touches you, beams whenever you're around. Like you're the only thing in the room he can see. Like you're all he *wants* to see."

"Oh my God, you're right, I think…I mean I do know." Katie squeezed Natalie's hand and giggled. "Holy shit, Leo Treversini loves me."

* * * *

At first Leo drove. He didn't remember where, his mind on autopilot while his heart slowly disintegrated. Now he was parked somewhere, hands resting on his steering wheel. They shook. He pulled them away like he'd been burned.

'I had my one true love.'

Where am I? The corner where his home and his dreams perched came into focus. *Fucking home. How did I get here?* He made it inside as far as the kitchen. Bright light poured in through the enormous windows and danced across the silvery gray paint Katie had chosen for the walls. Except this wasn't home anymore. Not with the colors she'd chosen. The gas range she'd drooled over, the damn chandelier over the nook that sparkled almost as much as her eyes.

Not with her scent permeating the walls and now scraping the back of his throat with its lingering damage. Not with images of her fused into every fucking inch of this place. He dragged himself around the room, legs sluggish and heavy. A numbness crept through is limbs. He didn't feel pain. He didn't feel anything, except he had trouble standing. He slid down to his butt and thumped his head back against the cabinet.

What the fuck happened?

Leo had gone into Gage's kitchen to wash the dirt and grime from his hands—he'd been working on Gage's bike. He'd heard her. She'd been crying, and he'd wanted to comfort her. Instinct had him turning in her direction, but then her words, '*I had my one true love...I feel guilty...*' slithered under his skin like leeches crawling from the swamp.

Fuck! What she had with Leo made her feel guilty. She'd already had her one true love long ago, while he felt as if he'd finally found his. His head swam. He'd barely made it to his truck.

Now, collapsed on his kitchen floor, alone, when the pain finally came rushing in, all the old betrayals smashed a hammer into his chest.

A tunneled windstorm raged and tossed him around inside it. He lost track of time. At some point he left and returned with cans of paint. Paint seemed to be the only thing he could focus on. Paint would fix it. A constant hollow humming in his head, like being underwater. The sounds shrouded around him. The storm of his life had unleashed, razing everything he thought he'd found, earned, loved. All of it destroyed. And the carnage wasn't done. The wind hovered in his mind, behind his eyes, in the layers of his skin, waiting, gathering strength.

He didn't bother protecting the floor or even stirring the paint cans. Instead, Leo did what he had to do. He started erasing every hint of Katie from his house.

Chapter Twenty-Four

Katie found him at home. Stuck and confused, she observed him through the windows. Curtainless, bare windows. Inside was alight. As a child she used to love seeing lights on in people's homes at night. As she'd peered in through windows, she'd conjured imaginary lives. A family celebrating a birthday together. A woman and her cat curled up in the armchair under a blanket reading a good book. Babies sleeping while a parent sang a lullaby. It had always brought her comfort, made her smile.

She wasn't smiling now.

Thank God he's okay! The relief nearly brought her legs out from under her. After losing John, well, she hadn't wanted to imagine any of the horrors of what could have happened to Leo when he'd stood her up. Even his phone was off.

Yet here he was working on his house. An activity they were supposed to do together tonight. And she knew he hadn't forgotten. The man forgot nothing.

She could see him, hug him, but her weird feeling tapped against her stomach like a bat trapped in an attic when she knocked and he didn't answer. Then she rang the doorbell and he ignored that too, ignored her. *Leo, what's going on?* But she wasn't here to wonder—she needed answers.

"Hey." She let herself inside. She walked slowly as if she'd done something wrong. Guilt and worry snaked around her bones. Leo was painting the walls, *her walls*, with a horrible greenish brown. *Huh?* Since when did he decide to change the kitchen color from the shimmery blue gray they'd picked out together?

Katie had always thought she wanted an all-white kitchen, but when Leo had shown her the navy cabinets paired with the nickel fittings, the super-cool industrial light fixtures and gorgeous yellow Moroccan tile to fill the entire backsplash, she'd tumbled into love. It was a big enough room with a sweeping high ceiling made for bold dramatic colors. They'd decided to go light on the paint and adorn the walls with framed artwork. They? Were they still a they? The walls were supposed to be a barely there color, not a shade of decomposing leaves.

What she should have found more worrisome was how Leo kept his back to her without any acknowledgment. She was too stupid in love with the kitchen design and at a loss for what the heck was happening.

"Why did you change the color?" She dropped her purse at the end of the counter. Paint struck her as the least important focus right now. Yet it held significance.

That was when he stopped. Not when she'd called and left ten thousand messages, not when she'd knocked, and not when she'd walked in and greeted him, but when she'd asked a ridiculous question about a crappy decorating choice.

"Got work to do. Shouldn't you be home with your girls?"

His words were a reprimand, a flat slap across her cheek. "What?" she said but the word didn't make it far. She'd been right about his power to hurt her. His dismissal in this moment, a million times worse than that scorching day in the sun baking on the hot asphalt of Trevi's when he'd been rude to her. So much worse. And this time she wasn't dizzy from the heat and flu, or confused by the rude behavior of a man she didn't know, but sharply aware he could land a punch without ever touching her.

She clung to the details, as if in grounding herself to the mahogany floors and the wide copper sink they'd found together, the too-bright lights, naked without their shades could all help her see what was going on. *He installed the lightbulbs.* The gorgeous antique lightbulbs she'd been so giddy to put in the huge industrial hanging lights. He'd done it without her. One more piece of her shoved aside. The counters were littered with the remains. Empty cartons and a few bulbs mocked her. In that instant she could nearly vomit at the sight of a fancy lightbulb.

For a few blurry images it all swam together. The caustic smell of paint crept up her nostrils so each breath she took burned on the intake and exhalation. Then, the burning led her straight to pissed off.

"You stood me up?" She was getting it now, confident in her discovery, and sick with it at the same time. "But why?"

"Didn't stand you up. Had work to do. You said it yourself, 'We're both busy.'" He kept painting a fine line of edging around the trim, so calm, so precise.

What the hell?

"You painted over my color. The one you let me choose. You put the lightbulbs in without me."

"It's paint and lightbulbs, nothing of consequence."

Like me.

"Leo!" she snapped and tried to ignore the lance of his words. He jerked his hand back. She desperately wanted to hide in her confused brain, like after she drank too much wine and hadn't had her coffee yet. But, at his dismissive tone, something in her gained momentum. Those snakes crawled out from under her skin now, yet she forced herself to focus on his words and not run fleeing into the night. "Didn't stand me up?" She pushed off the counter she'd sunk against and watched him calmly set the brush down in the sink.

"So, you call not picking me up for our date, not answering your phone the gazillions of times I called, ignoring me when I come over — worried out of my mind for you — and now acting like a dismissive jerk, *not* standing me up?" She shoved into his space and poked him in the chest.

He moved back like she'd burned him. Still he avoided her eyes.

"Leo, what the hell is going on?"

"Think you should go now. Get home to your kids."

"Oh, you do?" The blaze of anger licked at her mind. "How magnanimous of you. How all-knowing of Leo Treversini. My *kids* are at home with their uncle. Not at Gage and Natalie's for the fun night they had planned, because they are worried sick about you. But you can't comprehend what that's like would you? Having your dad leave the house one night for a surgery then not come home, *ever again* because that surgery was fucking *final*! Now worried about a man they've all fallen in love with who didn't show to pick up their mom, because something happened and he didn't have the decency to even *talk* to her."

"Katie," he sighed, patronizing, annoyed and reached out to her. And even with such a familiar gesture, he wasn't her Leo. He was a blank rock, unfeeling.

"Don't! You don't get to touch me now. I want an explanation. I deserve one. At least give me that and I'll make it easy for you. You'll never have to. Speak. To. Me. Again." *As if I could survive such a thing, never hearing his voice intended for me.*

"Katie, don't get mad. We need a break. I'm giving you time to get your life together."

"What the hell is going on?" She stepped back. She put her hand over her heart to keep all the shattering pieces in one spot. "Break? Time? What fucking bullshit! Clue, Leo Treversini, don't ever tell me when I can or can't get mad. I'm so far beyond mad right now, I could hit you. Would that even make a difference?" She could barely get the last few words out. Her throat closed up. Inside her heart, all her promises and dreams fractured. Her adrenaline spiked and fell so fast she could barely stay standing. Once more, her world was collapsing around her and she couldn't do a thing to hold it together.

She'd fallen so hard in love with this man, had thought they were in love with each other, dreamed of a future with him, felt safe and protected with him. And he was dismissing her. Was this it? Was he not going to fight for them? She couldn't even see him, the man she loved, in his eyes. He was blank. "Don't you dare criticize my life. I may have struggles, but I'm doing a damn fine job raising my three girls and running a business all by myself. You lied to me, Leo. You swore you'd be careful with my emotions. Were all your words and promises and feelings fake? Did I imagine these past few months, the connection we had, the—"

"A loose connection isn't everything, Katie." *Punch!* His hands were on his hips, his eyes on the floor.

That blow nearly crumpled her. "*Loose* is how you would describe it?" she whispered.

"I'm letting you go!" he yelled, his body taut, angry all the sudden. *What the hell is he angry about?* "I can't do this. I can't be him for you!"

"Him who?" Her poor scorched throat ached with each word.

"Your husband! The love of your life! I heard you," he bellowed and flung things off the counter. Bulbs and tools shattered to the floor. "I heard you talking to Natalie, when I was at Gage's. John, he was it for you. He was your one chance at true love. The chance you had...the man you buried, Katie. How you feel guilty being with me. I won't be someone's second-best ever again."

"Well," she whispered, taking in the once-beautiful, now-tragic scene around her. Katie breathed out her agony and exhaustion. Like losing a long fight and crumpling down on the bare ground. Like giving up. She stepped over, exhausted now, beaten down, to grab her purse from the wreckage. Broken shards of those beautiful tinted light bulbs, a hammer, the little silver key for opening paint cans. "It's a good thing you didn't stay and eavesdrop a few minutes longer,

Leo…" She gasped as a piece of glass sliced into her palm.

"Katie, Jesus, let me see—"

"Don't," she stumbled back, pulled her purse in front of her like a shield and cradled her wounded hand in the other.

"Don't be stupid, darlin'. Let me clean and bandage—"

"No!" she snapped and couldn't hold the tears back any longer. "Don't touch me. You don't get to call me darlin' and you don't get to touch me."

She ran-tripped to the front door and yanked it open. He was nearly to her when she reared back. "I don't feel guilty because of my love for John." She tried to wipe her face, but it didn't do any good. There were too many to catch. "I was trying to explain to Natalie how my love for you is so huge, so much grander, and wilder and so much *more* than anything I ever felt for my husband. My guilt, Leo Treversini, is how could I ever be blessed with something as exquisite as you in my life after I'd already been blessed with John. Guess I don't have to worry anymore." And she stumbled down the steps.

Chapter Twenty-Five

"What the fuck do you want?" Connor Duggan's curt voice vibrated with anger.

"Tell me she's okay," Leo said. "She ran out of here, bleeding. Didn't want me to touch her. Her car's still here."

"Not sure I owe the asshole who broke my sister's heart anything, but her hand should be fine." Connor's voice was deadly cold. "She was smart enough to know she was in no shape to drive so she walked to Ellie's clinic. Ellie sewed her up. Not sure how the rest of her will get put back together. But my sister's nothing if not strong. Jackson and Gage are on their way over to get her car. Gotta go."

"Fuck! Fuck it all!" He threw his phone across the room. What in the ever-loving hell had come over him and caused him to act like such an idiot? His heart. A place he'd buried long ago. He should have kept it that way. Only these past few months, letting Katie in, falling in love with her... He'd been lying to himself all those cold years. A buried heart might as well be a dead heart. Love, *her* love, was the best fucking thing that ever happened to him. Hers and her girls', and he let his own fear and past smash it to smithereens.

He sensed there was a fine place in hell for someone like him, the way he'd gutted her. Only he didn't have to go to hell to feel the force of his actions. He was living it. And it was worse than any heartbreak, any betrayal he'd survived. This time, *he'd* done it. He was at fault. From the haunted look on her face when she'd left, like she'd never recognize him again. He wasn't certain he could fix what he'd broken.

Leo was cleaning up the last of the glass shards when Jackson and Gage barged in. He might have been annoyed or concerned or confused, any number of emotions, but he was gutted. And all he could see through the beautiful pieces of broken orangish glass was the blood seeping out of Katie's hand when she ran. And the look on her face, shattered, bleeding in its own way.

"What the fuck is your problem, Doc?" Gage set a bottle of bourbon and paper cups on the counter, so Leo knew that even if his friend beat the shit out of him, which he deserved, he also aimed to patch him back up.

"I don't know you well yet," Jackson said, "But I am very protective of the women in my life. Katie's like a sister to me. Gage said something must be up, besides you being an asshole."

"Your woman is shattered, man. Natalie's ready to kill you, but I know you. I *know* you. So talk." Gage poured them each a shot of bourbon. Leo took a cup. He wasn't sure he could stomach it. As much as he wanted to get lost, he deserved the pain, every punch.

"Jackson?" Gage offered.

Jackson stood with his arms crossed and shook his head. "I have precious cargo to get home tonight once we're done. Not fucking around with alcohol."

Gage never drank when he was driving, either. "I have orders from Natalie not to leave until I sort your shit, which could take all night. I'll crash on your couch. Now, what the hell happened? One minute you were telling me how you were fixing up this old dame with Katie and her daughters in mind. You're finally fucking living life again with passion, happiness, in a way I haven't seen you do in ten years—maybe longer, if I'm honest. Because face it, man, your marriage to Monica wasn't great. The next thing I know, I have a pile of Russia-sized manure to deal with."

"I fucked up." Leo slumped onto one of the stools. "I heard her say she felt guilty for her feelings toward me. How could they be love when she'd already had that kind of beauty. Misinterpreted it. Thought she was putting up with me even though I could never be as good as her husband. Swore I'd never be someone's second best again. Got pissed and acted like an idiot."

"You got scared." Gage shook his head and drank his shot. "Brother, you have got to deal with your past, or you're never going to have a future. Especially not one with that gorgeous family. Does Katie know?"

Gage was the only one who knew the minute details about that horrible day in Leo's life. Not even his family had the whole story. He'd never had the stomach to tell them. The worst day of his life…although today was coming in a close second.

"Know what?" Jackson demanded.

"Leo's first wife cheated on him. Told him one evening she'd found someone better, Leo wasn't 'classy' enough for her, wasn't following the path she wanted him to. Then she drove away and got in an accident. She died at the hospital with Leo at her side and the doctor offering sympathy for the life of his wife and unborn child. She hadn't even told Leo she was pregnant."

"Fuck!" Jackson swore.

"Jesus Christ, Gage, not your story to tell." Leo ran his hands through his hair while pain swamped his heart. Now the pain wasn't so much about long-ago loss and betrayal anymore—it was about him and Katie.

"Time's up, Doc. If I've learned nothing in life, it's that you have not one single minute to waste. You not dealing with your past is partly why you're feeling like death. You might deserve a few punches, but I really don't want to have to clean up blood. Left that part of my life behind. You love her and you haven't told her what you went through. Tells me, A—you're stupider than I thought, or B—you still have trust issues."

"Both," Leo admitted. "Worse, she loves me."

"*Worse?*" Jackson hissed. "What the fuck?"

"I meant," Leo began, "what I thought I heard her say wasn't the whole truth. I got pissed and didn't stay to listen the rest. She feels guilty *toward* her dead husband for loving me. She *loves me,* and I shit all over it."

"You love her back?" Jackson asked.

"More than life. Loved her the first night I saw her, I think. It was like no one else was even there. I can't breathe without her. She and those girls are the most precious, beautiful things in this world to me."

"Hmm." Jackson took the stool next to him, poured Gage another shot and added some to Leo's cup. "Guess you better figure out how to untangle this mess you created." He patted Leo on the back. "Good thing you have some people to help you."

* * * *

Katie lay on her bed facing Brie. Cece sprawled across the foot. It always amazed Katie how much room her tiny child took up. Rosie had disappeared as soon as Ellie and Jackson had brought Katie home and she'd given them all a super-shortened version of what happened, that she and Leo were over. Then she'd promptly burst into tears.

Rosie, her daughter who for the past several months had shown hardly any emotion except surly, looked as if someone had killed Kitten. Then she'd stalked into her bedroom and slammed the door so hard Katie thought it might be broken.

Katie probably could have handled that incident better as a mother, but as a woman she was annihilated. And moments like this it was hard to separate all the different parts of herself. They all bled together. Her adrenaline had long since taken a nosedive while Ellie had stitched her up and Ellie's Rottweiler had snuggled her hip in comfort. By the time she had seen her girls' faces lit up with happy expectation, even Kitten sitting with her tongue hanging out, Katie had snapped like a branch cased in freezing ice. And, unfortunately, there was no taking it back. Now she had to try to explain to her girls when she didn't understand herself.

Where would she even start? *He thinks I don't love him enough? Or, he doesn't love us enough?* The truth was she felt both of those. Had he chickened out? Why hadn't he even had the courage to talk to her? He'd broken down all her barriers, promised to take care with her emotions. What was she to believe now?

She couldn't feel bad for loving him. After all she'd ultimately had no say in the matter. There was no choosing when hearts were involved There was only the free-dive off a cliff. Whether it splashed brilliantly into the warm springs or crash landed was a crap shoot each time. She'd thought they'd taken that dive together, and would be each other's safety net.

"How could he not want us?" Cece cried again. "I love him."

Makes two of us. Pain slashed through Katie's heart again. Over and over the whipping flayed her open. *God dammit!*

"I think something's wrong," Brie said.

Katie gripped her daughter's hand and closed her eyes. *Understatement of the year.*

"I mean with Leo."

Something was definitely wrong with him, but here she and her daughters were shredded by the aftermath. She wanted to smack him upside the head. "I'm sorry you girls are hurting. It's so hard to understand and I wish I could make it easier. I…" The lamest fucking excuse she could come up with. She didn't want to tell them how cold he'd been. How he'd turned himself off. Just because she was in hate with Leo Treversini didn't mean her daughters had to carry the same burden. But damn, carrying it alone sure sucked. No, it wasn't hate, not even close. Hate was one note, bland, dismissive. Not this all-consuming rupture allowing her insides to bleed out.

"No, Mom, Leo doesn't seem like the kind of guy to change his mind like that. And why all of a sudden? I see the way he is around you, like you light the world up for him. And the way he interacts with us. He's genuine. I think he got scared. Erika says when boys get scared, they do stupid things."

Huh? Her gorgeous middle kid, her smart, sensitive beauty. She and her friend Erika were right. Boys did stupid things. Weren't they supposed to grow out of that behavior? Her exhausted broken heart wondered.

He'd said he wouldn't be someone's second best ever again. *I don't understand.* Was that the heart of it? Looking back and taking her own feelings out of it, devastation had poured from him, not indifference as he'd tried to pretend. *But some fresh hell.* Had his wife not loved him with every cell in her body? Had the woman hurt him in some unforgivable way?

He'd overheard her talking about John and feeling guilty. Then he'd guessed wrong and made stupid assumptions instead of talking it out with her. If he had, he might have heard how great her love was for him. Now, now she didn't know what to think.

"He quit on us!" wailed Cece. She rolled off the bed and stormed out of the bedroom yelling, "I'm going to sleep with Kitten. She's the only one I'll ever trust."

Katie and her mid-kid giggled. "Our little drama queen," Brie said. "I'm sorry Leo hurt you, Mama."

"Oh, honey," Katie began and ran her hands through her daughter's hair. "I am too. The heart is strong and fragile at the same time, isn't it? The sucky part of life is there will be times you have to relearn it and re-feel it. But you may be right about Leo. He overheard me saying something to Natalie earlier today and he got mad and hurt. Instead of talking to me, he closed himself off. I think there's a heartbreak inside him that has nothing to do with me or you girls or his desire to be a family with us. In trying to protect himself, he unleashed on me. Sometimes we hurt the ones we love the most."

"Are you ever going to talk to him again? Maybe he would want to explain and apologize?" Brie asked with such hope in her voice. Her girls had fallen head over heels in love with Leo too. *Too bad falling in love sometimes opens the door for torment.*

Would she be brave enough to face him again? God, she wanted to smack him, but yes, she also wanted to talk. Only if he wanted to explain and apologize. Only if all four of them were as important to him as he was to them. God help her pick up the pieces if that wasn't the case. *There's only so much loss and recovery a person can handle in life.* "I don't know, baby. I hope so, but it's not my decision to make."

"I hope so too," Brie whispered.

Chapter Twenty-Six

Ten years since Leo had woken both hungover and shattered. Twice now, a woman had broken his heart. But the experiences couldn't be more different. Monica had betrayed him, but the way she'd shattered him paled now in comparison. A hangover he could handle. A shame-on-him broken heart hangover ate at his insides like a disease. He'd learned over the last few weeks that his love for Monica was nothing compared to anything about Katie, the light in his world. She'd given him back laughter, beauty and love. She'd healed the wounds inside him, allowing him belief, dreams and hope.

That she loved him more than she'd loved her husband, her first true love, and he'd stomped all over it, tried to toss it away because he was…he was scared fucking shitless. Guess he deserved to feel like he'd been burned alive without the numbness of death to soothe.

And this time he'd been the one to hurt another. He might not have cheated on Katie, but he'd betrayed her love and trust all the same. Worse, he'd betrayed her girls. Fear was a monster he'd had no idea had been lurking inside him.

Gage was right, smug bastard. Leo had never dealt with his past. Hell, he'd never told his family everything. It wasn't only fear holding him back—it was the inability to trust. Coming face to face with his demons, he realized he might as well have been the one who'd died on the side of the highway that horrible night.

How did one go about moving beyond a tragedy? Or, living with it, but moving on? Leo had to figure it out, because he wasn't about to lose the best thing that had ever happened to him.

Fully clothed and reeking like a cheap distillery, he dragged himself out of bed. Ugh, he was rank. Shower first, then coffee. Then he had a life to fix, not only one, but hopefully the lives of four very important ladies.

Leo was cleaning the kitchen to the aroma of coffee brewing when his mom arrived.

"Honey," she called from the front porch. "My hands are full—are you home? I can't reach the doorbell."

"Hey." Leo took the box of supplies from her hands and made way for her to enter.

"What happened?" His mom's face turned ashen, her mouth wide when she saw him. She didn't step inside, like she was afraid of a demon or blood bath. "You look like hell, Leo. Like somebody died. Tell me you're okay, Katie, her girls?"

Guess I'm done hiding my emotions. "Come on in." He shifted the box and put his arm around her shoulders.

But she was more stubborn than him and his siblings combined.

"Nope, tell me out here. Tell me no one's dead. I mean it. You look worse than when we arrived in Chicago after Monica died." His heart broke again at what he'd put his parents through. At how he'd then spent the last decade keeping everyone, including them, further than arm's length, more like a galaxy apart.

"No one's dead. But I could use your help. I made coffee and I have some of your polenta cake in the freezer."

Finally she walked in. "Don't placate me with my own cake. Tell me what's wrong. What the hell happened to the wall? You painted over a gorgeous silver gray with something resembling old puke?" She covered her eyes like she'd been blinded.

He felt like old puke. He should've known he couldn't paint over Katie's light.

"Wasn't silver Katie's choice? It was so perfect in here. Long night?" She pushed the empty bottle of bourbon and the shot glasses out of the way.

Longest fucking night of my life. He waited till he'd poured them each some coffee before he spoke. "I hurt Katie." Might as well get it all out. "I thought she couldn't love me the way she loved her first husband and I fucked up. Broke up with her. Told her we were through."

"What?" she whispered. "Leo, her love brought you back to life. And her girls…oh, honey, what happened? I'm sure she'll always love her husband, but she also seems like the type of woman to want to live life to the fullest. She glows around you. Is it about losing Monica? I…your father and I felt like you never got over her death. I can't begin to comprehend how losing her must have devastated you. We watched you, hoped you'd heal, but you never did fully, did you? At least I thought you hadn't until Katie."

Leo sipped his coffee which bubbled like acid in his stomach with what he was about to say. "Monica did destroy me, but not how you think. I never told you about that night. She ran out of the house after telling me she'd been having an affair."

"She *what*?" Shock laced her hushed retort. His mother was loud and brash and swore up a storm, but when she was disappointed-angry or hurt-angry, her quiet voice made them all fear the punishment. And now he was only going to make it worse. She came around the counter toward him.

Leo rubbed his hands over his eyes and held his head, which had grenades exploding inside, from the bourbon or from the shame, he wasn't altogether certain. "At the hospital, after she died, I found out she was almost four months pregnant." He bit back the tears, or tried to. Until he watched the details play out over his mom's face—anguish, pain, heartache. And when she wrapped her arms around him instead of calling him an idiot, Leo let his tears purge the old wounds.

He expected her recriminations for never telling her. Instead she gave him what she'd always given as a mother—love and acceptance. "Oh, Leo. I am so, so sorry. No wonder you were lost."

"I'm sorry I never told you guys," he said through a jagged breath. "It felt like I fell into a black hole and couldn't get out. Truth is, I didn't want to. Seemed easier than maybe ever being hurt again."

She squeezed him tight one last time then pulled herself together. "Well," she started and grabbed some tissues. "Aren't we a pair? Seems like the time for crying is over and you have more important things to accomplish."

"Yeah," he said and wiped his face. "I do. Probably the hardest task I've ever had in my life, fix four broken hearts."

"Yes." She nodded. "But also the most amazing thing you'll ever do, honey. Get those girls back. Because when I said this was a family house, I meant it. And you all make a gorgeous family. Plus, I am over the moon to have three instant grandkids. If they'll have me."

* * * *

Her phone went right to voicemail and he couldn't blame her. After talking with his mom, he'd gone to Katie immediately, but no one was home. Even Kitten didn't bark or rush the door. Empty, the house was fucking empty, as if they'd never been there in the first place. Finally getting hold of Gage, he'd learned they'd left town for a few days.

Fuck! He'd chased her away from everything she loved.

So he went to the one place he could breathe — work. He shut all noise out and began burning his way out of the darkness. Hours he sweated and created, dividing his energy between the labor and the creativity. Leo worked his ass off for two days. Cleaning out the second storefront, installing new floors, windows and overhead lights. At night he welded, created, and let his dreams back into his heart. He needed it, the ache, the physical awareness to beat down his painful ghosts. They had no place in his life with his girls. And he did consider them his. He had an enormous amount of groveling in his future, and it might take him the rest of his life to regain her trust, but he'd do whatever it took to assure Katie and her beautiful daughters that he would not let them down again.

When there was nothing left to do to his sculpture, he stood back and studied it. Now that his goddess was finished, he was shocked at how wrong he'd gotten it all. She wasn't the one who needed to be reborn. *He* was. And she'd saved him. Leo polished her outstretched arms, open in a pose not in searching as he'd originally thought, but to welcome, to offer her healing powers to the world. She'd healed herself, her daughters and now him.

Power surrounded her. Power she wielded. And power she gave. All in the form of love. Brilliance shimmered around her.

When his phone rang, he shoved his work gloves off and sagged with relief. "Katie." Fuck, he was so choked up, he couldn't talk. She'd called him back. He didn't think she would. He didn't deserve it. "You called."

"Life's too short to hold stuff in, I guess." Her voice had never sounded so hollow and exhausted.

He closed his eyes and tried to picture her. What was she thinking? What was going through her mind? "Where are you?"

"Connor drove us to my parents'. We…I had to…to do something. We didn't feel right. Connor thought a change of scenery would help. I'm not sure if it did or not."

Jesus. And her parents' for Thanksgiving? That must have cost her, from all she'd said about how cold her mother was and how much the woman hated to cook. He'd fucking ruined their holiday. He'd forgotten about Thanksgiving until his own mother and Natalie had tag-teamed him and dragged him to dinner. They'd threatened to bring the party to his house, sawdust and all.

"You hurt us, Leo." The catch in her voice was more painful than any wound he'd lived through in his life.

Fucking hell. He'd ruined more than their holiday. It took every ounce left in him not to bash the phone against the brick wall.

"Are you there?"

"Right here, Katie. Right here. I…darlin'…I am so, so sorry for how I treated you."

"Why, Leo? That's why I returned your call…your messages. I need to understand. I need to be able to tell the girls something more than you acted like an asshole. They loved you —" Her words sliced through him.

Fuck me. It's now or never. "I got scared. I…something from my past got triggered, something I kept at bay for a long time. And I couldn't stand the thought of not being enough for you. I've been broken for a long time. In denial about it. And you, *all four of you*, put me back together, darlin'. I want to tell you everything in person. I am so sorry. I hurt all of you."

"Yeah," she sighed and he thought he actually heard her swallow back her tears. Sucking in a breath, she continued, "The thing is, they've been hurt before. A lot, in life already. I don't know how much more they can take."

Jesus, she was killing him. The knife went deeper and deeper. He'd never hurt so many people at the same time. *I love you.* He wanted to say, but over the fucking phone? "Let me come to you. Please. You don't owe me anything. But I want the chance to apologize in person."

"I'm not sure, yet, Leo. I think I need more time. It's more than me I have to think about."

"Whatever you need. If you can, will you call or text when you get back?"

"I'll think about it. Goodnight, Leo."

The phone may be dead silent in his hand, her voice gone, but he refused to believe this was the end. She wanted, no, she *needed*, to trust him again, and he'd do everything he could to win her trust back. Her love and the love of her daughters was worth it.

Owe him? *Poor man.* Didn't he realize love wasn't about being in someone's debt? It was about wanting to be the best for each other, for all of them together as a family. They had become a family before her eyes. She felt it. She knew it. And she wanted to keep it.

Family. So many different ways to imagine it. Right now, she was hiding out in her girlhood bedroom while her daughters made cookies with their grandmother. Ha, that woman had never made cookies with Katie or Connor when they were kids. When they'd arrived two nights ago, Katie had wondered if she'd made a huge mistake. The last thing she needed in her fragile state was being around her mother. To be fair, Connor had packed them all up, including their Thanksgiving food, and brought them here. Katie'd merely fallen in line.

Unlike the restrained, matter-of-fact woman Katie's mother normally was, Anna Duggan had welcomed them in with smiles and hugs. Katie had almost started crying again right then, standing in her mom's arms, but she'd kept it together because there was no way she'd be able to explain her tears.

"Turkey's ready," her mother called from downstairs. Ugh, her mother's turkeys left a lot to be desired, like, say, everything. But Katie was trying to be grateful someone was able to cook.

"I miss Leo," Cece said first thing when they all sat around the table. "He's Mama's ex-boyfriend. He didn't want us." Then she burst into tears and flung herself into her grandmother's arms. "He was Leo, my lion, and I thought I was his firelight. I thought he loved us!" She wailed and clung to Katie's mom. It almost made Katie laugh to see her youngest wrapped around her mom, seeking comfort. If anyone could break down walls of propriety, her baby could.

"It's good you started dating again." He mother nodded her way. "The girls need a good man in their lives."

"Hey," Connor said. He held up his wineglass in cheers. "Who am I, Uncle Chopped Liver?" All three of Katie's girls giggled and clinked their glasses with his.

"You could use a good woman in your life too, young man."

Katie silently agreed with her mom on that front.

"Hey," her girls chimed in.

"We're the good women in his life, Nana," Brie said. She clinked her glass with her uncle's again and he leaned over and kissed her head.

God, now Katie wanted to cry again. Her girls were so amazing.

* * * *

"Please don't break up with anyone next year around Thanksgiving. I vow never again to choke down Mom's attempt at turkey." Connor sank onto the couch next to Katie with a huge bowl of popcorn. Everyone else had gone to bed.

"I didn't break up with him. He broke my heart."

He put his arm around her in a quick hug. "That's why I packed us all up and brought us here. It's not a spa, but as cold as she was with us growing up, Mom showers your girls with fun and affection."

"It's weird, isn't it?" she said, and put her wineglass down.

"Those kids have magical powers."

"Thank you, Connor. You always know what I need in times of crisis and heartbreak."

"I'm fucking awesome."

"Ha!" She smacked his chest. "Never getting close to someone again does not say, 'Awesome.'"

"Hey! I have you girls. I have an amazing career. I have Kitten."

Kitten was sprawled belly up on the floor, making her puppy snores and drooling. But as soon as Connor said her name, she woke and sniffed out the popcorn bowl, pining her eyes at them.

Katie stole some popcorn. "Yum. Lots of butter. Exactly what I needed. I mean someone special to you, Connor. Someone you can unleash your amazing, kind, sensitive heart on. You haven't found anyone since Nina."

"Please," he scoffed. "She wasn't special."

"She still hurt you. Walking away when she did."

"Yeah, well, I think any woman walking away while my brother-in-law was dying of cancer would sting."

"So, if she wasn't all that, why haven't you tried to find someone else?"

"I believe we're talking about your heart and second chances, not mine."

Ugh, men and their deflection, their ability to keep their emotions bottled up so tight. They'd been close as siblings, two sensitive kids raised by the most unemotional parents ever. John's death had broken something inside Connor, like it had broken the rest of them. And since then her brother had eschewed relationships. He was afraid, like Leo.

Heartbreak sucked, but it unfortunately went hand-in-hand with love. The alternative was a long, cold emotionless life. Too lonely for her. She didn't want to be like these men in her life, completely shut off from or afraid of any chance at love again. But putting herself out there meant being brave.

"I called him," she said quietly. "Or, returned his calls. He's been trying to get hold of me."

"You're a better man than I am," he said.

"Thank goodness I'm not a man. I couldn't handle all your brooding. He's hurting, Connor. I'm not saying he didn't smash my heart into a million pieces, but I don't think he meant to. I could feel his love. I wanted to know why he did what he did."

"You've always been brave and wise." Connor offered her more popcorn.

She smiled. "True. He apologized. Ghosts from his past, I guess. He feared not being good enough for us. Said he'd been broken for a long time and the girls and I put him back together." She was crying again. This time the tears were for her beautiful Leo. What had happened to make him feel not good enough? She wanted to wrap him up in her love and make it all better. *Am I brave enough to work things out with him? Give him my heart again?*

"He said we healed him, but I think he healed us too. I love him and I want to make a family with him,

Connor. He wants to tell me what happened in person and I need to give him a chance." She decided right then. "I thought, no, I'm certain I discovered an amazing love again. And I'm going to fight for him. For me and the girls."

Connor fist bumped her. They sat in silence for a bit. Her brother made the ridiculous puppy sit and tossed popcorn up for her to catch. "So, you're leaving me then, huh?" He clutched his heart in mock pain.

"I hope so, goofball. I hope so."

Connor launched popcorn at her, and Kitten, in all her oversized puppy wiggles, pounced.

Family. She'd wanted to make one with Leo. And she needed to know if he wanted the same. It wasn't about owing, but it also wasn't about letting things slip through her fingers in a passive way because she was hurting either. She had a duty to herself and her girls to give him one more chance. Maybe the word *owe* did apply in its own way. Her duty to her girls, to her own happiness…it wasn't so much a debt she was obligated to, but rather a seeing to their ultimate health and happiness. For all of them.

Chapter Twenty-Seven

"Hi," Katie said. She stood in Leo's doorway on Sunday evening. Somber eyes surrounded by dusky circles stood out against his tired skin. After deciding at her mother's that she would do whatever it took to salvage their relationship, even if she hadn't been the one to crack it, she could hardly wait to find him.

"Darlin'," he said like it was his last breath on earth. Like she was his salvation. She certainly felt like he was hers. He held out his hand to her.

She stepped into him and put her arms around him. "Leo."

"God, I love you." He wrapped her up in a tight hug, kicked the door shut and carried her inside. She met his embrace. *Love?* Yes, it surrounded her.

"I wanted to tell you on the phone. Hell, I've wanted to tell you a million times since I met you. Then I was an ass and hurt you. Please give me a chance to explain. I don't deserve it, but I need you to know how amazing you are. How much you mean to me. I want everything with you, with your wonderful girls. I want to give you the world. I am unbelievably sorry." He placed her on the kitchen counter and stood between her legs. Then he gently held her hand and inspected her wound. "It's healing."

When she took his face in her hands, peace washed over him. "You love me?"

"So fucking much."

She brought him closer, put her lips to his and whispered, "I love you, too."

"Please say it again." Leo basked under her touch.

"I love you, Leo Treversini. Huge, epic love. My heart started beating again when you came into our lives."

He took her mouth in a searing kiss, gripping her head with his massive, wonderful hands. Stealing her breath, soothing her heart, making the wings under her skin take flight. *Oh, my love.* "You're crying." Katie wiped a tear off his cheek.

He kept his eyes shut and leaned into her touch. "You are my light, my breath, my heart. I almost ruined the most amazing thing to ever happen to me. I need to tell you what happened. Will you come with me?"

"I'll go anywhere with you, Leo Treversini."

He carried her to his bedroom and took both their shoes off. Then Leo tucked them together under the covers.

Side-by-side, they faced each other and he held her around the waist. "I was married once a long time ago." Jagged edges laced his words, each one a wound, a sin, a regret. "We were young, and I thought we were in love. Although now that I have you, it's clear to me what Monica and I had wasn't this soul-deep beauty."

"What happened?"

"She wanted me to pursue the academic side of my art, to be a tenured professor, to be involved in all the bureaucratic bullshit of a large university, and I…only wanted to make art. I honestly don't know who did more damage to the other. I was always right, stubborn. Maybe I hurt her too, in a way, shut her out. She found someone else. Started having an affair."

She reached her hand into his hair to caress his head and watched him sigh in pleasure, in exhaustion. "Oh, Leo."

"She told me one night, flung it at me. I didn't say anything. I was so shocked, gutted. I didn't know people really did that kind of thing. She left. Drove away and got into an accident."

"What?" Katie gasped.

"I was at the hospital with her when she died. The doctors gave me condolences for the loss of my wife and my unborn child. She was about four months pregnant. She hadn't told me."

"No! Leo." Katie buried her face in his neck and let her own tears fall. "Oh, honey."

They lay tangled, holding each other. Leo's pulse calmed against her cheek and she gave him a gentle kiss on his neck. He let out a huge breath. "I never told anyone the entire story. Except Gage. We were neighbors back then and he heard me tearing apart my garage studio. My family only knew Monica died. I never told them the rest until this week. When I heard you talking to Natalie, when I was an ass and didn't stay to listen to the rest. Something broke in me, like I wasn't good enough for you to love me. All my shame and anger from ten years ago came crashing back. And I tried to push you away before you could hurt me."

She listened, snuggled into him, rubbed his back.

He rested his forehead against hers. "I promise. I will do everything in my power to take care of you and your girls and to make certain you all feel precious. I want to make a life with the four of you, here in this house. If you'll have me. Do you think the girls will forgive me? They're pretty fierce about their mama."

"Honestly, Brie and Cece will be easy. My oldest is an enigma to me these days, so she might be a tougher nut to crack, but I think we can bring her around. The person you might have to sweet talk is my brother."

"I'm ready. God, woman." He kissed her, first her eyes, then her cheeks and finally her lips. "How did I get so lucky?"

"We both got lucky."

"Mmm." He snuggled in. "I never want to let you go, but I bet you need to get home to your girls."

Katie sighed, "Well, they're all in bed, but I do have lunches to make, laundry to do and too many clients to cook for this week."

"Can I drive you home?"

"I need my van, possessed though she may be."

"All right," he said and helped her up. "I'll follow you."

"There's no need. Besides you're barely awake."

He leaned in and kissed her. "Indulge me while I make sure the love of my life gets home safe to her girls."

"Okay," she said after nearly swooning. *The love of my life.* She felt the same about him. Lucky indeed. "When you put it like that."

Chapter Twenty-Eight

Charlie? Rosie's old best friend was across the hall when Rosie exited the girls' restroom, but misery shrouded him like a guard. Skinny, dragging his feet, head down with greasy hair like he hadn't washed it in days. Charlie had never been any of those things. Big, boisterous, always clean and funny, and so enigmatic. The worst part? He looked right through her and not so much on purpose. He was simply empty.

She was startled to see him after school, since it was Monday and the only club meeting was the school newspaper. She'd made sure none of Sienna's activities overlapped.

Even by avoiding her, Rosie heard stuff. Sienna was now charging her friends to find them online boyfriends. The girls weren't allowed to see pictures of the guys. Could only talk to them via text, but were required to send photos of themselves, sexy photos. It made Rosie's stomach churn to think of taking pictures of herself in her underwear, let alone sharing them with anyone. She barely liked her own body and there was no way she wanted anyone else to see it, especially strange guys on the internet.

Cockroaches skittering around her bedroom would have made her feel more comfortable. She'd researched the website and it screamed icky. Eventually, when a bunch of girls from school were paired up with dates, everyone would get together at a secret meeting place for their first group date. Definite heebee jeebies!

Head down, Charlie slunk into the boys' bathroom.

What happened, Charlie? God, her heart hurt. He was her best friend, her first friend, or he had been. Now they were nothing. They hadn't spoken in months, not even after she'd severed her association with Sienna. He'd changed so much and refused to talk to her. Instead she'd watched him shrink in on himself more and more as the school year went on. He'd even quit newspaper she'd discovered when she went to her first meeting.

Maybe if she stood here and waited long enough when he came out she'd force him to talk to her. She'd yell an apology, any apology across the corridor. Maybe if it was loud enough and echoed off the lockers, he'd finally listen to her. She was determined to make him hear her.

For twenty minutes she waited, alternating between standing and sitting. Each time she sank down to the floor and got comfortable she'd jump back up in case he came out. He was still in there. No one else was around and she was missing newspaper. She let ten more minutes tick slowly by. Ten minutes seemed like forever when you were waiting, when you were worried.

"Rosie?" Leo stood at the end of the hall. Leo who'd broken her mom's heart. Who'd broken all their hearts. She'd ditched art today. It was the first time she'd ever skipped a class. It hurt too much, knowing he didn't really want them, when they'd all begun to like him, to trust him. She couldn't face him and started to walk away, but her worry for Charlie stopped her. *What if he's sick?*

"Everything okay? Did your mom tell you we talked last night?" He walked closer.

His words whooshed at her through a tunnel. A tunnel of anxiety and worry. She'd mostly tried to ignore her mom this morning. When she'd seen the devastation Leo had caused last week, Rosie had closed up. Easier to shut people out than feel pain.

"Something's wrong."

Yes.

She couldn't go in the boys' room, but he could.

"Do you need help? Rosie, I can—"

The words came out in a rush. "My friend went in there a long time ago. He hasn't come out and I'm worried."

Leo took one glance where she pointed and pushed in through the doors. "Rosie," he yelled from inside the bathroom.

She slammed through the door. Charlie was on the floor, an empty pill bottle next to him. "Charlie!" His name caught in her throat.

"Take my phone. Call nine-one-one, now," Leo said. "Tell them we need an ambulance. He's got a pulse, but he's barely responsive."

Charlie. No. No. No.

"You can do it, Rosie. I need you to help me. We need to get him to a hospital."

Her fingers shook as she dialed. But she found the words to speak.

"My friend Charlie collapsed. He took some pills. We need...we need an ambulance to Corvallis High School. Now, please hurry. I'm with him and one of our teachers, Leo Treversini."

"I can feel a pulse, but he's barely responding," Leo said. "Put it on speaker."

"Okay. Who am I speaking to?" the nine-one-one operator asked.

"Rosie Walsh."

"Okay, Rosie and Leo. We're sending an ambulance. Leo, I need you to gently roll Charlie to his side. Can you tell me what pills he took? And how long ago he might have taken them?"

Rosie fumbled for the bottle. "The bottle is Vicodin. It's been about fifty minutes. I was waiting for him, but he never came out."

"Rosie, you helped your friend. Where are you in the school?"

"In the boys' restroom on the main floor by the art classrooms," she said.

"Good. Now both of you are going to help us get to him. Leo, I need you to stay with Charlie. Do not try to make him throw up or drink anything. Rosie, I need you to go to the office and tell them what happened. Take the phone with you. We need to alert them. Can you do that? I'm going to stay on the phone with you. And when they arrive, you're going to guide them to your friend and Leo, okay?"

* * * *

"Jesus, honey. Are you okay?" Katie crushed her oldest in a hug outside the middle school. Rosie slumped against her chest and started sobbing.

"Oh, honey. Talk to me."

"It's Charlie, Mom. He took some pills and he wasn't awake and I don't—"

"Shh. You helped him. You were there in time for him."

"It was Leo. He helped. I was so stupid. I was just standing in the hall waiting."

"Of course you waited, honey. You didn't know what was going on. Charlie is lucky you were there for him."

The office had called her immediately after her brave daughter had helped guide the paramedics to Charlie. Katie'd broken most of the speed limits to get here.

Katie took a deep breath while she soothed her daughter and finally took in her surroundings. Several police cars, a paramedic truck, fire and rescue trucks and an ambulance lined the parent pick-up drive along the main school entrance. Emergency personnel and police officers spread over the lawn between a few teachers, administrators and a handful of students.

A parent's worst nightmare.

Two paramedics rolled a gurney outside and lifted it into the ambulance. Leo climbed inside with them. Right before they closed the doors, he met her eyes and gave a small wave. She and Rosie watched as the ambulance sped toward the hospital.

"What's gonna happen? They couldn't get hold of his dad. He's all by himself."

"Leo's with him. Let's see if we need to talk to anyone here then we'll go to the hospital and wait. Okay?"

* * * *

"I ignored you this morning when you told us about Leo." Rosie's voice was like a gunshot in the silent waiting room. They'd been waiting for two hours. Charlie's dad had arrived. Charlie was alive. They were waiting for any more details.

"I almost ignored him when he saw me in the hallway. I almost didn't ask him for help, Mom. I was so...angry, hurt..."

"Oh, honey." Katie put her arms around her first baby. So close to being all grown up, but in the moment, still young and scared. "It's going to take some time to heal, but none of this is on you. You were there. You did everything right. The police said how amazing and brave you were. And what happened with Leo last week hurt us all. I should have explained better this morning, but we were rushing and he was planning on talking to you girls tonight.

"Something really awful happened to Leo years ago. It made him think he wasn't good enough to be loved. And last week he thought he heard me saying I felt guilty for loving him, but the truth is I love him so so much. It was more like a betrayal to your dad."

"Yeah," Rosie said. "I guess you'll never really stop loving Dad, huh?"

"Never, honey. At the same time, I'm so lucky, *we're* lucky Leo came into our lives. He loves us so much and when he thought he wasn't good enough again he lashed out because he was trying to protect himself from getting hurt."

"I get that."

"I know you do. You're so smart, so amazing."

"I miss Charlie, Mom." Her words, like a ghost between them. "I'm so scared. Is he going to be okay?"

My precious girl. "Thanks to you, he's going to get help. I don't know what physical injuries he'll have, but I suspect he'll need lots of emotional and psychological help."

When John was sick, she'd been guided by a wonderful social worker who urged her to be frank and not lie to her girls about what was going on. But Katie was out of her league here.

"I hope he'll let me be his friend again. I knew something bad was going on." Katie barely heard Rosie's whisper.

"What, honey?"

"Some kids, Sienna and her gang were bullying him, Mom. I didn't know at first when I started being friends with her. Then when I figured out what she was doing and all the scary stuff she was into online I avoided her. She found out about Charlie."

"You mean about him being gay?"

"Yes. I think she told Charlie I outed him, even though I would never do that. He wouldn't talk to me, but I *knew* something was going on."

"Oh, honey. I'm so sorry for both of you. I had no idea. I'm so glad you told me Everything from here on out we can get through together. And we are all going to be there for Charlie and his dad too."

Katie gathered her daughter in a hug and held on tight. When Leo came through the hospital doors, Rosie jumped up and threw her arms around him. "Thank you. Thank you. Thank you," she whispered.

"Brave girl," Leo said. "Charlie is alive tonight because of you."

Katie crowded around them. "How is he?"

Leo cupped her face. "He's going to be okay. His dad is a mess and they have a long road of recovery ahead of them, but he's physically okay. I told them I'd stay for a bit in case they need anything. He wanted me to thank you, but the man can hardly talk. Do you want to go home and I'll meet you there in a bit?"

Katie nodded into his chest. "Thank you so much," Katie said. "For taking care of these kids."

"Anytime, love."

Chapter Twenty-Nine

Exhaustion battled with anticipation in Leo's entire body when he arrived at Katie's. What a shitty day for Charlie and his family. Thank God the kid was okay. Even though Leo needed a week's worth of sleep, nothing was going to keep him from his girls tonight. He needed to be folded back into their love. If they'd have him. He suspected Rosie would be okay now.

Katie opened the door before he could knock and Kitten barreled through, but after one tail-wagging greeting, took off into the front yard to chase a squirrel.

"Kitten, no!" Katie yelled. Cece was in her arms and the minute she saw Leo, she smiled and monkey-flung herself toward him. He could picture her jumping out of airplanes in the future, his little airborne daredevil.

Cece hugged his head, but then abruptly put her hands on his chest and yelled, "You made my mama cry! You made us all cry. Except for Brie. She's very stowid."

"Stoic?" Leo asked. And she nodded solemnly. The dog raced back inside, lunged into the living room and knocked over one of the side table lamps.

"Hey," he said and leaned over to kiss Katie on the cheek. He walked them all back inside. "Another quiet night at home. I see a vacation in our near future." He whispered the words so only she could hear them and cherished the small smile she gave in return.

"Don't tease a lady, Mr. Treversini."

"It's late, but I wanted to talk to your girls if it's okay."

"Absolutely. Girls, come down here please," she yelled.

"It is late." Connor's voice came from the kitchen. He leaned against the counter with his arms crossed. Well, shit. It seemed Katie was right about whose forgiveness was going to be the hardest to earn.

"Connor," Katie chastised him with one word.

"What do you want to talk to us about?" Cece asked, pulling his attention back to her. She rested her head on his shoulder. Her yawn rolled through her entire tiny body.

"I want to apologize for being a big jerk and hurting your mom's feelings. And I want to promise never to do that again. I was afraid of how big my love is for all of you and I didn't feel worthy." Honesty might ease the chill from Duggan. Either that or he'd freeze Leo into an ice sculpture.

"Oh, silly, Leo, my lion." Cece patted his chest. "Uncle Connor says anyone who doesn't want our love is a huge big fool. You probably just got scared a bit."

Connor cleared his throat. Leo thought the man might be holding back a laugh or choking on his own words tossed out by the mini-goddess.

"Yeah, firelight. Do you think you can forgive me for hurting you?"

"Mama says I'm super-good at forgiving. And I love you, Leo. I was hoping and hoping and hoping you'd come back to us."

How could a sprite like this get him choked up? Because she was as special as her mother. Leo squeezed her and whispered, "I love you too. I love all four of you."

"You love me?"

"To outer space, around all the planets, blazing by the sun and back."

"Wow," she whispered and closed her eyes.

Her body slumped against him. *Tired puppy.*

"Mom." Brie came rushing down the stairs. "Rosie's gone."

"What?" Katie said. Leo's body tensed.

"She left her chat open on her laptop. She went with Zachary somewhere, I think. Something bad is going on."

"Call her," Leo and Connor said in unison.

"Shit! She doesn't have her phone," Katie said. "I took it away."

Just then Katie's phone vibrated across the kitchen counter. "It's your name." She looked to Leo in confusion.

He felt his empty back pocket and swore silently. "Answer it. She has my phone from school."

"Put it on speaker," Connor said and they all gathered around the phone.

"Rosie?" Katie said.

"Mom, you're going to be mad, but I had to leave. I couldn't do *nothing* again. And I need your help. It's bad."

"Talk to me, honey. I'm not mad. I need to make sure you're okay. What's going on?"

"There's a group of girls from school who are supposed to meet some guys tonight, like a group first date. Sienna set it up. She's been working on it for months. But, Mom. I hacked into the site she's been using and I don't think it's guys our age at all. I think it's some older men and it's like gross, scary bad. The girls have been sending pictures of themselves over the internet, naked pictures."

"Christ!" Katie swore. "Honey! Where are you? We're going to come get you."

"I'm with Zach. We called the cops, but I had to come see if I could help these girls. I don't even think Sienna understands what she's gotten involved in."

"Zach Wilder?" Leo asked.

"Yeah, Mr. Treversini. I'm with her," Zach said. "She said she was going to go alone, and I didn't want that to happen. I picked her up. We thought we'd get to the girls and tell them, but a bunch of creepy vans with no windows just pulled up."

"Tell me where you are!" Leo ordered. "I'm coming to get you."

"Me too." Connor grabbed his coat and pocketed his own phone.

"We're hiding behind the dumpster at the gas station by the old Pie & Pint. I can hear the sirens," Rosie said.

Fuck. A seedy part of town if there ever was one.

"You two listen to me. If you can safely get back in Zach's car and lock the doors, do it now. If not, you stay hidden. Connor and I are on the way. He has his phone. Stay on the phone with your mom, Rosie. Unless you need to call the police again or your uncle. You hear me?"

"Yes, Leo. Hurry."

"We'll be there. Do whatever you can to stay safe."

* * * *

Leo had expected the freeze out to continue in the car. Apparently, he'd misjudged the man.

"Did you mean what you said back there, about loving them?" Connor asked.

"Absolutely. Do you need me to sign in blood?"

"Nope. We're good. Glad to see you drop-kicked your demons and stepped up. Now, let's get our girl. Katie told me what happened to Charlie. Jesus, he used to be at our house all the time. What the fuck, man?"

"Don't know the whole story. His dad said he'd been getting bullied, but the poor man had no idea things had gotten so bad."

"One shitstorm after another."

"Yeah," Leo agreed. It only took them ten minutes to get to the Pie & Pint. *Longest fucking minutes of my life.* He'd already had one too many heart attacks in the last week. How many could a man take?

"What the ever-loving hell?" Connor said. At least twenty police cars surrounded the bar. Four police vans, several K-9 units. Yellow tape blocked a lot of them in. Police, some in regular uniforms, others in riot gear swarmed the area.

Leo parked on the curb across the street. They rushed to the police tape.

"Gentlemen. I need you to step back." A tall black man wearing a bulletproof vest which read *Detective* on it held up his hand. "Connor Duggan?"

"Detective Naylor, my niece—"

"Leo! Uncle Connor!" They turned to see Rosie running toward them. Zach jogged up behind her. "Mom, they're here. We're okay," she said into the phone.

The detective still held his hand up. "Names and IDs," he ordered.

"You know me, Detective," Connor said.

"Going by the book tonight, gentlemen. Think you can appreciate the importance of that."

"I'm her legal guardian." Connor dug his license out. "And this is her soon-to-be-stepdad, Leo Treversini." He eyed Leo as if giving him a chance to deny it.

Leo might have smacked him if the situation wasn't so serious.

After checking their I.D.s, the detective lifted the tape. "Your niece is a hero, Duggan. Couldn't be prouder if she were my own."

Connor grabbed Rosie in a fierce hug. "Jesus Christ, kid. What the hell were you thinking?"

He set her down and she turned to hug Leo. "I had to do something."

"She and Zach prevented a lot of heartbreak for a group of extremely scared teenage girls," Detective Naylor said. "We'd like to ask her a few more questions. We have a warm van over here."

"I need to tell them what I know," Rosie said. "And I'm sorry I took your phone, Leo. I forgot to give it back to you earlier." She handed it to him.

"Damn good thing you still had it. Proud of you, kid." She beamed and turned to follow the detective.

"Katie," he said into his phone. "We've got her. She's okay. We're with the lead detective now."

"God! Leo. What is going on?"

"Nothing good, darlin'. Nothing good at all. Place is crawling with police, fire, detectives, and there are about twenty men face down, on the ground, in handcuffs. Whatever was going down here tonight makes my skin crawl. But she and Zach are fine. Connor and I'll bring her home."

"Promise?" she whispered and he sensed she was holding herself together.

"Promise. I love you."

"I love you too, Leo. God, I love you so much."

* * * *

It was hours before Leo and Connor brought everyone home, but they did. She was grateful they were able to. And wished like hell they'd never be put in that situation ever again.

As late as it was when they walked through the doors, Katie and Brie were still awake, waiting for them. Cece was passed out with Kitten on the dog bed. Connor made coffee while Katie held onto Rosie and listened to her explain.

"We sat in a police van while I told them everything I knew, which wasn't a whole lot."

"It was enough to save some families a whole bunch of heartache," Connor said and kissed her head. "Ruby's dad, Detective Naylor, was the lead. FBI showed up too. Apparently, these men from several states have been targeting high school girls for three years. Child porn, kidnapping, worse…" He let his words trail off. No one needed visuals.

But Jesus. Katie couldn't help but think of the families over the years whose daughters *had* gotten caught up in this horrible situation. The actual heartbreak. Lives ruined. Families destroyed.

"You should be proud of her." Leo interrupted her dark thoughts. "She didn't hold anything back, even details that could get her in trouble, like how she found out about tonight in the first place."

"I am so proud of you, honey." Katie wiped tears from her cheeks and wrapped Rosie in a hug. "But please, no more hacking. I don't think my heart can take it. And who is Zach?"

"He's a junior. We have art together. He's the one who got me on the newspaper," Rosie said.

"He's a good kid," Leo said. "Responsible, kind, whip smart."

"We waited for his parents to get there because the police wouldn't let him leave on his own or with us."

"They're being smart. I want to meet him —"

"Mom." Rosie flopped her head into her hands and sighed.

"I get to meet anyone in your life, whether you like it or not. I want to thank him for keeping you safe tonight. And explain if he ever picks you up for a secret scary mission involving a child kidnapping and porn ring again, he'll have to answer to me."

"And me," Connor chimed in.

"Yep, me too," Leo said.

"*Jeesh.* I guess I'm lucky you're all ganging up on me. Can we go to bed now?" Rosie dragged herself off the stool.

"You are lucky," Katie said. "Tomorrow we can talk about you getting your phone privileges back. You were brave and strong twice today, when it really mattered, honey."

Rosie kissed her mom on the cheek and headed toward the stairs. "I love you," she whispered.

"Love you too."

Eventually Leo carried Cece to her room, then found Katie, Brie and Rosie snuggled in Katie's bed together.

"Turns out it's not as easy as we thought to shove the nightmares away," she whispered.

"I should get going." He leaned over and put his lips against hers. Gentle, warm, loving man.

She pulled the covers back and leaned forward. "Will you stay? I could use my own nightmare buffer."

When Leo sighed, his gorgeous smile took over his entire face. "Yeah, darlin', I'd like to stay with you forever. If you'll have me." He took off his boots and climbed in behind her to hold her while she held her girls.

* * * *

Who in the world invented high-pitched blaring noises? Head still buried in her pillow, she shut off her alarm the next morning, dreaming of that vacation Leo had hinted at. She was alone in bed. Voices from downstairs met her ears. She couldn't make out exactly what they were saying, but there were words and giggles.

Boy, did she ever want to sneak back under the covers and sleep for like a year. Teenage trauma was not for the faint of heart. And all those people who claimed parenting got easier? *Liars, all of them.*

The scent of coffee was too much for her tired body to ignore. After a quick shower, she found all three girls and Leo in the kitchen making breakfast. *Family.*

"Morning," Leo said and handed her a steaming mug.

"God bless you," she whispered and took a sip. *Creamy, warm, strong.* "I almost feel human again. How's everyone else doing this morning?"

"Tired," Rosie said. She glanced up from her book, which was nice, rather than her usual ignoring all of them.

"Connor took Kitten with him to his job site," Leo said. He wrapped his arms gently around her, and she melted against his warmth.

"Mama, Leo made honey toast, hot tea *and* bacon!" Cece squealed.

"She's easy to please," Leo whispered.

"Uh huh. Wait until she wants to hold your welding torch, while it's *on.*"

"I'll tell her she has to be ten."

Katie patted him on the chest. "Good luck with that."

He teased her neck with his beard, winked at her and got back to cooking bacon.

"Mom, Leo asked us girls if we'd help him with a project after school this week." Brie tucked herself under Katie's arm and looped her small skinny ones around Katie's waist.

"Yeah," Cece said in wonder. "Then he wants us all to have a dinner date at his house on Saturday. Please say, 'Yes', Mama. It's my first dinner date with a boy ever."

Katie smiled at Leo. "Well I can't think of a better man to have your first date with, honey."

Chapter Thirty

Spending her evenings alone was an unfamiliar pleasure to Katie. But she took her duties seriously. Tuesday she came home from delivering food, flopped on the couch and watched three entire episodes of her favorite renovation show while savoring a glass of red wine and a toasted bagel. Wednesday she, Ellie, Ruby, Natalie and Sasha had met at Spa La La for manis and pedis and never-ending laughter. Thursday she almost, *almost*, started to feel lonely. But she put on music and caught up on her Pins for her dream café space she was determined to establish as reality one day. Friday afternoon she cleaned the house, because that was about as exciting as she needed her life to be after the last few weeks. Plus, it made her feel good. Even if the clean would go up in a puff of smoke as soon as the girls returned.

When the front door opened on Friday night with all kinds of people spilling in, she welcomed the noise and the companionship. Leo balanced a stack of pizzas leaning like the Tower of Pisa before he steadied them on the kitchen counter. Her girls carried grocery bags. Cece's was almost bigger than she was. Connor, Ellie, Jackson, Sasha, Gage, Natalie, their girls and Ruby filled the space quickly. *Too bad Lachlan's working.* Katie eyed Ruby. Jackson put Kitten, Chewie and Buffy out in the backyard, which calmed the chaos a smidgen, at least until they barreled back inside.

"Hi, Mrs. Walsh. I'm Zachary Wilder. Most people call me Zach."

"He's been helping us with Leo's project." Rosie beamed.

"The project everyone seems to be in on except me," Katie asked.

"Yep." Leo gave her his sexy piercing gaze from across the room with his wiggly eyebrows. "And we're not going to say anything else about that project tonight, are we?" He scooped Cece up and made goofy cross-eyed contact with her.

"I promise not to say anything about the painting," Cece whispered. "Until tomorrow when you said we could show Mama her surprise."

Laughter spread throughout the room but as curious as Katie was about their project, she was so happy to have them all together, safe, warm. *Family.*

* * * *

"Close your eyes, Mama," Cece said. "I'm so excited. I'm so excited."

"I'm wearing a blindfold, goofy. I can't see. I promise." Katie was excited too. She had no clue what they'd been working on, only that her girls and Leo had come home every night this past week wearing paint-splattered T-shirts. Cece of course had managed to get it in her red curls too. She called it fairy dust and wouldn't let anyone wash it out. Which was a good thing, because Katie had no idea how to get paint out of hair.

Leo had picked them all up Saturday at three. They'd blindfolded Katie and put her in his truck and now they were leading her down the sidewalk.

"Careful, darlin'. It's slippery." Leo held her by the arm.

"Oh," Brie exclaimed. "It's snowing."

Katie loved the awe in her daughter's voice. A voice so normally calm and rational. Snow did that to all her girls, brought out the dreamer in them with all its magical beauty. Cold flakes fell on her hair, her cheeks. They'd had such a long, lingering fall that she'd nearly forgotten about winter.

"Okay, okay, okay, we're here!" Katie could imagine her youngest bouncing up and down.

"Calm down, Cecelia Bo-belia."

Katie smiled. Cece loved it when Rosie used her nickname. Mmm, maybe she would stay blindfolded for a while longer. All her girls getting along. Each one happy and healthy. A wonderful man leading her to a surprise in the magical first snow of the season.

"And we're here," Leo said. He whipped the blindfold off her head and ushered her through the doorway, closing the cold behind them.

"Holy cannoli!" Katie said. *Oh, oh.* She put her hands over her eyes in case it was a dream, but when she pulled them away, the beautiful space remained.

The entire second storefront next to Leo's art studio had been fixed up. White paint graced the ceiling and the walls, save one which boasted the most amazing botanical wallpaper of huge green fern leaves. Large snake plants in copper pots stood in the corners. One amazing silver food display case stood against a wall and one single antique pine table sat in the middle with five mismatched chairs. Exact replicas of the oversized industrial-chic pendant lights from her Pinterest board hung from the ceiling.

"There's even a back room with three whole sinks right next to one another," Cece said. Who knew three sinks in a row could amaze her kid?

"It's not finished yet," Leo said. "Obviously. We want your input and I ordered the best appliances, but if you don't like them, we can get what you want. And more table and chairs. I'll build a counter out however you like. We spied on your Pinterest boards and got a head start."

"I didn't even have to hack anything to get to your Pinterest boards, Mom," Rosie teased.

"Funny, ha-ha," Katie said.

"My favorite part is Leo's art. See." Brie opened the front door again.

Katie spun around and followed her daughter outside to see an iron sculpture of a goddess with flowing hair, her arms outstretched. Pure serenity radiated from her face. It was the most gorgeous thing she'd ever seen. Flowers and vines wove in and out and created a wreath-like nest around the feet. The snow decorated it with a perfect sparkle and shine.

"It's gorgeous, like a siren or a goddess. You all are going to make me cry. Will it be okay in the weather?"

"Yeah, it'll tarnish, which will change it a bit, but it's supposed to," Leo said. "She'll get prettier as she ages."

"You did this for me?" She walked into Leo's arms.

"Yeah." He touched his forehead to hers. "We all did. Welcome to your new kitchen and café. Whatever you want it to be. It's yours."

"I love it so much. I can't believe you all worked so hard on this for me."

"I still have to make dinner, but I have lots of snacks upstairs and one more surprise for each of you ladies," Leo said.

* * * *

"A scavenger hunt!" Cece's screech was muffled by the fact that she clung like the monkey she was to the rail at the top of the stairs on the third floor while yelling down at them. This enormous house had more advantages than Katie first realized. Her eardrums were still intact.

"Yep, for each of you. But you have to start in the kitchen." Leo, his arms wrapped around her, spoke at a much lower decibel and her ears cheered at that too, but for completely different reasons. She sighed and mourned the loss of his warmth when he pulled away. *Guess he can't stay connected to me every single moment.* Leo put a small folded piece of paper in each of their hands, a different color for each girl.

Including her. "Me too?"

Leo nodded, his face awash in secrets and joy.

"Now, it's not a race, but there will be celebrating when you all find your prize." Leo clapped his hands together. "Go!"

It started as a mad scramble and eased into laughter, squeals of delight, socked feet sliding across the hardwood floors, people racing up and down the stairs, doors opening and shutting and cheers when clues were discovered.

Leo had drawn pictures for Cece's clues—thoughtful man—so she didn't need help reading difficult words. And little firelight, as Leo called her, was the first to finish. Katie found it odd that her daughter didn't run around screaming about coming in first, but she was having too much fun discovering her own clues to pay much attention. However, one by one, her girls each found their prize. Then the quiet did nag at her. *Odd.*

She was the last to find her prize. *Be fearless with me.* The words she found written on her last clue Leo had placed on the stairs leading up to the roof. On top of the world, dusk fell around her and city lights twinkled below them and danced with the snow. There stood Leo next to a heat lamp, his hands in the pockets of his jacket. Snowflakes dusted his black hat. Sparks flared in his eyes. His smile was beautiful, peaceful, all hers. Giggles came from behind her and she turned to see her three girls, arm in arm, each wearing a new winter hat and mittens, in their own special colors.

"Leo got us new necklaces with hearts on them," Cece said. When they surrounded her and ushered her closer to Leo, she found him down on one knee with another heart in his hand. A petite, satin heart-shaped box. He opened it to reveal a cluster of diamonds set on an antique rose-gold band.

"Leo," she whispered. Her words froze in her throat.

"It's so pretty. Look how it sparkles in the snowlight," Cece said.

"Hush." Brie gently put her mittened hand over Cece's mouth.

Her girls wrapped their arms around Katie and Leo took her hand. Tears warmed her cold cheeks.

"You are the most precious thing that's ever happened to me," he began. "All four of you are gifts. I don't know how I got so lucky to find you. I love you and vow to cherish all of you for the rest of my life if you'll have me. Katie Walsh, I want to make a family with you, here in this grand, ridiculous house. What do you say?"

"Yes!" Her girls screamed in unison, which made her and Leo laugh. Laughter and joyful tears. *Best combination ever.*

Katie wrapped her arms around him and swallowed back her happy tears. "Leo Treversini. I trust you with my heart and with my girls. I love you more than anything in the world and I'd be honored to marry you."

He lifted her up and twirled her around while her girls cheered and danced in the snowflakes.

Epilogue

Katie took in the scene before her. The weather, which had been plain old cranky and rotten chilly rain for weeks, had been snuffed out. At least for the day. People strolled the neighborhood, enjoying the cloudless blue sky and bright sun, warming themselves after a long hibernation. She'd had one of the busiest days ever at her café, Goddess Kitchen. It was awesome!

Towering over the shops stood their home. Theirs. She loved the way that made her feel. The renovations were almost finished. Her favorite part was the master bathroom she and Leo did in fact use often. Together. Sometimes with toys. Now, when thoughts of Leo worshipping her body made her cheeks redden, she soaked in the rush of warmth and love.

She brushed her hand over her new Nissan Pathfinder parked in front of her shop and Leo's studio. It had been a gift to herself in January when her van finally took its last breath. It was so much easier to stomach, knowing she didn't have to save for a new home or new kitchen space. They were planning a road trip in it to see Leo's sister and her wife this summer. She might loathe the car after spending two days with her minions in it, but for now, she was head over heels in love with it.

Inside Art Lion, as they'd finally named the studio, Leo was cleaning up after a welding class. Her girls were there too. Rosie stood at a table with Zach paging through Leo's old art textbooks. Even Charlie was here, putting welding equipment away. He looked so much better than he had that last week in November. Each time Katie saw him, he was healthier. Although, he'd never gotten his loud boisterous personality back. Maybe because of what had happened to him, what he'd survived, or merely maturity and changing with age.

"Sorry to burst everyone's happy art bubble, but we have to go," she said, pushing open the door.

"What? No!"

"Why?"

Voices begged for answers.

"I'm in the middle of a masterpiece, Mama."

"I promise it's worth it, Cece. Charlie and Zach can still come over later for dinner if they want."

"I need two more minutes to finish my sketch." Brie hadn't even looked up from her canvas. Knowing her, it would take her exactly two minutes.

Leo wrapped his arms around her from behind, kissed her ear — one of her favorite things he did to her — and asked, "Everything okay?"

Since her girls weren't paying attention, she turned in his arms and kissed him, long and deep. "Mmm, still tingling from our shower this morning," she whispered so only he could hear.

"Yeah? Glad I put in the bench?"

"That bench, whew!" she teased and kissed him again.

"No kissing! Gross." Cece gagged, which made Katie and Leo laugh. She loved holding him while he laughed, and she got to do it often these days. She never wanted to let go. The man was warm and hard and smelled so damn good.

"Well, I suppose you can all stay here if you want. Leo and I can take my beauty for a spin to the hospital to meet baby Alexander without you."

Even Brie's head shot up. "Ellie had her baby?"

"Yippee!" Cece yelled and did a running jump into Leo's arms. He'd had lots of practice catching her over the last few months. "I get to be an honorary auntie!"

"Sorry, guys. We have to go now." Rosie ushered her friends out of the door, but not before giving them both hugs and demanding they show up later to eat with them.

Her teenager was blooming, growing fast into a beautiful, compassionate, intelligent young woman. Katie was so glad Rosie had friends again, an old one who was healing slowly, and a new one, who, Katie suspected, might be turning into more than just a friend. She shook her head, totally not ready to deal with boyfriends yet. Thank goodness she had Leo to help her navigate that minefield. *Good thing we've had the sex and baby talk. A ton. Hopefully it made a dent in their heads and babies won't be a reality for any of my girls for the next millennium.*

She squeezed Leo's hand. *Babies.* She smiled through her sigh. The topic was certain to come up a lot more, if she and Leo got their wish. Late one night, when they'd moved her and the girls into the almost finished gorgeous home, Leo had held her naked body close after making love and asked her how she felt about having more kids. *A baby with Leo?* The man could probably get her pregnant with one sexy look. And she wanted that with him and *for* him.

But first she had a wedding to plan. A big celebration she hadn't had the first time, since she and John had been so afraid of their parents' reactions, they'd run off to the courthouse and gotten married in secret. What had they been thinking?

This time, she wanted a fancy party with all their friends. Plus, she wanted to stretch out each moment with Leo, enjoying his company, his body. Him enjoying her body before they tossed a pregnancy into their already crazy but wonderful lives.

She had a beautiful life with a new man who adored her and her girls and a thriving business she couldn't quit beaming over. Most of all she was surrounded by love every day. And she was going to enjoy every single second of it.

Graciella: Seducing the Dragonfly
Sara Ohlin

Excerpt

"We have five acquisitions in the works, including the two connecting properties in Bergmannkeiz. Those are going to be an albatross around our necks, or, preferably, like spinning thread into gold. Things are changing rapidly. We need to stay ahead of our competition and the trends. That's why we're successful. But we won't be if we keep slacking off. Gabe, make sure you're ready for our Frankfurt trip. Focus your research on demographic shifts and traffic patterns. I shouldn't have to tell you how to do your job." Turner barely looked at his staff as he gave them orders.

Nine a.m. and it feels like midnight. Routine Monday morning meeting and he could barely think straight. His agenda blurred in front of him.

"I need the financial analysis on the five acquisitions finished and on my desk at the end of the day. Rebecca, you're on Bergmannkeiz. I don't want your thoughts on the long-term profit strategy. I need data."

"The end of the day, sir? The entire analysis?"

Turner shot his eyes toward his best financial planner. "This is the second extension I've given you."

His temper shot like sparks through an electrical wire, angry, uncontrollable. Shit, he was tired. "Miss Graves, more coffee. Please," he yelled through the open door of his office. Not sleeping for several weeks was dragging him through the mud. Fucking nightmares of Brockman Farms. His own fucking albatross.

"Right, Mr. Brockman. You do remember we've been waiting for the tax assessment?" He *did* know that. Meeting Miss Graves halfway across the room, he took the mug she offered and faced the city.

From his wall of windows on the twenty-sixth floor of the Sony Center Office Tower in Berlin, Turner could see the red brick Kollhoff Tower and the city beyond. New Berlin, they called it, much of Potsdamer Platz having been rebuilt after the fall of the Berlin Wall. It was a modern city dominated by steel and glass, boasting four-star restaurants, world-class shopping, glitzy hotels and apartments.

With his keen sense of planning, design and eye for location, Turner had worked with the top architects and business developers to polish Berlin's shiny new look. This job provided him with an office at the top, more money than he knew what to do with and a sense of power.

Power. Something he'd been searching for his entire life. Something he'd never had at the farm.

No matter how far he got, how hard he tried, he could never purge the small town of Graciella, Oregon, from his mind. He'd been all over the world searching for control, and he'd found it, commanded it, buried his memories in it, because he'd been powerless in the one place it mattered, against his father. Now he felt the frayed edges of his conscience coming undone. For Christ's sake, he was yelling at his team. And his team was amazing. They could do his job for him.

Turner had no intention of ever seeing Brockman Farms again, even now, with his father dead and buried months ago. Unfortunately, he'd been plagued by insomnia, a bastard of a headache and memories of Graciella every night for the past three weeks. Memories he would have sworn he'd annihilated.

"Mr. Brockman—"

"What?" he snapped at his secretary before he could rein in his emotions. He rubbed his temples and forced a calmness he didn't feel into his tone. "I'm sorry, Miss Graves, what did you need?"

"Mr. Klein would like to see you in his office. Now, sir."

"Right." He followed her out and strode down the hall to the office of Hans Klein, his boss and CEO of Klein Development Strategies.

"Ah, Turner. Have a seat," Hans said. An imposing man in his late fifties, at six feet tall, two hundred pounds and with silver hair, it was the sly gleam in his eyes that had people snapping to attention in his presence. Hans was known internationally for being one of the top business developers, shrewd and cunning with his eye on absolute success and profit. Turner was one of the few who knew there was a softer side to the man, that he enjoyed playing with his grandchildren more than designing stunning office towers, for instance. In turn, Hans was one of a handful of people Turner trusted.

"How's Melanie?" Turner asked.

Hans' smile warmed. "Lovely as ever. We're going sailing this weekend. She asked if you'd join us. I told her you wouldn't be available."

"I'd love to...what? We don't start work on the new residential development until Monday. Do you need me in Frankfurt early?"

Hans sat on the edge of his desk, facing Turner. "You're not going to Frankfurt. You're going home to Oregon."

Uncrossing his legs and standing gave Turner the few seconds he needed to maintain a sense of calm. But he barely controlled the anger and confusion in the glare he tossed at Hans.

"Oh, don't pull that warrior bullshit with me, Turner," Hans said. "I know you're stronger than me. There's no denying you're younger. And those ruthless looks might get you far in business dealings, but you can't intimidate me. I know you too well."

"Care to tell me what this is about?" Turner said.

"I know your father died."

Jolted, Turner said, "How? I've never spoken of my family. No one knows who my father is."

"I'm not an idiot, son. T.D. Brockman was well known in the international business world. The infamous 'soulless' Brockman brought down in an instant by a heart attack. I can only imagine what your childhood was like. I see how detached you are. Not getting close to anyone. Melanie and I feel lucky you've shared what you have with us over the years."

"You've been good to me," Turner began, struggling to find his words. "But I can't go back. Not now. I don't know if I ever can."

"You will. Even if only to blast through the ghosts and get on with your life. It's obvious you're not sleeping. You're being an asshole to your staff. And if you snap at your secretary one more time, she's liable to quit. Face the past, Turner. It will eat away at you if you don't. You'll find your e-ticket in your email."

"You're my boss, not my father," Turner said, the steel in his voice matching his eyes. One last attempt to deflect.

"I'm your friend, you idiot. And I care about you."

One sentence was all it took to deflate Turner's temper. Hans was one of the only friends Turner had. He ran his hands through his hair and sighed. God, he felt fifty pounds heavier. It was a struggle to stay awake at his desk. Even work couldn't keep the memories at bay.

"I don't know if I can." Deep inside, a coil of fear tightened in his chest, but that was something he wouldn't admit to anyone. He'd spent years putting distance between himself and Graciella, between himself and the people he loved. Every step he'd climbed had been with the intention of banishing his past. All of it. Including the bond with his brothers and the love for his mother, because he'd let them all down. Because the truth was, even though he'd finally grown to hate T.D., as a child he'd craved the man's approval, wanted to be just like him. How sick was that? It wasn't only memories of T.D. he ran from, it was his own shame in loving his father. He'd loved a tyrant, longed for his love in return. How could he ever reconcile that?

"You can and you will. Your flight leaves tonight at seven." Hans busied himself with his papers. "Your job will be here when you return. Now I'm late for a meeting." He smiled and strode out of the office. Even with the friendship they'd formed over the years, Turner knew when Hans meant business.

Hell! Turner thought, closing his eyes to the memories trying to purge themselves from his gut. Fine. He'd go back to Graciella, confront his ghosts, try to apologize. Then move on to the next development deal up the ladder in his career. A career that had never disappointed him…at least where power and money were concerned.

Home of Erotic Romance

Sign up for our newsletter and find out about all our romance book releases, eBook sales and promotions, sneak peeks and FREE romance books!

About the Author

Sara Ohlin has lived all over the United States, but her heart keeps getting pulled back to the Pacific Northwest where it belongs. For years she has been writing creative non-fiction and memoir and feels that writing helps her make sense of this crazy world. She devours books and can often be found shushing her two hilarious kids so that she can finish reading. When she isn't reading or writing, she'll most likely be in the kitchen cooking up something scrumptious, a French macaron, shrimp scampi, a fun date-night-in dinner with her sexy husband, or perhaps her next love story.

Sara loves to hear from readers. You can find her contact information, website details and author profile page at https://www.totallybound.com